Without Reserve

A Novel of the War on Terror
Second Edition

by
Steven B. Howery

Khukuri Publishing
Littleton, Colorado

To my extraordinary wife and three incredible children, who've borne with me the honor of serving my country.

Dedicated with greatest respect and admiration to the people of the Republic of Singapore, whose strength and dignity have earned my everlasting affection.

With profound thanks to those exceptional men and women who serve in the armed forces of the United States.

———

Without Reserve was submitted for review for classified content and has been cleared for publication by the Special Security Office, Chief of Naval Operations, Washington, DC

———

Though Without Reserve is based, in part, on actual events and living historical individuals, it is a work of fiction. The words, thoughts and actions of historical figures described in this story are also fictional. The remaining characters are composites of individuals the author has encountered throughout his career. Therefore similarity to any single individual, living or dead, is purely coincidental.

Without Reserve, a Novel of the War on Terror
© Copyright 2007 (1st Ed.) & 2015 (2nd Ed.)
by Steven B. Howery, All Rights Reserved.

ISBN 13: 978-0-9793274-2-1
ISBN 10: 0-9793274-2-3

Library of Congress Control Number: 2016900392

Printed in the United States of America

PROLOGUE

Colonel Mok glances at his watch. *What's a nice Muslim boy doing out so late on a Saturday night?*

It's sweltering inside the van; he's ordered the driver to kill the engine - hence the air conditioner - to make the vehicle less obvious. He realizes the junior officers stuck in the van with him silently curse his precautions.

He takes a long drag from his cigarette and exhales the smoke through his nostrils into the humid evening air, the opaque wisps encircling his balding pate before fading into the blackness. As he leans forward and wipes the fog from the glass to peer through the mirrored window, an excited voice suddenly erupts in his earpiece.

"Target acquired," it rasps. "Comfort Taxi 0499. Approaching from the West."

It's the voice of Captain Peter Chang, one of his finest special operations team leaders. The Colonel presses the side of his face against the cool glass, staring back down the block to see a single, light blue taxi approach the home of Kastari bin Ali, a Muslim extremist with purported ties to Osama bin Laden's Al Qa'ida terror network.

Colonel Mok grinds his cigarette absently into the ashtray and raises the walkie-talkie to his lips. "Wait until he exits the vehicle. We don't want any innocent casualties," he orders.

"Yes Sir," responds Chang tersely.

The taxi rolls to a stop and the rear passenger door swings open. Ali appears, peering warily around the quiet street before turning to help the woman emerging from the taxi, her face hidden within the shadow of a black hijab.

"Go!" hisses the colonel into his walkie-talkie; the team springs to action. A plainclothes sergeant emerges from the dark alley and quietly approaches Ali.

Reaching to help the woman from the car, Ali catches a glimpse of the figure moving toward him. The sergeant lunges and Ali spins sideways, sending him crashing into the woman, knocking her with a strangled scream against the side of the car.

Captain Chang and one of his officers spring from a parked car in front of the condo, MP5 submachine guns trained on their quarry, beams from barrel-mounted flashlights crisscrossing in the mist. Two more officers emerge from the rear of the colonel's van.

"Halt, Police!" shouts Captain Chang. As the officers close in, Ali's eyes anxiously seek an escape route. Spotting his only chance, he turns and sprints down the alley, the officers clattering after him.

"Damn!" swears the colonel. "Get to the other side of the block," he snaps to his driver. The van lurches forward and speeds a half a block, screeching around the corner, its open back doors swinging wildly. At the end of the next block, the van cuts left and the colonel spots Ali emerge from the alley and hesitate, his wild eyes flashing in the headlights of the approaching van.

"Stop!" rasps the colonel as the van skids toward a halt ten feet from Ali. Before the van came to a complete stop, the colonel rolls from the passenger seat and lands at a crouch in the street, his pistol drawn on the terrorist. Emerging from the alley behind Ali, Captain Chang and another officer slam into Ali from behind, knocking him to the ground and piling atop the struggling man.

Two more officers emerge from the alley, submachine guns at the ready as they shuffle cautiously toward the tangle of bodies grappling in the street. Captain Chang rolls Ali onto his back then leaps back in horror. His eyes snap toward the colonel, the color draining from his face.

A blood-curdling *"Allahu Akbar!"* erupts from Ali's lips, echoing between the concrete and glass buildings.

"Oh, God. No," rasps the colonel. He flings his arms over his face as five pounds of plastique strapped to Ali's torso explodes with an earsplitting *"Crump!"* Captain Chang and his brother officer disintegrate along with their suspect; the colonel and remainder of his team are slammed violently to the ground and peppered with flying debris as they scramble to escape the blast.

Several officers stumble from the rear of the shattered van and drag their wounded colonel to safety. Sirens shrill through the night air as backup units from Singapore's National Police speed toward the scene of carnage.

"The woman! Where's the woman?" coughs the colonel.

An officer hisses into his walkie-talkie and raises it to his ear for a response. His eyes cut to the officer beside him. Without a word, they abandon their injured colonel and sprint into the darkness to where the taxi remains, engine idling, at the far end of the alley.

Against the curb, they discover Sergeant Khan's body lying in a puddle of blood beneath the taxi's open door. Weapons raised, they shuffle cautiously around the exterior of the car. Submachine gun trained on the driver's door, an officer seizes the handle and jerks. The door creaks open to reveal the driver slumped over the steering wheel, bloody gray brain matter and bits of shattered skull splattered across the windshield from the bullet that entered from the base of his spine and exploded from his forehead.

The woman is gone.

"Stay here," the senior officer breathes, his eyes warily sweeping the empty street. "I'll inform the colonel."

The young officer gulps nervously, "yes Sir." He hunkers down beside the taxi, peering over his submachinegun's open sights into the darkness beyond.

As the senior officer emerges from the alley, he spots the colonel propped with his back against the van, grimacing as a paramedic cuts away his pants leg and attempts to stanch the bleeding from his shrapnel-torn thigh.

The look of despair on the approaching officer's pallid, sweating face speaks volumes.

"They can't be here," rasps Colonel Mok, eyes rolling back in his skull as the shock of his wounds overwhelm him.

"Not here..."

CHAPTER 1

There's a chill in the early morning breeze, a hint the autumn of an era is fast approaching. Leaves explode in hues of bullion and burgundy as Chris Gates jogs lost in thought along the trail hugging Cherry Creek. Traffic congeals on downtown streets following the meandering course of the stream. From beneath the eastern horizon, a glow backlights Denver's skyscrapers, casting shadows forming long black fingers closing unnoticed around him.

War never begins the way you'd expect.

After three miles he slows to a brisk walk, panting in long, controlled breaths as he crosses the street amid the irate honking of passing vehicles and enters his high-rise. Hopping the elevator, he rides the empty car toward the 12th floor, swaying hypnotically as he stares absently at the ascending numbers. The doors rumble open and he shoulders his way past anonymous neighbors crowding into the elevator, strolls down the hallway, and enters his condo. Tossing his keys on the bar, he grabs a bottle of water and a cup of coffee and heads for the bedroom, nudging the door open with his elbow.

"Hey," he announces. "It's after seven. You gotta be someplace this morning?"

Linda, his occasional girlfriend, stirs beneath the sheets, eyes peering tiredly between strands of tousled blond hair.

She yawns lustily and reaches for the proffered cup. The sheet slides away to reveal her pale, nude body.

"Manna from heaven," she groans appreciatively, brushing the tangled hair from her face. After a long sip she cradles the cup blessedly in her hands. "What the hell was I drinking last night, anyway?"

"Dirty Martinis," he replies as he strides into the bathroom and starts the shower. "Shaken, not stirred."

"Feels more like beaten..." she mumbles as she hears the shower door slam. Glancing around the bedroom, she locates the television remote half-buried beneath a discarded pair of panties and presses the "on" button.

Five minutes later, Chris finishes showering and is toweling his hair dry as he returns to the bedroom. The television blares in the background as he slides open the closet door and runs his fingers along the line of freshly pressed dark suits hanging in neat rows. He selects a charcoal gray single-breasted Armani, a starched white shirt and thumbs through the rack before settling on a conservative blue and silver silk regimental tie.

Brushing aside Linda's wadded-up cocktail dress, he drapes his suit neatly across the foot of the bed. He glances around the room, noting with irritation the remainder of Linda's clothes strewn haphazardly across the floor, a strapless brassiere hanging from the lampshade on his nightstand. His gaze leads to Linda who lies on her stomach in bed, her willowy nude body half-concealed beneath the mussed sheets. Gawking at the television, her brow is furrowed in concentration. He lifts the bra from the lampshade and drapes it over her head, trying to spur a reaction. She merely reaches up and pulls it absently from her hair, discarding it on the floor beside the bed without comment; her eyes never leaving the screen.

"What's so fascinating?" he asks casually as he flops beside her and runs his finger lightly down her spine.

She shivers. "Sorry," she replies distractedly. "I was just watching the news..." her eyes return to the television. "There's been a terrible accident..."

"What?" Directing his attention to the image of smoke billowing from what he recognizes as the North tower of the World Trade Center, he snatches the remote and crushes the volume button.

The news channel is running an un-narrated close-up of the tower, flames and smoke billowing from a long horizontal gash. He aims the remote at the screen and insistently presses the volume button, but to no avail. The only sounds are distant sirens and muffled conversations of bystanders off-screen.

"How the hell...?" The sound of a hurtling freight train draws his attention back to the screen. Camera panning unsteadily from the building, its operator fumbles erratically for the source of the roar. From the left edge of the frame, a blue and gray airliner streaks into view and slams into the South tower, liquid fire spurting from the opposite side of the building. Onlookers scream as the second tower bursts into flames.

Linda gasps. Chris sits up abruptly.

"Al Qa'ida," he breathes.

"Huh?" she asks.

The cell phone on Chris' nightstand chirps. Checking the caller ID, he hesitates momentarily, sighs and flips open the cover.

"Captain Gates," he replies briskly. Linda does a double take, staring at him quizzically as she attempts to follow his conversation.

"Yes, Sir," replies Chris curtly. He nods several times and ends the call with, "Okay. I'll be available 24/7 by cell phone."

He disconnects the call and slips the cell phone into the pocket of the suit jacket lying across the foot of his bed.

"*Captain*?" she mocks. "Who the hell is *Captain* Gates?"

Glancing at the half-dozen framed photos on his bedroom wall, he selects a picture of three soldiers in muddy camouflage, white teeth and eyes glowing beneath camouflage paint appearing in shades of gray on the black and white photo. The three men have their arms draped across each other's shoulders, M-16A1s dangling in their hands. A husky man in the center carries a chopped-down M-60 machine gun slung from his shoulder. A faint smile creases Chris' lips, evaporating as he wipes his hand across the dusty glass and drops the photo on the bed.

"He's the guy on the right," he murmurs, beginning to dress as he watches her reaction from the corner of his eye.

She retrieves the photo and examines it closely. She shoots a glance at him then back at the photo. "Oh my God, that's you!" she gasps. "Where was this taken?"

"El Salvador, 1986," he shrugs.

"Where?"

"El... in Latin America," he stammers. "You know: the civil war in the 1980s?"

She stares back blankly.

"It was a war no one ever heard of, okay? I was a sergeant with Special Forces back then."

"And now?"

He shrugs and retrieved the photo. "I'm an intelligence officer in the army reserve." He nods toward the phone hidden in his pocket. "That was my detachment commander. Looks like I'm going back."

"'Back' where?" she asks.

"If he's right about what just occurred, I'm going back to war."

"Ladies and Gentlemen, we'll be landing in approximately ten minutes. You will notice the captain has turned on the seat belt sign. Please return to your seats and fasten your seat belts..."

The flight attendant's voice fades from Chris' consciousness as he slips off his headphones and peers out the window at the aqua-blue ocean rushing beneath the descending aircraft. The smell of damp, re-circulated air tinged with the odor of jet fuel make his stomach squirm.

"On behalf of the entire flight crew," the flight attendant continues, "I want to thank you for flying United Airlines and welcome you to Honolulu, Hawaii. Mahalo."

The Boeing 767 banks, its wheels rumbling into position beneath the fuselage as the distinctive outline of Pearl Harbor slides into view. Set off from the ships, cranes and warehouses he spots the gleaming white USS Arizona Memorial resting serenely above the decaying mass grave where 1200 souls perished in the last attack on American soil nearly 60 years before. The aircraft's wings level, the runway races into view as Chris cranes his neck, spotting the adjacent Hickam Air Force Base, it's massive, ghoulish gray aerial refueling tankers parked in martial rows along the tarmac.

"How the hell am I supposed to fight a war from *here*," he grumbles.

The airliner rolls along on the shimmering tarmac and pulls up alongside the jet way. As the plane creaks to a halt, the clap of metal buckles rippling through the aircraft like so many falling dominoes as passengers spring to their feet in desperation to beat others to the aircraft's exit. He glances up at the fasten seat belt sign, chuckling as it belatedly blinks-off.

Filtering among the throng of travelers, he gathers his laptop computer from the overhead compartment and joins the mass flowing inside the terminal and surging toward the baggage claim area. He recovers his suitcase and wanders over to a solitary stand marked "Military Arrivals." A crew-cut Marine in a razor creased tan and blue uniform mans the station; rather unusually, a Beretta M9 pistol was strapped to his hip. Chris drops his luggage in a heap and digs into his back pocket. He flips open his wallet and displays his Military ID. The Marine straightens. "Yes Sir."

"Lance Corporal, what's the best way to get over to Pearl Harbor?"

"Sir, all military facilities are at THREATCON DELTA. Everything's locked down tight," he snaps in crisp, factual manner.

"That's not what I asked. I have orders to report to Joint Intelligence Center, Pacific at 0700." He passes the Marine his orders.

"Yes, Sir," the Marine confirms, glancing at, then handing back, the document. "I suggest you arrive at least two hours early if you plan to report by 0700. Since 9/11, clearing security takes forever."

An interminable three months later, Chris hears his boss, Major Greg "Bear" Berewood clomping down the hall long before he enters the room. The major snatches a chair from another cubicle and heaves it into Chris' cramped space.

"Morning, Bear," Chris grins as he leans back and stretches. "What brings you up here to the sun deck?"

The major drops into the borrowed chair and leans forward, his voice lowered conspiratorially. "How'd you like to go to Singapore?"

Chris eyes him warily. "Uh, huh. What for?"

"Hey, ever since arriving you've been complaining about being 'sentenced' to the backwater of the war on terrorism," he replies with a shrug. "You wanna be a player or not?"

"Sure. When do I leave?" asks Chris, still uncertain if Bear is joking. He takes a gulp from his Diet Pepsi.

"Well, after you meet with the J2 this morning, I'd say first thing tomorrow."

Gagging, Chris spews soda over his computer screen. "*What*!?" He sputters, coughing, as he grabs a paper towel and dabs soda from his keyboard. "You better not be shittin' me..."

Bear laughs heartily. "We received a requirement to provide a liaison to Singapore for some sort of intelligence exchange."

"So, why me?" asks Chris suspiciously. "You've got a room full of careerists down there in the basement. Why the skuzzy reservist?"

The chair groans as Bear leans back and holds up a massive hand. "First," he replies, beginning to tick-off fingers. "It has to be an officer – *Captain*. We have what, maybe eight regular officers in the CT shop? Second, the officer has to know the Jemmah Islamiya inside and out - *that's definitely you*. Third, it's semi-undercover. No uniforms. *And no one in his right mind would mistake you for an Army guy*," he grunts derisively. "Fourth, it's gotta be someone who can deal diplomatically with the Sings. *I'm reasonably certain you're house broken...*"

"... And fifth," Chris interrupts, "none of your 'climbers' want to be too far from the flagpole."

"Not true. Not true," pleads Bear, stretching out his ape-like arms in a mock plea of innocence. "Commander Giles is chompin' at the bit. But of course he's a team chief and can't be spared..."

Bear notes the disbelief on Chris' face and shrugs indifferently. "Okay," he admits. "The guy's a moron and I'm not putting *him* in front of the Sings. We've got enough troubles without fuckin' over our friends, too."

Chris thinks for a few moments. "So what's the deal with the Admiral?"

"The Sings are quietly rounding-up the JI cell identified from the video tape our SOF guys discovered in Afghanistan. Their intelligence services are gonna crack these guys like an egg. She sees it as an opportunity for direct contact with a key player in the region."

"Makes sense," agrees Chris. "What now?"

Bear glances at his watch. "You meet with the Admiral at 1000, buddy. Better get cleaned up," he replies as he slaps Chris' shoulder and rises to leave. "And wear your 'Bs'," he advises with a nod toward Chris' camouflaged BDUs, "with ribbons. Gotta show her you earned that gray hair legitimately."

Bear extends his hand. "If I don't see you before you leave, have a great trip and don't forget to bring me back some Tiger Beer."

Chris sprints the quarter mile to his room at the Makalapa Visiting Officer's Quarters located in the dormant volcano crater behind the headquarters building.

After his second quick shower of the day, he grabs his freshly pressed Class "B" uniform and slaps five rows of ribbons over the left breast pocket. The ribbons symbolize nearly 16 years military experience, the top two ribbons representing the Silver Star for valor in combat and a Purple Heart for having been wounded in action. Then he pulls on his beret and troops down to the old blue Jeep he purchased at the "Lemon Lot" at nearby Hickam Field. Guiding the vehicle through the crater, he dodges between the zigzag barriers protecting the headquarters and past the guard post onto King Kamehameha Highway heading north.

The J2's office is located at the Marine Corps' Camp Smith in the lush, towering hills overlooking Pearl Harbor. Visitors hate being summoned "uphill" because parking is a nightmare. Chris wheels around the peaks and valleys searching unsuccessfully for a place to leave his Jeep. *It's*

1000 hrs NOW, he realizes before deciding to gamble and park in a space near the main building marked "Reserved for O6 & Above" - as an "O3" he's parking well beyond his pay grade. *What the hell?* He decides. *It's better than pissing-off the admiral.*

He bursts into the Admiral's outer office, the crisp creases in his uniform fading; dark stains forming beneath his armpits as he belatedly snatches the sweat-soaked wool beret from his head. "Captain Gates to see Admiral Lang," he blurts to the admiral's aide, a prim, attractive female Navy ensign.

"She's expecting you, Sir. You're late," she informs him prissily as she rises and opens the Admiral's door to announce him.

"Parking..." Chris mumbles lamely as he follows her into the Admiral's cavernous office. He's seen dozens like it before: the flag officers' "ego" wall of plaques and signed photos of influential military and political leaders; the usual glass topped table display of "coins" presented by key commands; the Turkish rug, Ming vase, or beer stein evincing previous worldwide assignments.

He snaps to attention and salutes. "Captain Chris Gates reporting as ordered, Ma'am."

Admiral Lang rises from behind her wide Teak desk and tosses a casual return salute. A tall, tanned woman in her mid-50s, she's legendary for her caustic temper and intolerance for bullshit. After a cursory handshake, she motions him to the sofa and drops into the overstuffed leather chair behind her desk.

"Bear speaks highly of you, Captain," she drawls, examining him over the top of her half-moon reading glasses. "Now I need to figure out if it's just because you're a fellow snake-eater or if you're the person for the job."

He realizes a response is in order. "I'm no snake eater, Ma'am," he chuckles. "I'm a lawyer."

"JAG?"

"No Ma'am. Intelligence. Well, actually I'm a corporate attorney from Colorado."

Her heavily lined face darkens. "Reservist?"

He nods.

"I told them 'active duty only'," she growls.

Chris shifts uncomfortably in his chair. This isn't the first time he's had to overcome the stigma of being a reservist. Despite its "Minuteman" heritage, the active duty military resents it when reservists emerge during times of crisis to "threaten their rice bowls" – Vietnam-era military vernacular for stealing the choice jobs.

"Ma'am. Reservists *are* the JICPAC counter-terrorism office," he responds defiantly. "In fact the only active duty personnel working CT are the department heads. So unless you want to jerk a SWO off some destroyer..."

"Really," she interrupts skeptically. "I didn't realize that." She reaches across her desk and flips the switch on her speakerphone. "Get JICPAC-CT on the line. I want to speak with Colonel Davis."

Chris clears his throat. "You know he's a reservist," he offers, realizing he and the others had been mobilized *before* the admiral took over as J2.

"No. I didn't," she replies flatly.

"Yes Ma'am," he responds and, seeing his opportunity, persists. "So are LTC Darwin and CDR Foreman and MAJs Schmidt and Berewood," he explains, rattling-off her entire counter-terrorism staff. "And all the NCOs," he adds.

The Admiral contemplates him for a moment, then leans forward and keys the speakerphone again. "Belay that call," she tells her aide. She leans back in her chair and motions ostentatiously to Chris. "All right, Captain. Tell me why I should send you to Singapore."

"Well, Ma'am. I know the extremist groups in the region. I've been tracking their bank accounts, shipping sources, and weapons suppliers for three months," he explains. "Singapore is the only truly multicultural, secular country in the region... AND," he adds significantly, "it's surrounded by hostile states with restless Muslim majorities. Singapore's survival is at stake."

"Agreed. But why *you*?" she asks with an encouraging twinkle in her eye.

He changes tacks. "Ma'am, as an attorney, I work for a company that does business in Asia. I've negotiated contracts over there and I know how to get things done." He throws up his hands in resignation. "If you send some tight-assed, um... I mean... active duty officer over there, he'll spend the next three months negotiating the agenda."

The admiral snorts her grudging agreement.

"Captain," she begins tentatively, her stern demeanor fading as she suddenly appears ill at ease. "Since you're a reservist, I'm not privy to your personnel file," she admits as she toys with the pen between her fingers. "So, please indulge me..."

"Of course Ma'am," he agrees, though he realizes she is hardly asking permission.

"You've obviously 'been around,'" she observes, nodding toward the five rows of awards and service ribbons on his uniform. "May I ask how it is you're only a Captain?"

"I'm a mustang, Ma'am," he responds, hoping the answer will suffice.

It doesn't. She motions for him to continue.

He sighs and proceeds. "I was an NCO with 7th Group, Army Special Forces in the 1980s. I served in Honduras, El Salvador... and, uh, other places in Central America," he explains vaguely.

She nods. If he'd said "South America" or even "Latin America," she would have assumed he meant counter-drug operations. But in the 1980s, Central America was purely the stuff of civil war.

"Counter-insurgency operations," she confirms.

"Yes Ma'am."

A lengthy silence ensues. The Admiral clears her throat and speaks. "Captain. You seem reluctant to talk about your past," she observes with irritation, taking off her glasses and wiping them on a small cloth. "Why is that?"

"I suppose its habit Ma'am," he replies after some hesitation. "Most of the operations I was involved with remain classified. The people I worked for wanted them to remain that way and I respect that."

She cringes inwardly, eyes wandering momentarily to a framed photo on the wall beside her desk - a picture of a young sailor, a Navy SEAL, standing cockily against the helm of an unnamed ship. Below the photo hangs the single Purple Heart presented at her only son's funeral - a casualty of an unknown battle in a war that never occurred.

Her mind made-up, the admiral slides a file across her desk. "Read this."

Chris withdraws a multi-page message composed in the irritating, difficult to read "all caps" format in which intelligence message traffic is compiled. He reads and rereads it several times.

The message informs him a routine inventory revealed 4-tons out of a 300-ton shipment of Ammonium Nitrate has gone missing from the container transshipment storage area at the Port of Surabaya on the southern tip of the island of Java, Indonesia. The cargo was offloaded on October 18, 2001 and part of it was discovered missing on January 6th. The reporting officer concedes the missing 4 tons could be a clerical error, but concludes it probably isn't. Recent satellite phone intercepts indicate the Indonesian born bomb-maker, known only as Khalid and last known operating in Singapore in December 2001, is organizing an attack somewhere in Indonesia.

"Share whatever intelligence you deem necessary," orders the admiral. "And concentrate on locating Khalid and the Ammonium Nitrate."

"What about the Foreign Disclosure Office?"

"Clear what you can and pass it through official channels," she responds before lapsing into a considered silence. "But if you need bargaining power, pass whatever you need in order to get cooperation. Do you understand what I'm saying?"

"Nothing in writing?"

"Nothing in writing."

Chris nods.

Admiral Lang passes a sealed envelope across the desk. "If you need something to break the ice with the Sings, you might use that," she recommends. "But be careful how you deliver it; it may ruffle some feathers." Leaning forward she palms him a piece of notepaper like a drug dealer closing a transaction. "Here's Colonel Mok's number," adds the admiral. "He's head of SID's CT office. Call him when you arrive."

"Should I set a meeting with him?" asks Chris.

The admiral smiles wanly. "No. You'll probably never actually meet the colonel," she observes. "Few people have. He's kind of like the old West German spymaster Reinhard Gehlen – known but never seen. Colonel Mok's a ghost; a myth. But if we're going to succeed against Al Qa'ida in Southeast Asia, he'll be the reason.

"His people will arrange an apartment for you," she explains before hesitating and fixing him sternly in her stare. "Expect it to be bugged."

"I thought we were allies."

She smiles wryly, a twitch in her grim smile. "There are no such things as allies; only interests. So, like I said..."

"... Expect it to be bugged," he repeats.

CHAPTER 2

It's nearing midnight when Chris arrives at Singapore's Changi Airport after sixteen hours and a layover at Japan's Narita Airport in Tokyo. A tall attractive young woman of Indian descent intercepts him as he emerges groggily from the customs clearing station.

"Captain Gates. I'm Shikha Patel of the Ministry of Defense," she introduces herself while handing him a generic business card. "I'm to ensure you get settled into your apartment."

"I have an apartment?" he asks coyly.

She flashes a vague, tolerant smile. "Yes. Would you please follow me? Your luggage has already been taken care of," she adds blithely. He follows her from the terminal to a Toyota van parked illegally in the passenger pickup area.

Racing down the deserted East Coast Parkway, she maintains a running tutorial on Singapore's modern infrastructure.

"Look, I appreciate the tour," Chris interrupts politely when she pauses for a breath. "But I've been here before, so please don't feel it's necessary."

Shikha lapses into a sullen silence.

"Yes. I realize you've been here before, *Captain*," she replies finally. "But then you were a '*businessman*'." she announces with a smirk, watching him closely for a reaction.

"I was – I am – a businessman," yawns Chris. "My company was bidding on a contract to provide billing system integration services to SingTel."

She snorts dismissively, her eyes surveying the road ahead.

"Shikha, my country's at war," he sighs. "I happen to be here now as a mobilized reservist. Don't be paranoid."

"Fine," she replies with exaggerated condescension. After several more minutes of silence, she continues. "Strangely, *our* records indicate Centennial Systems never *did* business in Singapore, *Captain*."

"It's called 'losing the bid', Shikha," he snaps. "If you'd spend some time in the private sector you'd understand the concept. ...And I would appreciate it if you would stop repeating *Captain* as if it's a nasty word. It's rude."

"Excuse me, S*ir*," she replies and falls silent. Chris watches her, eyes fixed on the road as if she's merely a disinterested chauffer. He reaches into his pocket and withdraws the card she handed him at the airport. It contains no job title.

"So, Shikha. What do you do for the Ministry of Defense?" he mocks. "*Protocol*?"

"Touché," she replies with a smirk. "Mainly I babysit foreign spies."

Chris chuckles. "Well that's a relief. Good of you to help-out on your night off."

Moments later the car draws into the circular driveway of Fraser Suites, an elegant high-rise apartment building. "This apartment building caters to foreign corporate executives," she explains as he emerges from the car. "So please introduce yourself using your cover."

Chris rolls his eyes in exasperation.

"Aren't you coming up to tuck me in?" he chides.

"A car from SID will retrieve you from the American Embassy tomorrow morning at 08:00," she replies dryly. "Is there anything you'd like me to keep under lock and key for you?"

"No thank you. You've been *most* helpful," he declares. The van pulls away and disappears down the abandoned street. He turns and recovers his luggage, heading for the front desk to check-in.

Alone in his apartment, Chris explores his new home. Furnished in classic European decor, it has blonde hardwood floors and modern Scandinavian-style furniture. Glancing up at the ornate light fixture in the ceiling, he wonders if someone really *is* recording his actions and immediately decides not to sleep in the nude. The idea of some police bureaucrat reviewing nude tapes of him leaves a sour feeling in the pit of his stomach.

He unzips his suit bag and arranges his clothes in a built-in armoire covering one entire wall of his bedroom. Then he reaches into his pocket, withdraws his cell phone and passes through the sliding glass doors onto the balcony. Even at this early hour of the morning the humidity is stifling.

Dialing a special U.S. Embassy number, he places the phone to his ear. He hears several clicks followed by a steady tone. Using the keypad, he inputs a series of numbers, disconnecting when the tone changes to a beep. The numerically-coded message is simple: I've arrived.

Monday morning, SID provides an unmarked car and driver to retrieve Chris from the palatial Mandarin building that serves as the U.S. Embassy. He slips into the back seat with a locked briefcase containing the classified briefing. The car moves nimbly through the early morning traffic with an ease that makes him wonder if there is some discreet marking on the vehicle that encourages others to move from its path. Beside him on the seat rests the English language Indonesian newspaper, The Jakarta Post. Glancing at the front page, he wonders if it was left intentionally:

SINGAPORE ROUNDS UP ALLEGED TERRORISTS

(AP) JAKARTA – Based on information supplied by U.S. intelligence, Singapore has been arresting Al Qa'ida linked extremists, said an unnamed U.S. official.

The information, allegedly contained in videotape discovered by U.S. troops in Afghanistan, purports to show American facilities in Singapore being cased by members of a previously unknown group called Jemmah Islamiya...

He sighs and shakes his head – there's been a leak. "This is going to be a long fucking day," he sighs.

"Sir?" asks the driver.

"Nothing," responds Chris. "I'm just wondering what time I'll need to leave to catch the next flight back to Honolulu."

The car rolls through a residential neighborhood filled with high-rise apartments and into a large, well-kept commons. Winding through the tree-lined park, it draws up in front of what appears to be a plantation surrounded by tall, dense hedges. A military policeman, assault rifle dangling from a sling over his shoulder, steps from the guardhouse, checks the driver's ID card, and waves them smartly through.

As they proceed up the curved driveway a large, modern white marble and glass office complex comes into view.

Uniformed and civilian personnel walk purposefully between the buildings. A sign to the right of the driveway indicates they have arrived at Headquarters, Singapore Ministry of Defense. As Chris studies the scene, the car slows and abruptly dodges left into an unmarked opening in one of the dissecting hedges. Another MP waves the car into a clearing filled with parked vehicles surrounding an unadorned white building.

This is SID headquarters.

As Chris emerges from the car, a tall, austere-looking man steps forward and offers his hand.

"Captain Gates?" he asks crisply.

"Yes, Sir," replies Chris as he shakes the man's hand.

"I'll be your escort. Please follow me." He escorts Chris through security and into a three-story atrium to a bank of elevators. As they await the elevator, Chris examines the two-story floor to ceiling abstract painting dominating the atrium.

"Intriguing, isn't it?" observes his escort. "It represents the many facets of intelligence."

"Yes, quite," agrees Chris, not entirely sure what the grids, dots and squiggly lines are meant to represent. He assumes that *is* the point.

The elevator carries them several levels below ground, where he follows his host to a large, high-tech conference room.

Several people mill around a stainless steel teacart laden with coffee, tea and small cakes. He recognizes one of them.

"Hi Shikha," murmurs Chris as he slips-up beside her and grasps a pastry. "Seen any spies lately?" he asks conspiratorially. She flashes him a sour look and shakes his hand.

"*Captain*," she mocks with a smile at their mutual joke and introduces him to the others.

They seem quite young. *Probably their second-string*, Chris notes with well-concealed disappointment as he alternately shakes hands and bows to his counterparts. Besides Shikha, only one of the remaining five analysts is female. All appear to be of Chinese or Indian descent, he observes. None are Malay, the dominant ancestry on the peninsula. He can't help but wonder at the significance.

Fortunately, he soon discovers his assumptions are incorrect. These *are* the senior analysts, each a specialist on nations of interest to Singapore. He recalls reading somewhere youth is a valued commodity in the Republic. While the elders retain quiet overall control, young people are rapidly placed in positions of responsibility. The relative youth standing around him seems to confirm it.

He also realizes the Chinese woman is in charge - clearly, sexism isn't an issue at SID. She introduces herself as Jessica Ling, the senior Indonesia analyst.

Encased in a smart navy blue suit and high heels, her lithe body moves like a cat as she steps from the darkened room to the floodlit podium to formally open the session. As she speaks in a British-educated accent, he's distracted by the way her high, elegant cheekbones bracket expressive almond shaped eyes; her full, slightly pouting lips move sensuously, in strange contrast to the academic tenor of her presentation. Her short jet-black hair makes her appear younger than what he supposes is her thirty-five years, but as an elegantly-manicured hand sweeps across the pages of her notes, she slips-on a pair of reading glasses that provides her an older, more intellectual air.

Despite her beauty, there is something intimidating about her, aloof, not quite cold but definitely on the chilly side - like some stern headmistress at an English girl's school. In his trance, he misses all but the gist of her few, perfunctory comments regarding shared values and the common threat before realizing she's turning the podium over to him.

Approaching the front of the room, he becomes painfully conscious of her eyes fixed critically upon him. He stumbles uneasily over his opening comments, noting the restrained smirk on her face. Finally overcoming his unease, he directs his attention to the other analysts who are leaning forward in their seats, soaking in every detail as he presents what the U.S. knows of the scattered remnants of the JI organization.

"On a related matter," Chris announces as he withdraws a report from within the specially marked envelope the admiral provided. "We understand there was a recent 'incident' resulting in the deaths of several SID operatives." The flashing eyes and sudden murmurs filling the room confirm he is indeed treading in sensitive territory.

Jessica pales. "Your information is incorrect," she declares icily. "There has been no 'incident' in Singapore."

"I'm glad to hear it," he responds softly. "Then presenting my report on the source of the explosives would be unnecessary." He slides the report back into its plain brown wrapper. Jessica glances sharply at Shikha, who shrugs helplessly.

"Of course, if there are explosives known to be circulating in the region, we would be interested in knowing where they came from," announces Jessica.

Chris nods and reproduces the report. "The explosive is Semtex, a Czech-made product created by combining Cyclonite and Pentaerythrite into a relatively stable gelatinized explosive," he reads. "Based on the metallic and odor 'fingerprint' associated with each lot, the explosive believed used in ... recent events," he explains generically, "was produced by Synthesia in 1996." He turns the page, glancing up at the uneasy stares of the assembled analysts.

"The 10-metric ton lot was delivered to the Republic of Iraq in 1998," he continues, "allegedly for use in oil exploration and demolition of structures left 'unstable' as a result of the 1991 Gulf War. We believe that in July of 2001, a portion of the lot was shipped from Basra, Iraq on the Cypriot-owned, Cambodian flagged vessel M.V. Arassa, arriving at Port Klang, Malaysia on August 5th. Through a series of cutouts, it appears the JI bomb-maker, Khalid, obtained 226 Kilograms of the Semtex from a contact at the port authority. He had the explosives woven inside lightweight vests by a tailor in Kulai."

He glances up from his notes. From the tragic expressions on the faces of his fellow analysts, Chris realizes he's struck fertile ground. "We believe the vests were delivered by truck across the Johor causeway to a Singaporean import/export company called East Asia Imports, owned by an Indonesian national named Kastari Bin Ali."

When he finishes speaking, the analysts turn imploringly to Jessica. "I have only one question," she announces.

"Yes?"

"What is the date of your information?"

He flips to the back page and reads the 'Information Cutoff Date'. "Three days ago," he replies.

Jessica nods and sighs, "thank you."

Chris departs the podium, drops into his seat and glances up expectantly, prepared for the reciprocal briefing. But to his surprise, the analysts stand as one, smile tensely and disappear single-file from the room, leaving Chris alone with his escort.

"What now?" asks Chris, staring blankly around the empty conference room.

"We are through," announces the man.

Chris rises. "No," he replies. "I don't think we are."

The man limps forward from the shadows, his craggy face sharpening as he steps into the light. "Pardon?"

"This was to be an *exchange*," insists Chris, anger rising in his voice. "No such thing has taken place."

Taken aback at Chris' brusqueness, the man blurts something in Mandarin before catching himself and switching quickly back to English. "It will take time," he purrs soothingly. "This was a *good start*."

"For you, yes," replies Chris coldly. "For the United States, I'd say it's been a waste of effort."

The man goes rigid. "Well. Your – people – haven't shown themselves particularly adept at keeping secrets, have they?"

Realizing his mission is in jeopardy; Chris casts caution to the wind.

"Sir, you know the leak didn't come from Pacific Command," he explains, attempting to control his temper as he slides his notes into the envelope marked SECRET//REL SGP. "It came from some publicity-seeking politician."

"None-the-less," interrupts the man. "That 'premature' revelation exposed an ongoing operation. Suspects fled. That *cannot* happen again!"

"Look, I can't fix what's happened in the past. I was sent to ensure information *you* provide goes only to the J2. That's as compartmentalized as it can be. If Colonel Mok trusts her, you'll have to trust me."

"He may trust her, but he doesn't *know* you."

"Then I'd say the relationship is over before it's started."

"That's is not for you to decide, *Captain*," scoffs the man.

Chris frowns and leans across the table, fixing his host with steely blue eyes.

"Sir," he replies. "I'm a reservist. If the Admiral wants to send me home to my comfortable civilian job, that's her privilege. I'm here because a bunch of extremists declared war on my country – *and yours*. My job is to exchange intelligence and if you don't want to play, I have damned little to lose by telling you to *get stuffed*."

He stuffs the classified briefing into his briefcase and stalks to the door.

"*Now* I'm ready to leave, Sir," he announces, eyes focused on the exit.

His escort remains motionless.

Chris chances a look over his shoulder. "Sir?" he asks.

"Sit down, Chris," sighs the man, motioning to Chris' previously occupied seat. Chris detects a hint of amusement in the old man's expressive eyes.

After glaring at his host for a few seconds, Chris returns slowly to his seat. The man presses a button on a speaker box, saying nothing. Moments later, the six analysts return to the room. A PowerPoint briefing flashes on the luminous screen at the front of the room. As if without interruption, Jessica draws a telescoping pointer from her jacket pocket and steps to the podium.

"We agree with your assessment that Khalid was operating in Johor. However, recent information places several of his confederates here..."

After a meticulous briefing, the analysts shake hands with Chris and bow politely, broad smiles all around. Jessica offers her hand; he is surprised by the firmness of her grip.

"Well done, Captain," she offers. "Your agency seems to have overcome its chronic ignorance of the threats against you."

He stares at her, stunned by her backhanded compliment. "*My* agency?"

"Yes. CIA," she challenges.

"I'm Army, Ms. Ling," he corrects.

"Of course you are," she purrs condescendingly before turning and strolling out the door.

As the last of the analysts leave the room, Shikha takes up the rear, winking conspiratorially at Chris, conveying in her own way the exchange is a success.

"Come," insists the old man, slipping his arm through Chris'. He leads Chris upstairs through security into the sweltering afternoon sun. As they stand outside in the tropical heat awaiting the car and driver from the SID motor pool, the man turns and peers wryly at Chris.

"Chris, you remind me of a quality I so much admire in Americans," he announces.

"What's that, Sir?"

"No 'bullshit,'" he replies with a grin.

Chris stares bemusedly at the craggy old man.

"Who *are* you?' he asks.

The old man looks up with a twinkle in his hawk-like eyes.

"My name is Mok," he replies. "Colonel Jimmy Mok."

From that point forward the exchange burgeons.

Chris soon realizes most significant intelligence is passed informally, usually under the guise of a casual conversation over drinks at any one of a number of bars in Singapore's fashionable Marina district.

It's during these exchanges Chris' control over his mission begins to slip imperceptibly from his grasp.

Were he not so desperately lonely, he might never have stumbled over the chink in Jessica's formidable armor. But over the course of numerous "unofficial" gatherings with the SID analysts, he notices her painfully appropriate demeanor begin to soften. On several occasions, he's embarrassed when she catches him watching her. But instead of the withering stare he expects, she blushes and glances away with uncharacteristic timidity.

Scenes of Jessica begin to invade his sleep; shocking, intimate dreams bleeding over into his otherwise public encounters with her and the other analysts. He becomes self-conscious, fearing she might sense his growing obsession. But the admiral was explicit – be wary of SID. So he checks his libido and focusses on the mission.

One evening the group meets on Clarke Quay at a nightclub clearly geared for more youthful clientele. Shikha is the instigator, declaring they need a *real* night on the town – no business; just play.

Arriving outside the bar that evening, Chris is stunned by the appearance of the attractive Indian analyst with the alluring brown eyes and puckish sense of humor. Already tall, her height is accented by high-heeled sandals and a pair of hip-hugging jeans clinging to her long, shapely legs. Smooth cocoa colored abs and a pierced navel peek from beneath her short tank top.

Jessica's conservative slacks and silk blouse, if not accenting her feminine form, do nothing to disguise her svelte runner's body. He wonders if her ubiquitous spiked heels are an affectation to close the height difference between them, but quickly dismisses such thoughts as figments of his own unrealized fantasies.

Soon after the group secures a table at the edge of the dance floor, Jessica's cell phone rings. She bends low to the table, pressing the device to her ear and plugging the other with her finger in a futile bid for silence.

"Come," purrs Shikha, grasping Chris' hand and dragging him toward the dance floor. "Let's dance. We'll see if we can make your Jessica jealous."

"What?" asks Chris in bewilderment as he stumbles reluctantly toward the crowd gyrating on the parquet floor. "*My* Jessica? What the hell are you talking about?"

Shikha laughs, drapes her arms loosely around his neck, and sways her hips alluringly to the music. "You're two of a kind," she teases. "Neither of you belong in a place like this," she observes, surveying the neon lights and lasers.

"You can't even dance," she laughs throatily. "But you never miss an opportunity to go out with us – especially when Jessica's along."

He feels his face burn. "Maybe it's my job," he growls defensively.

"You sound just like her," she laughs. "I've seen the way you look at each other when the other isn't watching. She's beautiful, isn't she?"

He doesn't answer at first, glaring defiantly at his tormentor. Then, "Yes," he admits finally.

"She shouldn't be alone anymore," announces Shikha vaguely. "God gives food to every bird, but does not throw it into the nest."

Chris peers at her inquiringly. "What's that supposed to mean?"

"It's an old Hindi proverb," she explains. "You're a bright guy. Figure it out." She pulls him closer and writhes in his arms.

Her eyes cut back to the table. "She's watching us now," murmurs Shikha. "What are you going to do?"

"What am I *supposed* to do?" he hisses.

Her eyes keep wandering to where Jessica is sitting before flitting inquisitively back to him. Finally, he can no longer resist. He glances toward the table in time to see Jessica stand up, sling her purse over her shoulder and stalk purposefully toward the exit.

"Damn!" he swears and slides from Shikha's arms, fighting his way through the crowd in pursuit of Jessica. Over the heads of the crowd on the dance floor, he spots her closing rapidly on the front door.

"Excuse me," he blurts as he stumbles into a small clutch of girls dancing together. A young woman grasps his arm and urges him back toward the writhing mass. "Please, I..." Mercifully his arm slides from her sweaty grip and he bolts toward the doors through which Jessica disappeared.

He bursts onto the crowded quay, glancing rabidly across a sea of late night partiers. He spots her standing at a quayside railing, staring across the water at the reflected lights of the city.

He takes several deep breaths and approaches her cautiously; unsure what to do next. "Jessica?" he asks in a low voice as he steps beside her and leans on the railing. She glances at him, and turns away.

"Jessica. Why did you leave?" he asks.

She shakes her head, still avoiding his gaze. "It's late," she responds with a lame shrug. "I have to go." As she turns to leave, he reaches out and grasps her arm. In a blinding flash, she spins, knocking loose his grip in one smooth professional blocking movement. He deflects her follow-up slap.

Plastic chairs clatter onto the cobblestone quay. People seated nearby stare in muted shock at the sudden eruption. Chris and Jessica stand glaring at each other.

"What do you *want* from me?" she demands.

"Just you," he replies softly. "Only you."

Breathing heavily, her eyes fix upon him. "*Why?*" she implores.

He shakes his head, amazed it isn't obvious in the way he looks at her, the way he becomes tongue-tied in her presence. "Because you're homely and stupid," he replies.

Her eyes widen as she stifles a startled laugh.

"And because when I close my eyes I can feel the subtle curve of your spine against my fingers; smell the musk of your arousal; taste the sweet perspiration inside your thigh..."

Her hand moves slowly to her gaping mouth as he continues.

"But mainly because I see you here and I can't touch you," he whispers, "though I want to desperately."

Her hand drops from her mouth; she licks her lips nervously. Staring into his honest, strikingly blue eyes she mutters weakly, "I'm not allowed."

"Neither am I," he replies, placing his hand cautiously on her arm. Her muscles tense beneath her sleeve then go suddenly slack.

"Where do you want to go?" she breathes.

"Anywhere," he moans.

Taking his hand in her sweating palm, "Come. I know a place," she announces huskily and leads him across the quay toward her parked car.

CHAPTER 3

"Anh khoé khô" the ambassador announces as he steps from behind his ornate, hand carved desk to greet his visitor.

"Khoé cám o'n," responds Major Tran Minh, U.S. Army Special Forces. "You still speak it well, Sir. Perhaps you'd like me to conduct the briefing in Vietnamese."

"No, Tran," laughs the ambassador. "It's been an awfully long time since the Mekong Delta." He turns to his secretary. "Ms. Garrett. Would you please get us a couple of coffees and see we're not disturbed?"

"Decaf, for me," adds Tran. "I'm still battling jet lag – I don't want to take sides."

The ambassador pushes the door shut and drops into the well-worn overstuffed burgundy leather chair beside a matching sofa.

"So what has Special Operations Command got you doing these days?"

"'Snoopin' and poopin'," chuckles Tran. "We're trying to determine whether China will play with us in the war on terror."

The ambassador nods knowingly. Parts of America's old Cold War adversaries – the former Soviet Union and Peoples' Republic of China – contain large Muslim majorities that serve as breeding grounds for Al Qa'ida.

Those states' cooperation in what is becoming known as the "War on Terrorism" will be critical.

"I'm on the flip side of a trip to Jining and Kashgar in Northwestern China," explains Tran as he selects an antique swagger stick from the ambassador's collection displayed on the mahogany bookcase. He reaches across the sofa and traces an imaginary circle around a portion of the map of Asia covering the wall of the ambassador's office. "We're trying to assess China's ability to stem Muslim extremist activity in the Xinjiang Province."

"Was this an 'official' visit?" asks the ambassador.

"Ah... no," replies Tran.

"I see. So, how's it looking?"

Tran peers at the spot on the map as if awaiting some sort of mystical inspiration from the innocuous orange blot representing China. Receiving no new wisdom he merely shrugs. "If we don't hammer on them too much about civil rights, they'll keep the extremists in check. But don't look for any kind of reconciliation."

The heavy, dark paneled office door slides quietly open and Ms. Garrett slips inside with a tray of coffee. "Mr. Ambassador," she interrupts smoothly as she places the silver tray on the table. "This classified message just arrived for you," she explains, laying a brown envelope on the tray.

"Can't it wait?" snaps the ambassador.

"No Sir. It's urgent from Admiral Lang at Pacific Command and pertains to Major Minh's presence."

The ambassador retrieves the envelope and reviews the message carefully, raising one eyebrow before passing it to Tran.

"That's the strangest Operations Order I've ever read," he admits. Tran reads the message with a similar startled reaction and hands it back.

"Pretty vague. It says I'm to advise 'current assets in place' for an operation into Kalimantan; Singapore will provide support," Tran announces. "Whose operation is this?"

"Actually, Major," corrects the ambassador, "I believe the term 'current assets' refers to the admiral's Counter-Terrorism liaison here in Singapore. It appears she wants you to... 'lend your expertise' to his operation," he clarifies.

Major Minh glances at him inquiringly. "Who is this 'liaison'?"

"I don't really know much about him," admits the ambassador. "He just comes and goes between our secure communications center and SID."

"Sir, he's in the outer office," adds the secretary. "He's the one who delivered the admiral's message."

Tran's face wrinkles as if he smells something bad. "Well let's see what they've gotten me into," he announces dubiously. The secretary opens the office door and motions to the silent figure seated on an elegant oriental sofa in the outer office.

A tall, 40-ish man in gray tropical wool slacks, blue and white striped Brooks Brother's shirt, and silk Jerry Garcia tie enters the office. The ambassador offers his hand. "Good to see you again, Chris." He motions toward the man standing beside the sofa. "Captain Chris Gates. I'd like you to meet Major Tran Minh."

The men turn to greet each other. A stunned expression erupts on Tran's face, contrasting with Chris' surprised grin. "I'll be damned," Tran mutters.

"Hi 'LT'," Chris announces as he offers his hand. "Long time, no see."

Tran's mouth work dumbly, he's speechless, as though staring at a ghost. "My God!" he replies finally, grasping Chris' hand in an anxious grip. "I thought you'd dropped off the end of the earth."

"Rumors of my demise are greatly exaggerated," Replies Chris grimly. His half-smile fades. "It's great to see you again, Sir," he adds. The two men stare silently at each other as the ambassador and his secretary look-on in amused confusion.

"So I take it you gentlemen have met before," the ambassador chides.

"Um... yes," Tran stammers, his face turning toward the ambassador but his eyes remaining locked on Chris as if afraid by switching his gaze the apparition might vanish.

"Sergeant... I mean Captain Gates and I served together in the '80s," Tran explains as his eyes break reluctantly from Chris. "I was a young lieutenant back then," he explains to the ambassador. "He kept me out of trouble more often than I care to admit." His attention returns to Chris.

"I lost track of you after El Paraiso..." His voice fades and he glances around sheepishly, realizing no one else in the room would have ever heard of the backward, anonymous village in northern El Salvador.

Several hours later, an unmarked van rolls slowly up to a seldom-used gate at Changi Naval Base. The guards, on a heightened state of alert due to recent terrorist events, shift their MP5 submachine guns nervously toward the vehicle. The sergeant of the guard steps cautiously to the van's window and asks the driver for identification. A civilian in the passenger seat reached across the driver and passes the sergeant a laminated ID card. He's rewarded with marked change in the sergeant's demeanor.

"Yes Sir," he barks, snapping to attention.

"Area 5," announces the man. "No escort."

"Yes Sir," repeats the sergeant. He turns, motions discreetly for the guards to lower their weapons and steps into the concrete blockhouse. After a brief, terse phone conversation the reinforced chain-link electronic gates creak open and the retractable barrier collapses into the ground.

Once inside the facility, the panel van rolls past sleek, gray patrol boats swaying gently alongside immaculate, freshly painted piers. Navy trainees jog past in formation paying scant attention as the unmarked van winds its way through the narrow streets of the whitewashed training area and disappears over a small rise.

On the opposite side of the hill at the end of a short, seldom used dirt road stands a sun-bleached two-story concrete warehouse and several piers surrounded by a razor wire topped fence. The foreboding structure stands aloof, orphaned from the remainder of the base like some insane relative thought too unstable to be exposed to polite company. The van stops at the gate and a member of Singapore's elite Guards unit appears from inside a lonely gray concrete blockhouse to open the barrier.

As the van continues through the gate and down the driveway toward the seemingly abandoned warehouse, two more soldiers wrest open the building's doors to allow the van to enter, then immediately slide the doors shut and resume their walking patrol.

Colonel Mok steps with a limp from the passenger seat and raps on the side of the van. As head of SID Counter-Terrorism Strike Force, he carries the weight of the world on his narrow shoulders. With more than 40-years conducting special operations in Southeast Asia, he's protected Singapore as it evolved - as Senior Minister Lee Kuan Yew called it - from Third World to First. Now his challenge is to ensure Muslim extremists operating in Malaysia, Indonesia, and the southern Philippines don't ply their trade in the Lion City. It's becoming an increasingly awesome responsibility.

Responding to his knock, the back door of the van pops open and out clatter three men in civilian clothes. They immediately begin unloading their equipment as Colonel

Mok stands watching quietly, an oddly paternal look on his normally impassive face.

A civilian rushes into the cavernous bay and strides purposefully to the colonel, thrusting a message into his outstretched hand. "From the American Embassy, Sir," he reports. The colonel eyes the self-important young man, snatches the note and nods, acknowledging receipt and dismissing the courier. His left eye twitches as he scrutinizes the message. A thin smile creases his weathered face.

"Looks like you get to go on a boat trip," he announces with a grin, handing the note to Tran. "Operation Gold Leaf is a 'go'."

Tran reads the message and grunts his acknowledgement, passing it without comment to Chris, who reviews the message. "I didn't realize we were this desperate," Chris mumbles

Tran response with a strained smile. "TF 510 is tied up with the Abu Sayyef in the Philippines," he announces. "It's us or nothing."

"Like I said…"

"Aw, come-on, Admiral Lang says you've been whining about going operational ever since you arrived in her command."

"You talked to Lang?"

"I spoke briefly on the STU-III from the Embassy. She doesn't like it, but gave her blessing."

"God help us," Chris grunts. He grasps the handle on one end of a long green fiberglass case. "Jon!" he shouts to the third man who's climbed from the back of the van. "Give me a hand getting this to the boat."

They half-carry, half-drag the heavy container full of weapons to a dilapidated civilian boat and heave it over the rail onto the scarred deck.

Singapore's Coast Guard confiscated the 75-foot Indonesian fishing vessel from its previous owner for illegally running counterfeit cigarettes through the Strait of Singapore. Despite outward appearances, it has a reinforced hull and is outfitted with powerful new engines, allowing it to outrun the patrol boats used by most Southeast Asian police forces. Now in the hands of Singapore's special operations directorate, it's equipped for "special duty," frequently with a false name, hull number and national flag.

Chris glances at the plaque above the cabin and notes the boat had "morphed" into the Indonesian flagged vessel "Prince Hidayat." The new sign is suitably weathered to match the rough wood exterior and faded, chipped paint in colors Chris assumes had once been gaudy, upbeat hues but which have since run to the depressing pallor of fruit rotting untended on the vine. Nevertheless, the Prince Hidayat is mechanically sound and utterly seaworthy, its frank banality permitting it to mingle unnoticed among the other unremarkable vessels plying local waters.

He enters the small weather-beaten pilothouse and conducts a radio check. As with the boat's other features, the powerful transmitter/receiver has been modified within its unassuming box, the antennae concealed in the aging vessel's upper deck. In keeping with the boat's covert role, the cabin is artfully strewn with empty Bintang and Bali Hai beer bottles, Asam Garan cigarette butts and tattered charts of the Java Sea and Strait of Malacca. The cabin reeks of stale cigarette smoke and the stench of rotting fish.

He rummages through a small compartment to the right of the throttle and withdraws a World War I-era Colt M1911 model .45 caliber automatic pistol, its once matte-gray finish worn shiny by years of careless concealment. The venerable .45 is as commonplace as piracy in Southeast Asian waters. Its easy access near the helm is reassuring and its presence on the vessel will not raise suspicion if the boat is searched. He removes the magazine and jacks-back the slide. After quick inspection, he reinserts the magazine, chambers a round, and carefully lowers the hammer.

"Sir?" The unexpected interruption startles Chris. He slips the .45 back into the compartment and turns to Jon, his Gurkha bodyguard. Jon stands nearly at attention – a habit Chris had tried unsuccessfully to break for several months. Even clad in civilian baggy black shorts and shirt there is no mistaking his military bearing.

"Jeez, Jon," laughs Chris. "You look like a VC."

"VC?"

"'Viet Cong'," elaborates Chris. Jon's frown makes clear his disdain for the association. "I'm just kidding," Chris sighs. "What is it?"

"Colonel Mok is ready for the final brief, Sir," he announces crisply as if reporting that all troops are present and accounted for.

"Right," replies Chris and follows Jon out the cabin door. As they cross a deck cluttered with fishing nets and other innocent paraphernalia, Chris spots the brass tip of a Khukuri sheath hanging slightly below Jon's shirttail. The Khukuri, an 18" curve bladed machete, is traditionally carried by the Nepalese Gurkhas. Now under cover, Jon is wearing his beneath his baggy civilian shirt.

Chris takes several exaggerated steps, closing quickly with the smaller man. "You shouldn't be carrying that," he mumbles over Jon's shoulder as he thumps the back of the sheath.

"Yes, Sir," Jon replies, but makes no attempt to remove it.

Chris grins. *Pure Gurkha. I'll bet he sleeps with it.*

Charged with Chris' security, Singapore takes no chances. When he travels through the region, it's Jon's job to keep him from harm. Though Jon usually travels without a weapon, his hand-to-hand combat skills are exceptional and his willingness to sacrifice himself, unshakable. Protecting

Chris is more than his duty; it's a point of honor Jon traces without question to generations of Gurkha warriors before him.

Jon isn't his bodyguard's real name. It's a bastardized pronunciation of "Jambulung." Unlike most of the Gurkha mercenaries employed by Singapore's national police, Jon actually served at one time in the British Army's Gurkha Brigade. A long scar on the left side of his face bears witness to hostile action. Chris would like to know how Jon received the wound, but soldiers don't ask each other such questions. And, truth be told, he's afraid the answer will be a disappointment.

Chris follows Jon to the entrance of a large briefing room situated in the corner of the warehouse. Entering the room, Chris encounters the efforts of an anemic air conditioner wheezing miserably from a hole in the wall, filling the room with damp, barely cooled air reeking of Freon and stale seawater. Posted on a long whitewashed wall are several oversized nautical charts and enlarged aerial photographs. Tran is already seated, as are several Republic of Singaporean Navy (RSN) officers and Colonel Mok. Jon closes the door behind Chris and does not join them in the room.

"Good afternoon, Gentlemen," announces Jessica Ling. Chris smiles at the sight of her. After all, there's something exhilarating about encountering her innocently among colleagues when her musk still lingers on his breath.

"I apologize for the delay," Jessica continues. "But some new information has come in from your JICPAC," she announces, presenting a one-page message to Chris. As he scans the message, Jessica provides a summary for Tran and Colonel Mok.

"Your contacts were nearly apprehended by the Indonesian paramilitary police in Palankaraya this afternoon. There were apparently shots fired and your agent was wounded. Extraction must proceed immediately or we'll lose the opportunity."

She approaches the map board and traces the contour of the south-central part of the island with her finger, resting it on a small nipple of terrain jutting into the Java Strait.

"Pacific Command has arranged a new pickup site south of Kendawangan on the Sembar Peninsula." She opens her folder and hands them each an 8"x10" aerial photo.

"I didn't have time to have them enlarged, but you can clearly see a radio tower quite near the coast. There will be your landmark," she explains. "Here are the geo coordinates." She hands Chris a small piece of paper. He glances at it and slides it into his pocket without comment.

"Because the extraction point is nearly one hundred miles further east than originally planned, you'll need extra time to reach it." She glances at her watch. "Extraction has been pushed-out to 0600."

"Shit," declares Tran. "It puts us in hostile waters in daylight!"

"Fate has intervened, my friend," interjects Colonel Mok, stepping away from the wall against which he was leaning and placing his hands solemnly on the edge of the table. "You have at least one wounded; your people must be withdrawn immediately."

"The encounter with the POLRI delayed them," adds Jessica, "but they can neither make it to West Kalimantan nor wait until tomorrow night. The Jihadists have the scent, so unless you're willing to write-off your agent..."

"Fine," concludes Chris, abruptly ending the discussion. Tran glances at him darkly and shakes his head without comment. "Tran, we're on an Indonesian boat," explains Chris, trying to put a positive spin on the information. "We'll be fine." Tran appears skeptical but remains silent. Jessica continues.

"Of course it means your rendezvous time with the naval escort on the return will change also. Make it 09:15. Questions?"

"Just one," asks Tran. "Who's our control?" The control officer will coordinate the mission from start to finish, providing whatever support necessary to conduct the operation.

Jessica defers to Colonel Mok.

"Ms. Ling," he replies, nodding toward Jessica.

Chris glances at her sharply. *So she's not just an analyst,* he notes.

She ignores the look on his face and immediately takes charge. "Okay," she announces. "Strip!"

Chris' head snaps up. "What?!"

"Sterilization..."

"No thanks," mutters Chris. "I still plan to have children."

"This is a black op," she replies, a hint of rebuke in her otherwise professional tone. "There must be nothing to connect you with your country - or mine."

Chris eyes her skeptically.

"Standard precautions," she adds innocently, handing out plastic zip lock bags in which to place their personal items and identification.

While they empty their pockets, she lays out their new credentials on the table before them.

Chris sorts through the documents and holds up his new passport. "I'm German?" he asks dubiously.

"Well you certainly don't look Indonesian," snorts Jessica. "Besides your dossier says you speak the language."

"My dossier? Why Ms. Ling, are you keeping tabs on me?"

"Like you're not keeping them on *me*," she grunts.

Chris laughs politely. *Actually, no I'm not,* he admits to himself. *But I apparently should.* He fingers the passport uneasily. "What if we get picked up by the Indonesian authorities?" he pursues. "My cover won't make it past the German Embassy."

She rolls her eyes. "If you get picked up by the POLRI, you'll have a hell of lot more to worry about than your national identity. These things," she announces, waving her hand across the documents on the table, "are to help keep you *out* of the hands of the authorities."

Chris shrugs his acceptance and sifts through the remaining documents. Besides the passport, he has a driver's license with a Heidelberg address, business cards identifying him as a visiting professor at the intercultural Goethe Institut Jakarta, some Euros, and several hundred thousand Indonesian Rupiah. Behind the money clip is a dog-eared photo of someone's children with their German names scrawled by hand on the back. "Nice touch," he comments.

"We find people are less suspicious of family men," she explains patiently. "If asked, you should also say you're divorced or widowed. It helps with women," she adds.

"You sound like my pimp," he observes dryly.

"No," she smiles sweetly, folding his wallet closed and handing it back to him, "just your control officer."

"What about Jon and Mr. Soo?" asks Tran.

"They have their usual covers," she replies dismissively as she places a large plastic tub full of clothes on the conference table. "Now get changed."

Tran rummages through the container, grabbing a pair of brown shorts and a black shirt, both of Indonesian manufacture.

"Where do we change?" he asks.

"Here," replies Jessica. "We have to ensure you are not *accidentally* hiding anything that might compromise you."

"Okay!" he announces enthusiastically. He slips out of his Wranglers and Tiger Beer T-shirt, then turns with uncharacteristic shyness and steps out of his American-made underwear.

While Tran dresses in the "sterile" clothes provided, Chris digs through the pile. "Um. No offense, but this is all Asian-sized," he observes, dropping a pair of ridiculously small shorts back into the tub.

"I hadn't thought of that," admits Jessica. "Sir?" she asks turning to Colonel Mok, "he's definitely larger than our average agent."

The colonel glances at his watch. "You have two hours. I suppose you had better take him shopping."

"On 'The Department?'" asks Chris coyly.

Colonel Mok nods and tosses the van keys to Jessica. "Keep him out of sight until you're off base," he reminds her.

The van skids to a stop at a roadside rest area just beyond the base gate. Chris hears keys rattle in the lock and the back door pops open.

"Want to ride up front like a civilized person?" asks Jessica.

"Sure," replies Chris as he stumbles from the van and snatches the keys from her hand. "But I'm driving – you drive like shit." She kicks him playfully in the backside. "Bastard," she swears with a disarming smile.

He loves the way she draws-out the letter "a." *So I'm a baaaastard now*, he thinks with a grin as he proceeds toward the driver's side while she climbs into the passenger seat. He starts the engine and pops the clutch, sending the van careening onto the East Expressway toward the Orchard Road shopping area.

"Why don't we try Manchester United?" he asks, referring to the clothier named for the famous British soccer team. "That should cost the Department some bucks."

"Hmmm. A bit too fashionable," she replies analytically. "Not bloody likely to be found on an Indonesian fishing boat." She reaches beneath the seat and retrieves a sack. "Here," she announces offhandedly, dropping the package unceremoniously into his lap.

"What's this?" he asks, trying to keep his eyes on the road as he fumbled to open the sack.

"Your clothes," she replies simply. "Exit at the next left," she directed.

"My...?"

"We're not going shopping," she announces. "I've already got something for you to wear."

"Then...?"

"We're going to the safe house on Napier Road."

"What's there?"

"Just us."

CHAPTER 4

The "safe house" is actually a second-story apartment nestled at the end of a cul-de-sac on a small street off Napier Road, not far from the Embassy. They have barely entered the apartment when Jessica pins Chris against the foyer wall and pulls his lips down to hers. The kiss is deep and passionate, like a woman saying farewell.

She struggles to unbuckle his belt. "The damned air's off," she moans as the stifling heat washes over them.

"I love it when you talk dirty," he chuckles, his hands sliding down her sides as he jerks the silk blouse from her pants and pulls it up over her head, exposing small round breasts encased in a black satin bra. He reaches to release her brassiere.

"Stop it," she giggles and slaps his hands out of the way. She jerks his Polo shirt over his head and flings it to the floor, then rips his belt from its loops and tosses it across the hall. Working frantically, she unbuttons his pants and let them drop around his ankles.

She reaches down and grabs him.

"Here?" he asks, glancing anxiously around the foyer.

"MmmmHmmm..." she pants.

Nearly forty-five minutes later, they stand together in the shower, cool water flowing over their intertwined bodies.

Something occurs to him.

"You said this is a safe-house," he recalls.

"Yes," she replies reaching for the shampoo. "We use it to debrief agents coming in from the field. Why?"

"So it's wired, isn't it?"

She draws away and looks him in the eye. "Very good, Chris. Yes, usually. But the system is off right now."

"Too bad," he chuckles.

"Ah!" she gasps. "You're such a pervert."

"Glad you noticed."

She has just finished drying her hair when she glances down at her watch on the vanity. "Oh, hell!" she curses, reading the time. "We've got to get back!"

"Do we?" he replies, placing his hands on her shoulders and lightly kissing the back of her neck. Shivers crawl down her spine as she shrinks from his grasp.

"Yes," she laughs. "People are waiting."

"But won't someone notice the towel bar missing?" he asks teasingly, pointing to the recent damage to the shower stall.

"Fog of war. You surprised me," she chortles, tucking the blouse into her slacks and stepping into her high heels.

"I didn't hear any complaints," he goads.

She tosses him a pair of hiking boots. "God, no..." she purrs, a crooked smile on her lips. Watching him fumble with his pants, she becomes annoyed. "Let me help," she insists as she finishes buttoning his Malaysian-made black cotton shirt.

Moments later, Chris bounds out the front door, taking the stairs two at a time, his old clothes wadded up in the shopping bag swinging wildly in his hand. Jessica locks the apartment door and hesitates.

"I'll be right back," she shouts from the top of the stairs. He throws his hands in the air and mouths, "what?" She waves him off impatiently and disappears inside the apartment.

In a coat closet off the foyer, she removes the false front from the fuse box and switches off the video and audio recording devices. She comes galloping down the stairs, her high heels clicking loudly on the concrete steps. She pulls open the driver's side door. "Get in back," she orders breathlessly. "We won't have time to switch later."

"Why'd you go back inside?" asks Chris as he slides from the driver's seat and she replaces him behind the wheel.

"I forgot to turn on the alarm system," she lies. He climbs into the back of the van, having barely shut the doors when Jessica grinds the van into gear and lurches out of the driveway.

"I'm jealous," quips Tran as Chris climbs unsteadily from the rear of the van.

"Don't be. That was the most horrifying ride of my life," Chris laughs, despite a guilty smirk on his face.

"It may get worse," advises Tran, nodding toward a navy colonel that has appeared in Chris' absence – it is a constant enigma to Chris why, unlike the rest of the world, Singapore insists on its naval officers using army ranks. But at least it avoids confusion over seniority. The officer is standing by the conference room door, speaking solemnly with Colonel Mok.

"Problem?"

"Seems there are weather issues," Tran mumbles as they walk together toward the conference room.

"Good afternoon, Sir," Chris greets the navy officer. "Come to see us off?"

The colonel looks at him and replies brusquely, "Perhaps *not.*"

Tran and Chris follow the two colonels into the conference room where Jessica is already studying a typed one-page report. She glances up as they enter. "Does this mean the mission's off?" she asks.

"Off?" snaps Chris. "I don't think so!" He reaches for the report and Jessica reluctantly passes it to him. He scans it quickly.

"What's the bottom line, Sir?"

"A low pressure zone is widening, moving south and east..." the navy officer begins.

"So?" interrupts Chris.

"I don't recommend going under these circumstances," he announces flatly. "*Our* vessels will be restricted to the Strait for the next 48 hours."

Chris looks to Tran for guidance. To his relief, Tran nods for Chris to say what was on his mind. He fixes his stare upon the officer.

"Sir," he begins, picking his words carefully. "The 'circumstances' are we have agents out there on the run and apparently shot to hell." His voice begins to rise. "They have critical information and if we don't go, they're dead. Now, in light of those '*circumstances*'," he snaps with a little more sarcasm than intended. "Is it still possible for us to get there and back in THIS weather," he asks, holding up the report. "And in THAT boat?" he growls, motioning toward the docks.

The colonel purses his lips but hesitates to respond. Major Lim, commander of their naval escort, springs to his feet. "Sir," he announces. "I am confident Dominion can get these gentlemen to the rendezvous and back, despite the weather."

The colonel shoots him an angry look. "Our vessels are not going anywhere, Major!"

Colonel Mok has been leaning against the doorjamb watching the exchange.

"Colonel," he announces quietly. "It's no longer your decision." He walks slowly into the room, his head bowed as he ponders his team's predicament. The navy colonel opens his mouth to argue, but Colonel Mok raises a cautionary hand. "If these gentlemen are still willing to go, the Republic will provide full support."

Realizing Colonel Mok is speaking on the authority of the Ministry of Defense, the navy officer demurs.

Chris thinks for a moment before addressing Jessica. "Look, if the weather is going to get ugly, why doesn't Jon stay behind? I don't need a bodyguard out there anyway."

Jessica looks to Colonel Mok. "Sir?"

"No," replies the colonel firmly. "Jon's a good man and you may find need of him."

Chris shrugs. "Okay. But if the weather turns out to be as bad as predicted, he's gonna *hate* you after this."

As Chris and Tran depart to complete the boat's load-out, the door creaks slowly shut behind them.

"He doesn't realize the extent of Jon's role, does he?" asks Jessica in monotone.

"Of course not," responds Colonel Mok quietly.

Major Lim's Fearless Class Missile Patrol Boat, RSS Dominion, escorts the Prince Hidayat down the inlet from Changi to the Strait of Singapore. Beneath iron skies they navigate still calm waters, weaving between ships and tankers floating at anchor inside the harbor. Chris stands on the quarterdeck enjoying the fresh sea air and peering out over the most heavily transited seaport in the world.

Cargo vessels vie for anchorage alongside massive container ships that await unloading and transshipment of cargoes to other ports throughout the world. Mammoth supertankers and LPG vessels lay at anchor in the distance, far from the populated area.

Visible behind towering cranes and stacked cargo containers is the island city-state of Singapore, its immense ultra-modern glass buildings set among the manicured foliage of once-dense jungle. Chris turns and peers south toward Indonesia and is immediately struck by the contrast between the beckoning safety of his 'home port' and the threatening skies ahead.

Beyond the anchorage, the two boats cross the international transit lane and skirt Indonesian waters near the island of Pulau Batam where, as prearranged, the Prince Hidayat takes the lead. Dominion shadows a quarter mile behind and several hundred meters off the port quarter. Bearing south-southeast, they proceed toward the coast of Kalimantan.

After five hours at sea, the sky becomes pitch-black but for occasional eruptions of blinding white lightning. The pilothouse is lit solely by the eerie green glow emanating from the instruments on the helm. No one has spoken for at least an hour, each man lost in his own thoughts. Finally Tran catches Chris' attention and motions silently toward the ladder leading below deck. Chris nods and follows him into the bowels of the boat.

Tran closes the wardroom door and turns on the dim yellow light. Nearby, Jon lay snoring lightly in a swaying hammock strung in the shadows between two beams, his Khukuri cocked sideways and hanging off to one side. *I'll be damned, he does sleep with it,* Chris reflects with a smile. The Prince Hidayat rocks forward and back then keels sideways, alternating erratically as the bow rises and falls, waves slamming into the starboard side and tossing the boat like a toy in a rambunctious child's bath.

"So are you going to tell me?" asks Tran.

Chris looks back at him in bewilderment. "Tell you what?"

Tran leans against the worn wooden table mounted to the bulkhead. He frowns momentarily then elaborates. "Are you going to tell me about these 'people' we are going to recover?"

Chris is stunned, assuming the Admiral briefed Tran about their mission. Fortunately his astonishment appears obvious to Tran, who smiles when he realizes Chris is not merely being coy. Chris' eyes cut to Jon still snoring in his hammock. He steps closer to Tran, his hand braced on an overhead beam, steadying himself against the effects of a violent sea. His voice is barely audible over the roar of the engines and crashing waves.

"They're Defense HUMINT 'assets'," he murmurs.

Tran nods for Chris to continue.

"It's an Indonesian couple," Chris explains. "He's in the lumber business in Balikpapan and she works for a maritime insurance company."

"You've been running agents?" asks Tran. "I thought you said you were here as 'liaison'."

"Actually I inherited them," explains Chris, side-stepping the awkward distinction Tran is attempting to draw.

"They've been on DIA's payroll for a long time," Chris continues, "mainly reporting on corruption in the Kalimantan lumber industry and commercial piracy stuff in the region. But last month, *he* showed up at the embassy in Singapore and demanded to see a DIA rep. They turned him over to me."

"But you're not an agency guy," observes Tran. "Are you?" he adds as an afterthought.

"Well. No. But he didn't need to know," Chris shrugs. "After all, a contact is a contact. The point is he had urgent information he needed to sell."

"Which was?"

Chris glances again at the sleeping Gurkha. He lowers his voice another octave and murmurs, "Khalid." Having spoken the forbidden word, he reclines against the bulkhead and continues. "Our guy spotted him in a Kalimantan village about a hundred miles northwest of Samirinda."

Tran lets out a low whistle.

"No kidding," snorts Chris. "JICPAC scrambled to get some cash and have me send him back to locate the son-of-a-bitch. SOCPAC wanted to send a team to conduct a snatch operation once we have his location pinned-down. My guy was just supposed to find out what he could about Khalid's whereabouts. But a few days ago he got too inquisitive and blew his cover. He's been on the run ever since."

"So did he locate Khalid?" asks Tran.

"He says so. But he won't tell us anything until we get him and his wife safely off the island".

"How did the Sings get involved?" asks Tran.

"We had to move fast and, as you said, Special Ops got tied up in the Philippines," explains Chris. "So Singapore's the only game in town. Well," he corrects. "Singapore and us."

"What do the Sings get out of it?" Tran wonders aloud.

"The info and the agent."

"But if he's blown, what good is he to them?"

Chris smiles cynically. "My bet is he's been playing a double game, so they probably don't want him in the hands of Indonesian authorities any more than we do. Besides, SID probably wants to pump him dry of whatever information remains."

Tran considers this for a moment then smiles. "I like this guy already," he chuckles.

"Well, it might not come to anything," warns Chris. "As Jessica said, the POLRI nearly nailed them in Palangkaraya last night. Now he's wounded and his wife is our main point of contact."

"The JI are connected with the national police?"

"According to our guy, the local POLRI commander is on the Jemmah Islamiya payroll."

"Damn!" swears Tran. "What about the rest of the government?"

Chris shrugs. "Some are with us. Some are against us. The problem is we don't know who *they* are. So the bottom line is: we're on our own."

Soon after the Prince Hidayat disappears over the hazy horizon, Jessica moves her team's operations to Changi's sophisticated communications center. To minimize the risk of communications intercept, they're tracking the Prince Hidayat passively through its GPS transceiver. If movement ceases before the boat reaches its destination, Jessica will know the vessel is in trouble. If so, Mr. Soo will break radio silence and signal Dominion for help – at least so long as they remain in international waters.

"Where are they now, Mr. Namur?" Jessica asks the communications sergeant for the hundredth time in the last 15 hours. She's as exhausted as she appears. Her silk blouse hangs un-tucked from her slacks and a strand of hair keeps falling irritatingly over one eye. She brushes the hair absently out the way and peers over the sergeant's shoulder at the map on his monitor.

"Here, Ma'am," he replies, indicating a position off the southwest coast of Kalimantan, "about an hour from landfall." As instructed, Jessica picks up the phone and dials a familiar number.

"Sir, our guests have reached the 'hotel,'" she announces elliptically, though they were on a secure line.

"Fine," responds Colonel Mok casually. "Keep me posted."

"Yes Sir," she replies drearily.

He detects the tone of her voice. "It's in fate's hands now, child," he reminds her gently.

"Yes, Sir. Goodnight." She drops the phone into its cradle and sighs heavily.

"I'm going out for some air, Mr. Namur," she announces suddenly, as if the thought has just occurred to her. She walks aimlessly from the secure room and out of the communications center before deciding to head upstairs to the galley, kept open 24 hours to accommodate personnel working the night shift. She orders a bowl of char kuey teow and carries it through sliding glass doors onto the balcony, where she leans on the railing and gazes out at the southern sky, picking absently at her meal.

The skies are clear over Singapore, but distant flashes illuminate for fleeting moments the dense, ominous clouds over Indonesia. Despite the 80-degree evening, she shivers at the thought of what it must be like in a small fishing vessel at sea in such dreadful weather.

A sultry breeze wafts into shore as she closes her eyes and recalls the events of the past year; events that shattered her life, shook her confidence and raised passions she'd never known existed.

Her mind drifts back to an incident last year when she was assigned to collect intelligence against a member of the People's Republic of China's embassy staff.

SID believed the man's position as clerk in the consular department was a cover for intelligence activities. The Chinese of course recognized people were their weakest link, so all except the ambassador and certain trusted members of the staff were required to live in a dormitory on embassy grounds where each was kept carefully under observation.

SID's "watchers" kept the embassy under surveillance around the clock, notifying Jessica whenever her target left the compound. She tailed him for several months, studying his interests and habits before making her approach. Her reconnaissance finally paid off when she discovered he was a collector of Western classical music.

One afternoon at Tanglin Mall, just blocks from the embassy, she managed to insert herself into a conversation he was having with a clerk at the music store.

"No. No. Bach is far superior to Mozart," he was insisting to an intransigent clerk.

"I particularly love Bach's organ pieces," Jessica interjected as she placed a boxed collection of Bach's fugues on the black marble counter. "They're probably the greatest compositions ever written."

He turned with a start to the woman who'd so rudely interrupted, fully intending to tell her to mind her own business. But her disarming smile left him speechless.

"Really?" he asked in a mocking voice. "*You* know Bach?"

"Of course," she announced with an air of juvenile arrogance. "I'm a graduate music student at the National University." She offered her hand. "I'm Susan Yip."

He smiled widely, providing his Embassy cover name before launching into a soliloquy on the finer points of Bach's compositions. Jessica forced herself to gaze adoringly into his eyes, like an addict inhaling an intoxicating drug.

"Wow, you really are an aficionado," she giggled. The squat, aging clerk in the shiny blue slacks and frayed short-sleeved white button-down beamed with benign superiority.

She met his piggish eyes, suddenly averting her gaze shyly to the floor as she carefully staged the "hook" to draw him into her trap. "There's a music festival at University Cultural Center next week," she said tentatively. "Might you like to join me?"

He stiffened. "Well. I'm... I'm not sure of my schedule," he stammered, caught off guard by the young beauty making an apparent pass at him.

"It's all right," she gushed, scrawling her cell phone number on the back of her receipt and forcing it into his reluctant hands. "Please," she implored. "If you can make it. We can meet there."

As the festival drew near, he still hadn't called. Shikha took particular pleasure needling her friend.

"Don't worry," she purred as she leaned against Jessica's desk, her long, cocoa legs bare beneath her conservative skirt. "Maybe you're just not his type," she chided with an unconscious shake of her glimmering black waist-length hair.

Jessica peered sourly over the tops of her reading glasses as she removed her target's photo from the case file and tossed the folder aside. She presented the photo and Shikha cringed.

"Maybe I should have blacked out some teeth and padded my hips," Jessica scoffed.

Shikha laughed. "Maybe grown a penis, too," she added and the women burst out laughing.

"I'm out of ideas," Jessica admitted. "You're welcome to make the next play," she snorted in frustration. "Besides, Peter doesn't like me using my body for recruiting purposes."

"I can't imagine he would," Shikha snorted.

"*So*, I have these tickets to this great music festival," Jessica announced in an artificially cheery voice. "Want to join me?"

Shikha laughed. "He'll call. He's just being male..."

Jessica's cell phone began to chirp. She glanced at the caller ID and grinned, holding up a hand for silence as she placed the phone onto its recording cradle and slipped-on the headset. Pushing "Record," she leaned back in her chair.

"Hello? This is Susan," she answered innocently, casting an arrogant expression of triumph at her friend.

A hesitant voice on the other end of the call began by thanking her for the invitation, "But..."

He's trying to slip off the hook, she realized. *Just a push*, she decided. *Something to sweeten the deal.*

"A friend just provided me orchestra-level seats," Jessica gushed. "Eighth row center!" Overwhelmed by her girlish enthusiasm, he quickly agreed to meet her.

Throughout the series of concerts she hung continuously on his arm, touching him affectionately and laughing with delight at his otherwise tedious stories. Strangers looked-on with unabashed envy as the squat, aging clerk swept the beautiful young woman off her feet. Unaccustomed to such envy, he reveled in the onlookers' esteem.

While at dinner at an Indian restaurant that evening, she slipped sodium amytal into his cardamom tea, making him utterly pliable as she lured him to the apartment off Napier Road. It was of course the "corporate" apartment - owned by SID and fully wired for sound and video. There, she attempted to seduce him. But it quickly became apparent it was her company, not the drug, lowering his libido.

"It's all right," she purred understandingly, cradling him tenderly and soothing him while he tried to explain his love for women, but his attraction to men.

"Perhaps you need a combination of both," she said consolingly.

He squinted up at her through teary eyes. "Yes! Yes!" he sobbed, relieved someone finally understood.

She smiled warmly and slid from the sofa to make a discreet phone call, desperately relieved she was not going to have to sleep with him to close the trap.

Moments after receiving Jessica's call, her control officer slipped from the apartment next door, cursing as he hastened several blocks toward Orchard Towers, a building so crammed with discos and prostitutes it was well known throughout Asia as the "Four Floors of Whores." After a quick search, he hired a tall leather-clad Thai transvestite who appeared at Jessica's door within the half-hour, fully paid and prepared to work - a hefty bonus having been offered for a successful seduction.

The clerk's libido returned when the visitor entered the room. "Would you like to join us?" rasped the elegant, hip-booted transvestite as he slowly uncoiled a long black leather bullwhip from within his oversized purse and tossed a pair of handcuffs onto the bed. Jessica stifled a surprised gasp and politely excused herself before disappearing into the kitchen and pulling a Tiger beer from the icebox.

Attempting to ignore the sounds of violent ecstasy emanating from the bedroom, she collapsed onto the overstuffed sofa and took a long pull from her beer. She sighed and relaxed, closing her eyes and trying to obscure the disturbing images floating through her mind. Her respite was interrupted a few minutes later when the door swung open and the sweating, half-naked transvestite stalked from the room, the dangling whip snaking across the floor behind him.

"Do you have any candles?" he asked abruptly.

Jessica motioned toward the kitchen, "try the cupboard beside the sink." As the transvestite disappeared momentarily into the kitchen, Jessica chanced a glance through the open bedroom door. From this angle she could see the naked Chinese officer bent over the back of a chair, ankles bound to the wooden legs, his backside covered with long red welts and a strange, foreign object...

"Sure you don't want to join us?" interrupted a sultry voice from beside the kitchen door. Jessica's eyes cut to the transvestite who stood in the doorway, an arrogant smirk on his face.

Jessica flushed. "No, of course not," she snapped. "You have a job to do. Get on with it!"

With a submissive nod he slinked exaggeratedly past her, entering the bedroom with a last, passing glance before closing the door behind him. Jessica sighed and, as an afterthought, peered up at one of the hidden cameras behind the mirror over the bar and flipped-off her control officer, whom she was certain was watching, disappointed Jessica had declined the perverse ménage a'trois.

Without her assistance, the encounter in the bedroom unfolded pretty much as expected.

After several more such carefully orchestrated evenings, she'd dropped the façade and merely arranged for the embassy official's "date" to meet him at the apartment.

When finally confronted with evidence of his indiscretions, he was unsurprised and expressed his gratitude for her "understanding" by exposing Chinese operatives in place in Singapore, Kuala Lumpur and Jakarta. He remained her most successful recruitment, lasting nearly a year until he inexplicably missed a late night contact.

"So how long *did* you wait?" Colonel Mok growled as Jessica's surveillance team sat in sullen silence in the cramped office at SID's headquarters.

Jessica turned to her lead watcher. "Ben?"

He thumbed through the tattered case file, seeking the written details so meticulously recorded.

"Weren't you *there*?" Colonel Mok snapped irritably.

"I... Well, yes. Of course," Ben stammered. "We remained in-place for about four hours beyond the scheduled time." The note miraculously appeared beneath his trembling fingers. "Until 03:18," he said with relieved confidence confirmed by his notation. "We couldn't remain at the club once it began to close," he explained reasonably.

Colonel Mok sighed. "We'll have to reload the dead drop and watch it for a few days," he decided. "Just in case Chinese intelligence..." He halted abruptly in mid-sentence, raising a bony finger toward the muted television balanced atop a pile of files stacked on the cabinet behind Jessica. There appeared a grainy image of a two gurneys being wheeled from the lobby of a seedy hotel in the Little India section of town.

"Turn that up," he insisted. Jessica twisted the volume.

"... in what police report as a bizarre double-suicide," sniffed the reporter in what she supposed to be an appropriately disapproving tone. "The bodies of a couple were found this morning in a Gelong hotel room hanging from the sprinkler system pipes."

"I think we've found your agent," Colonel Mok observed dryly.

"The couple?" scoffed one of Jessica's team members. "Boy is *that* coroner in for a surprise," he chuckled. His laughter faded under Jessica's withering stare.

"The MSS?" Jessica asked, referring to China's Ministry of State Security.

"Probably," responded Colonel Mok. "Cleaning house and sending messages." He saw Jessica's jaw tighten as her usually tanned face drained of color.

"Gentlemen," he sighed, rubbing his forehead. "Please leave us." Jessica's team slunk from the room and disappeared into the dark, cavernous hallway, their whispers fading in the distance.

Jessica rose silently to her feet and switched off the television, standing for a few moments and breathing slowly, her head bowed in contemplation. There was really nothing to say.

"It happens," Colonel Mok offered lamely. "He knew the risks..."

"The *risks*?" She erupted. "He was just some freaky little man looking for a thrill. He wasn't thinking of risks!"

"He did..." the colonel began as she continued to rant.

"He did!" he repeated, loudly enough to stem her tirade. "The moment he agreed to meet you for an 'innocent' concert and intentionally hid it from his superiors, he accepted the risk."

"He... he..." Her voice faded as her rage fizzled to blackness.

Colonel Mok picked up her agent's thick file and flipped absently through the pages, glancing without seeing the volumes of contact reports.

"That 'freaky little man' was a colonel in Chinese intelligence, Jessica," he growled contemptuously. "He betrayed his country in exchange for some perverted weekly tryst!" Colonel Mok let the file drop onto her desk, a portion of the contents sliding from the manila folder onto the floor. "He let his emotions overcome his better judgment," he said pointedly. "A lesson from which *you* would do well to learn."

She stared at him blankly, her jaw slack before tightening suddenly. "I want out," she blurted. "I can't do this anymore!"

He recoiled as if he'd been slapped. "Jessica..." he began, checking his anger. *This was her first high-level recruitment*, he reminded himself. Though she found her agent repugnant, she quite rationally felt responsible for his death. *Time*, he realized. *She just needs time.*

"I'll take you off operational status for six months," he offered. He watched her shrink into her chair, staring sullenly at the white Styrofoam cup on her desk.

"This country – *I* - have a significant investment in your career, Captain Ling," he reminded her as he stopped in the doorway. "Now go home," he mumbled. "Get some sleep."

A mere three months into her sabbatical, the bloody failed arrest of Kastari bin Ali brought Jessica back to "operational" status at her own request. But the injured

Colonel Mok, condemned and ornery in his bleak hospital bed, refused to return her to the field in what he called "her fragile emotional state."

She vented her anger to her best friend.

"Liaison!" she raged. "I'm one of the most successful case officers in the department and he wants me to babysit some... some *American*," she spat. "Americans," she repeated bleakly. "They're so... *parochial!*"

Shikha laughed sympathetically. "Well, they've certainly acquitted themselves well in Afghanistan," she observed. "Maybe they're not so reckless after all." She thumbed through a dossier and held up a photo taken by Singapore's immigration department several years before.

"Besides. He's a good looking guy," she commented, sliding the photo across the table. "It says in his file he's a corporate attorney - looks wealthy," she added naughtily.

Jessica snatched the photo and examined it skeptically. "You don't really believe...," she reviewed the name on the file. "This 'Chris Gates' is some sort of reservist, do you?"

"No. He's probably CIA. But he's 'declared', so just get close enough to see what information becomes available. It's a low-risk op. The department doesn't want you to attempt to turn him. Give him a chance. He might lead us to Khalid."

Jessica nodded deliberately, her eyes tearing. "Yes," she said firmly, "*anything* to get Khalid."

Awaking from her daydream, she glances guiltily around the terrace as if afraid a passing onlooker may be reading her mind. A flash of lightning draws her attention offshore, the subsequent rumble barely audible in the distance.

"Not again," she murmurs in solitary prayer. "Never again..."

CHAPTER 5

The rain ceases, yet the seas continue to churn. Major Lim, captain of the RSS Dominion, peers across the blackness, awaiting Prince Hidayat's radioed acknowledgement to the signal he has reached the extent of his escort. Moments later, the appropriate squawks - two long, one short, one long – Morse Code for the letter "Q" – come over the radio in reply.

The major orders Dominion to turn about and take up a patrol pattern bringing it back to the same location for rendezvous within three hours. He's proud that, despite the raging storm, his ship has successfully escorted its charge to the correct location nearly on schedule. A steward presents him a cup of tea as the patrol boat swings onto its new course. He has just taken his first sip when the Combat Information Center buzzes him.

"Sir," sings the voice of Third Sergeant Han, his lead sonar operator. "We have two surface contacts bearing 181-degrees and closing at 28 knots. Range, three kilometers."

"I'll be right down," Major Lim sighs, wedging his mug into the cup holder. "Mr. Bhanu, you have the con," he announces to his executive officer. He slides down the ladder to the CIC and approaches his surface radar operator.

"What do you have Li?" he asks, placing his hand paternally on the young sailor's shoulder.

"Sir, we have several surface contacts, but these two seem to be making straight toward us."

"Can you make out the type of vessels?" asks the major in an even tone.

"No Sir, but based on their speed and the way they're deployed, I'd say they're definitely naval contacts."

"National pride is a sticky thing, Li," Major Lim counsels the young sailor. "The TNI-AL doesn't like us operating in its back yard, even if we *are* in international waters. We'll send the usual message of peaceful intent and a polite warning not to commit 'acts dangerous to maritime safety'."

He retrieves the intercom handset. "Mr. Bhanu, prepare to warn off..."

"What the hell?" grunts Tran, jerking upright from his half-sleep on the floor of the cabin. Chris sprints through the door onto the deck. He peers intently toward a glow on the horizon; the blood drains from his face.

"Dominion," replies Chris in a hollow voice. "She's exploded." In the dim light, he can just make out at least one... no, two, vessels closing on the wreck. "Indonesian patrol boats! It's a fuckin' ambush," he shouts as he rips open the pilothouse door. "Get us the hell out of here, Mr. Soo!"

The boat rears-up as Mr. Soo shoves the throttles forward. Chris grapples for the door frame and heaves himself into the pilothouse. He climbs up the bucking deck to the chart table to locate the landing area on the map. Tran appears at his shoulder.

"If they knew about Dominion, they're probably waiting for us there," Tran observes professionally, his finger tapping the Sembar Peninsula.

"Well, that leaves running like hell or landing somewhere else," Chris admits in a shaking voice. *Calm down! Think*, he scolds himself. He glances over his shoulder at the receding light from the fire as the Prince Hidayat roars away from the scene of the attack. "We can't go back there," he admits, realizing the attacking patrol boats have probably switched their pursuit to the Prince Hidayat. He turns to Tran. "How do you like our odds on dry ground?"

Tran nods grimly. "We stay on this hunk of junk, we're toast."

"My feelings exactly." Chris turns to the coxswain. "Mr. Soo! Get us as far up the coast as you can, then beach this fucker!"

Mr. Soo nods his silent acknowledgement.

Tran thrusts his head into the ship's hold. "Jon! Get up here! We're abandoning ship!" Jon scrambles up the ladder and through the hatchway into the pilothouse, still wiping the sleep from his eyes.

"It's an ambush!" Chris yells over the roar of the engines. "Help the major gather up all the weapons and ammunition." Jon freezes. His hand slides behind his belt as he feels for his Khukuri.

"JON! We're going ashore! *Move!*" Chris roars. Responding to the order, Jon darts onto the deck to assist Tran. Groping their way through the darkness, the men wrench open side boards and retrieve the automatic rifles concealed within, slinging the weapons over their shoulders and jamming the extra magazines into their waistbands and baggy pockets. The two men return to the cabin and begin to distribute their booty.

"Shit! I forgot about the machine gun." Tran shouts and starts to return to the deck.

"No! They're too close," Chris shouts over the roar of the engines. Tran peers off the fantail; tiny flashes blink back at him, the laser-like tracers groping for the small vessel.

Instantaneously, he hears the telltale *"SLAP! SLAP! SLAP!"* as bullets splinter the rear of the pilothouse, showering him with wood fragments and shards of glass. He drops onto the quavering deck and crawls through the shattered door.

"That was a shitty idea," he laughs tensely. Chris flashes him a nervous grin.

Responding to the machine gun fire, Mr. Soo flings the boat into evasive maneuvers, cutting and weaving erratically across the waves to throw off their pursuer's aim, the boat bounding over the swells in search of safety.

As they near shore, Mr. Soo shrieks something in Mandarin. Chris and Tran grapple for handholds as the Prince Hidayat rockets at an angle up the sandy beach and plows into an embankment, flinging the crew violently to the deck. The stricken boat shudders as the engines continue running full open, spraying a geyser of mud and saltwater as the diesels continue trying unsuccessfully to propel the boat forward through the mire.

Mr. Soo springs to the helm and kills the shrieking engines; the patrol boats are rapidly closing. "Get out! Get out!" he rasps as he kicks open the port side escape hatch.

"Shit!" Chris curses as he scrambles around the darkness groping for his dropped weapon. Tran slips through the opening first, reaching back to help the next man in line. Finally Chris locates his weapon and hisses to Jon, "Go!"

Jon reaches out his hand. "No, Sir. You first," he replies evenly.

Chris curses again and grasps Jon's hand. With a mighty tug, the Gurkha draws Chris to his feet. "Okay! Okay! Let's go!" Chris shouts. Passing the helm, he hesitates, reaches into the cabinet, withdraws the pistol and drops it into his cargo pocket. Seizing Tran's proffered hand, he's drawn through the opening. Turning to assist Jon, he discovers the wiry Gurkha already emerging onto the mangled deck through the shattered front windscreen.

The men drop onto the sandy beach and glance around frantically. Tran spots a small opening in the thick foliage. "Follow me," he rasps and bolts for the comparative safety of the jungle. The crew collects a dozen yards inside the thick undergrowth, gasping lustily as they adjust to their new surroundings. The lead patrol boat is just coming into sight when it suddenly veers to port, turning parallel to the beach and sliding slowly past the wreck.

"Do you figure they have troops aboard?" asks Chris.

"I doubt it," replies Tran, peering between the leaves of a massive plant. He checks his compass then stares into the darkness beyond. "We better get inshore. Everyone ready?"

Mr. Soo slithers onto the Prince Hidayat's twisted deck, his movement masked by the enclosed stern. He works loose a section of deck and drags the well-oiled MAG-58 machine gun from its hold. His experienced hands massage the weapon with the intimate familiarity of a lover. He locates the release and opens the receiver. Sliding the belt of 7.62 mm ammo into the feed tray, he quietly presses the receiver closed. Carefully, he draws the charging handle to the rear.

A second patrol boat slides slowly past, its searchlight sweeping the wreck. As the beam passes and begins to illuminate the edge of the jungle, Mr. Soo releases the machine gun's charging handle, chambering the first round with a loud metallic *clank!* He heaves the machine gun onto the railing, pops up quickly behind it, and squeezes the trigger. Flame erupts from the barrel sending a line of green tracers raking the side of the patrol boat.

From cover of the jungle, the crew of the Prince Hidayat hears the bark of Mr. Soo's weapon and shrieks of shock and pain from the patrol boat's crew before the cries of the wounded are drowned-out by a roar of engines. As the boat sprints out of range, the tracers from Mr. Soo's machine gun claw into the darkness in pursuit.

"Let's go help him!" Tran shouts over the firing; he raises his weapon and starts for the boat. Chris springs to his feet to follow.

Jon blocks their path. "No! He covers *us*. We move out NOW!" he shouts, pointing into the jungle.

Tran starts to push past angrily, freezing when he hears the familiar "*Pop! Pop! Pop!*" of a Mark 19 automatic grenade launcher aboard one of the patrol boats.

"Down!" he shouts and tackles Jon and Chris. A line of stubby 40mm high explosive grenades crash in rapid succession against the Prince Hidayat's twisted wooden hull. Mr. Soo's machine gun ceases firing. The survivors glance at each other, realizing there's only one option left.

In unison, they leap to their feet and sprint away from the scene, stumbling through the thick jungle as they put as much distance as possible between themselves and the beach. Zigzagging northward up the peninsula for a half-hour, they finally collapse in an exhausted heap at the foot of a massive fallen tree, gasping-in the sultry air.

"Ma'am?"

The communication sergeant's voice startles Jessica.

"Ma'am?" he calls a second time before she realizes she's been alseep.

"What is it Mr. Namur?" She asks, noting with alarm the confused expression on the sergeant's face.

"Ma'am, my calculations show Prince Hidayat has made landfall," he reports, his voice pregnant with uncertainty. "But they're in the wrong place."

"Check your coordinates, Mr. Namur," she orders sternly, now wide-awake and looming menacingly over his shoulder. He reviews the data and declares the position accurate.

"Where the hell did they land?" she demands.

The sergeant manipulates the image, zooming-in on a point on the Kalimantan coast. "Here, Ma'am. South of Matua – they're one peninsula east of where they should be."

"Those *idiots!*" she rages. "What the hell do they need to find their LZ, *a bonfire*?" She seizes the secure phone. Colonel Mok's imperturbable voice responds immediately.

"Sir! They've..." she catches herself. "There's a problem. It appears our visitors have arrived at the wrong resort."

"Jessica, we're on a secure line. You can tell *me*," responds Colonel Mok tiredly.

She feels her face flush. "They landed one peninsula east of Sambar," she blurts. "They're in the wrong place!" There's a long delay on the other end of the line.

"Break radio silence. Contact Dominion," he replies finally. "Have them raise Prince Hidayat."

CHAPTER 6

Sweat stings Chris' eyes as he squints at the fading numerals on his watch; it's nearing dawn. Quietly, Tran reaches into his backpack and withdraws a worn map of Kalimantan. Spreading it on the ground before them, he cups his hand around his red-filtered penlight and locates their approximate position.

"Based on our direction and erratic rate of travel, we should be about here," he estimates, "a couple of klicks South of Matua – if we landed where we think we did. Without the boat, we've got no comms," he observes flatly. "We're going to have to get to a phone."

"They'll be looking for us in Matua," warns Chris. "We're gonna have to bypass it."

Tran returns his attention to the map. "It's mostly swamp, marsh, and jungle for the next ten or fifteen kilometers," he observes. He squints at the faded label identifying a river running north to south. "Whatever river this is," he observes, tracing it northward. "The village of Sukamara is upstream. Maybe we can locate a phone there."

Chris nods his agreement. "I can get us around Matua," he appraises. "But one of you is probably going to have to go into Sukamara."

A quiet argument erupts over who should take the point.

"Look, we've got two issues," explains Chris patiently. "We've got to avoid the POLRI patrols *and* we have to make contact with our agents. I was a grunt – a million years ago – but I still know how to walk point. So I won't get us ambushed."

Jon shakes his head vehemently. "No! I should be walking point. You're officers."

"Jon, we need to find out if our people are still in the neighborhood," explains Chris. He motions vaguely toward the two Asians. "They'll lay low if they see either of you sneaking through the bush. You look too much like locals," he observes. "They may recognize me."

"So what you're saying," replies Tran with a wry grin, "is you can avoid being spotted, but if you *are*, it might not be so bad..."

"Yeah. Something like that."

"Sir," Jon pleads. "*You* are not expendable. *I* am."

"Expendability is not the issue, *Jon*," replies Chris irritably. "The mission is to recover our agents and get them the hell out of here." The expression on Jon's face tells Chris he resents being spoken to in such a manner.

"Look, why don't you follow me and the Major here can bring up the rear."

"I remind you - now that we're on the ground I'm in command, Chris," Tran interjects testily.

"Yes Sir, you are." The two men stare at each other, trying to decide if the matter was worth fighting over. "So?"

Tran waves his hand dismissively. "Go. Take the point," he snorts.

Chris peers at his compass, listens carefully for movement nearby, and silently rises to his feet and moves off along the overgrown trail, his weapon at the ready.

In the darkness, the narrow path fades repeatedly from beneath his feet, only to reappear further along. He moves slowly, placing each foot carefully as he steps, trying to avoid producing the telltale snap of a twig or muddy splash that might alert a nearby listening post or patrol. He isn't concerned about booby traps because he is not in a country at war – at least not one *it* was aware of. As he moves up the trail, he halts and listens periodically, peering down the murky path ahead. He rotates his head side to side in slow, sweeping movements, scanning for movement in his peripheral vision. The assault rifle is slick in his sweaty palms. Beneath the jungle canopy there's no breeze, in fact the air doesn't move at all. It's like breathing water: stale, stagnant, moldy water. He quietly wraps the canvas-webbed sling around the plastic fore stock and secures his grip before continuing up the trail.

Dawn nears, the triple canopy acting as a sieve against the light. After nearly 45 minutes of tense, arduous movement, he detects the faint sound of voices in the distance. Not the sounds of soldiers shouting commands, but the chatter of people doing everyday things. Civilian sounds; a village awaking. As he edges forward, the jungle thins, the trail becoming more pronounced as light filters through the canopy. He drops exhaustedly to one knee and waits for Jon and Tran to catch up.

"Matua," he whispers. Tran nods and leads the team forward for a better look. It isn't much of a town, mainly a depressing gaggle of misshapen wooden plank buildings, walls constructed from salvaged lumber and roofs of palm thatch or rusting corrugated tin. The team skirts south of the village, arriving at a dirt road running east to west across a ramshackle bridge.

Silently, Tran signals for Chris' and Jon's attention, pointing a knife-edged hand toward the bridge and shaking his head exaggeratedly from side-to-side, indicating they are not going to cross it. He gestures instead to a field of tall grass across the road, signaling they should take up positions on the other side.

One by one, each man crosses the road at 30-second intervals. They drop prone, forming a loose semi-circle in the weeds, weapons pointing in three directions of the compass. They lay motionless, familiarizing themselves with the sights and sounds around them. Tran taps Chris' leg and motions him to follow at a low crawl toward the riverbank. Once concealed in the thick vegetation, he whispers to Chris, "Get us upstream about a half-mile and find a suitable place to cross."

Chris nods and takes the point on a muddy trail on the left bank of the river. Clouds hang low in the sky; a heavy mist embraces the lowlands. Discovering a suitable ford, he motions for the group to assemble at the riverbank so they can cover each other as each slip one by one into the water and cross the chest-deep stream.

As Chris emerges on the opposite side of the river a rumble in the distance foretells the coming of rain. *Good*, he decides. *That'll keep the locals indoors*. But when the rain arrives it comes like shards of glass broken over their heads, blinding, painful, distracting, and oppressive. Movement becomes much more complicated as the trail becomes a tributary, awash with muddy brown paste flowing downhill. He slips and falls several times before halting to allow the team to regroup deep inside the jungle. The crash of the rain on the leaves drowns out all attempts to whisper; Chris cups his hand over Tran's ear and speaks as loudly as he dares. "We're probably two klicks from Sukamara," he announces, sounding out each word distinctly. "Why don't you take the point?"

With an exaggerated nod, Tran slips into the lead as the team moves north toward Sukamara and, hopefully, a telephone.

"Still no response from Dominion Ma'am," reports the signals sergeant. "Do you want me to keep trying?"

Jessica hesitates then mumbles a halfhearted "no." Something tells her it will be wasted effort; there will be no contact. The mood in the room is funereal.

The silence is broken when Colonel Mok bursts through the door and strides into the room. Unusually, he is in full uniform; his starched khaki shirt and olive green pants identify him as an Army officer. He wears no ribbons, for unlike its neighbors, Singapore does not gratuitously award medals. But his parachutist and master diver badges are clearly apparent.

"Status?" he demands as he approaches the gaggle of SID officers encircling Jessica and the communications sergeant.

"We still can't raise Dominion," announces Jessica, massaging the throbbing pain in her forehead, "and we have no word from the Prince Hidayat."

"Atmospherics?" he asks.

"Maybe. But something's not right. I don't think Prince Hidayat landed where it did by mistake."

Colonel Mok raises an eyebrow in question.

"Sir. On my own authority, I've requested this evening's voice intercepts from our station at Sentosa," she announces. "The recordings will be here within the hour." She hesitates, studying Colonel Mok's expression, trying to decide if she should pursue her line of thinking.

"Sir, I think we may have lost Dominion."

The thought has been lingering at the back of everyone's minds. Upon hearing the unthinkable spoken aloud, the other officers gasp collectively. Strangely, Colonel Mok doesn't appear shocked in the least.

"You mean sunk," he replies in monotone.

"Yes Sir."

He strokes his chin thoughtfully. "You realize the implication if that's the case?"

"Yes Sir."

Thirty-five minutes later an Air Force warrant officer enters the communications office carrying a locked aluminum briefcase. After signing for the contents, the watch officer receives a single CD ROM. Jessica snatches the disc and follows Colonel Mok down stairs to the analysis cell beneath the communications center.

An eternity passes as the analysts isolate and begin translating the evening's intercepts. To speed the process, they divide digitalized segments between four analysts, each intimate with dialects commonly used in Indonesian military communications. Colonel Mok lounges at the conference table drinking tea and gazing serenely into the distance as Jessica stalks slowly along behind the line of seated analysts, staring at the backs of their heads as if by so doing she can read their minds.

One of the analysts shifts in his chair.

"*What*?" she snaps. The analyst shakes his head, meekly indicating he is merely adjusting his seat.

Twenty-five minutes later a small, frail looking analyst with owlish glasses turns slowly in his chair, agape.

"Sir! We have something!" announces Jessica.

Colonel Mok slams his cup onto the table, springs from his seat and approaches the console. The analyst slips off his headphones, sweat beading on his brow. "Sir. I believe we have tactical channel traffic confirming a naval engagement."

"Put it on speaker," the colonel snaps.

"Sir, it's in Javanese..."

"Do it!"

The analyst replays the garbled radio message. For the benefit of those who don't speak Javanese, Colonel Mok translates.

"Nala to garbled... Fearless Class patrol boat... garbled," he translates.

Those listening intently to the recording hear cheering in the background – or is it static?

"Yani Base to Nala. Confirm destroyed," the colonel continues. "Destroyed as ordered." At this, Colonel Mok flinches.

"Yani to 'garbled'... Survivors." He listens intently then shakes his head in frustration. "What did he say? I can't understand that part," he growls to the analyst.

"Sir," replies the analyst. "I believe he said 'ensure there are no survivors'."

Jessica's head snaps toward the colonel, whose eyes shift momentarily toward her then back to the speaker on the wall.

"Here's something about 'another boat'," mutters Colonel Mok, resuming his translation. "They're asking about the other boat," he repeats.

Jessica's heart is pounding. She wipes her sweating palms unconsciously on the legs of her slacks. Her insides squirm as she begins to feel dizzy. A long, slow, controlled exhale escapes from her parted lips as she forces herself to resume breathing.

"He repeats only one confirmed. More static. Garbled. Something... will be pleased."

"Who will be pleased?" asks Jessica, incredulously.

"It sounds like he said 'the admiral'," translates Colonel Mok then raises his hand to preclude further questions. He continues to translate.

"Mandau gave chase... beached. The civilian boat is beached," he reports. "The patrol boats came under fire and they destroyed it on the beach."

"So we don't know if they got out alive," announces Jessica.

Colonel Mok shakes his head.

"Is that all?" he asks the analyst, who nods grimly in response.

"I want a typed transcript of the segment ready in 15 minutes," demands Colonel Mok as he reaches for the secure phone. Waiting for an answer on the other end of the line, his eyes lock with Jessica's.

"Watch Desk," answers a curt voice.

"This is Colonel Mok at Changi Station. Connect me with the Defense Minister, immediately!"

CHAPTER 7

It's early afternoon when Tran, Chris and Jon arrive near Sukamara. Along the way they successfully sidestep POLRI patrols and avoid drawing undue attention to themselves. Now they lay-up in the center of an abandoned rubber plantation, its blighted trees aligned in neat rows, unused taps obscured by coagulated sap. Each man takes his turn sleeping on rotting leaves beneath branches swaying in an afternoon breeze that drives away – for the moment – the low clouds that have been their companions all morning. They agree Tran will enter the village at dusk, using his cover as a buyer for a Chinese rubber merchant.

"I can call special operations command," announces Tran. "But we already know they don't have assets in the area."

Chris shakes his head. "No. We need to get in touch with our control. She's our first line of support out here."

Tran and Jon nod in agreement.

"Do you have a contact number?" asks Tran as he leans against the rubber tree, withdraws a pen from his shirt pocket, and rips the back off a small cardboard box found in a heap of rotting leaves.

Chris dictates a Singapore phone number.

"What's that, the operations center?" asks Tran as he slips the pen back into his pocket.

"Uh. No. It's Jessica's home number," replies Chris.

Tran studies him closely. Chris actually blushes. "You prick," grumbles Tran as he shoves the piece of paper into his pocket.

Chris shrugs and changes subjects. "So how do you want to do this?"

"While you were sleeping, I did a local recon. There's a heavily traveled macadam road about a quarter mile that way," announces Tran, gesturing vaguely to the north. "I saw buses traveling in both directions. I'll just walk toward Sukamara until one comes along and take it into town."

"Won't it be dangerous?"

Tran chuckles. "No, Chris. Being stranded in enemy territory without an armored division is dangerous. But a bus ride? Not so much..."

"Well, here," snorts Chris as he slides the worn .45 automatic from his pants pocket. "Better take this anyway." Tran passes his rifle to Jon and accepts the proffered pistol. He slips it into the waistband at the small of his back and tugs his shirt tail over it.

As he stands to leave, Jon steps forward and brushes the leaves and dirt from Tran's civilian clothes. "Thanks, mom," jokes Tran. He turns to Chris. "Give me twelve hours. If I'm not back by then, you and Jon head due east to Pangkalanbun and try to contact your *girlfriend*."

He reaches into his backpack, pulls out several bags of dried fruits and fish products and passes them to Chris. "That's breakfast, lunch and dinner," he announces. "Make it last." He slings the pack onto his shoulder and strikes out across the plantation.

Watching Tran walk away, Chris' stomach drops. *Twelve hours?* He shakes his head, trying to clear the negative possibilities floating through his mind. Jon is watching him.

"Dinner?" asks Chris, tossing him a bag of dried fish.

Tran arrives at the road ten minutes after leaving the plantation and turns east toward Sukamara. Rounding a bend he spots the back of a rickety bus balanced precariously on the shoulder of the crumbling road. Its passengers are rolling up their thatched prayer mats. He glances at his watch and realizes it's time for ISHaa, the evening Muslim prayers. The bus has pulled-over to allow its passengers to make their last prayer of the evening.

He approaches casually, bowing effusively to the passengers as he walks to the front of the bus. The driver is a large man with a traditional black peci perched on his massive head and a jovial smile on his round face. Tran catches the driver's attention as he hefts his bulk into the cab. The driver asks something in Katingan, the local dialect; Tran responds in Mandarin. The driver smiles benignly and shakes his head, indicating he doesn't understand, and motions for Tran to take a seat in the rear of the truck.

The bus has been converted from a flatbed truck by adding a canvas roof and benches down the middle and both sides. Years of hard use has reduced the roof to a hodgepodge of overlapping plastic sheets and the benches to slabs of smooth wood, contoured at intervals to the approximate shapes of the passengers' backsides. More than a dozen people are crowded aboard, but they don't seem to mind his intrusion as they squeeze together to make room for the new passenger. Tran smiles and greets his fellow passengers with a few appropriate Mandarin phrases, the meaning of which is lost to them, but the intent of which is clearly friendly.

As the bus nears the outskirts of Sukamara, the traffic congeals to a halt. Tran climbs onto the edge of the tailgate and peers over the roof. His blood runs cold. Just around the curve a squad of POLRI has established a roadblock and is stopping and searching traffic entering town. The forged documents he carries are good, but he isn't anxious to test them. After the bus crawls forward a single car length in ten minutes, he throws his hands in the air and, with a rush of Mandarin expletives, tosses his pack onto the road and drops off the tailgate after it. Several passengers wave as they watch him recover his pack and stalk toward the checkpoint. Clearly he is a man in a hurry.

Rounding the curve, his pace slackens as he appraises the situation. There are five POLRI he can identify. The one obviously in charge supervises the other four, who are busily interviewing passengers, digging through automobile trunks and rummaging haphazardly through truck beds. The senior man intervenes in a loud dispute between a driver and one of the cops. With the squad thus distracted, Tran glances around casually and ducks quickly into the foliage by the side of the road. He squats in the bush for a few minutes to determine if his disappearance has attracted interest. Confident he hasn't been noticed, he rises and moves cautiously through the jungle, working his way around the roadblock and emerging a quarter mile past to resume his lonely trek into town.

Despite the shanty homes on the outskirts, Sukamara proper is a well-maintained village alive with commerce. He shuffles up the main street, hands thrust indifferently in his pockets as he scrutinizes the rooftops, looking for tell-tale phone lines. A long "beeeeeeeeeep!" brings him to his senses and he springs off the road. A beat-up white Land Rover flies by, its rear wheel disappearing into a shallow puddle and showering Tran with muddy water. Cursing in Mandarin, Tran slaps the mud from his shirt and again begins to cross the street when he spots the Land Rover skid to a stop in front of a small white building at the end of the block.

The driver pounds the horn, oblivious to the annoyed glances of the passers-by. "Hey, mate! Come on, I'm 'ungry!" he shouts, leaning out the window. A large middle-aged white man with a massive beer gut waddles from the building and hefts himself into the Land Rover. The driver guns the engine and powers a 180-degree turn in the middle of the narrow road, spraying mud and sending pedestrians scurrying for cover. As the truck speeds past, Tran notices a company logo on the door. It reads: "Kali Lumber, LTD."

He approaches the building from which the fat man emerged and realizes it is the lumber company's local office. Circling the structure, he spots what he's looking for: a telephone line extending from the side of the building.

As darkness descends, he purchases dinner at a roadside kiosk and squats on his haunches until night drives the local population indoors.

Floodlights light the front of the whitewashed wooden plank building, so he circles to where angular shadows cut nearly to the street. He ducks into the shadows, seeking refuge beneath the eaves at the rear of the building. Like the other structures in town, the lumber company's offices are not air conditioned, relying instead on tall airy windows to keep the building habitable. The offices closed for the evening, all the windows are shuttered, with large slats allowing air and insects to enter, but little else. On his third attempt, he locates a loose shutter, carefully wrests it open, and hauls himself through the window. The heat inside is oppressive.

The office is comprised of a single large high-ceilinged room crammed with a dozen shabby wooden desks. Six rusted ceiling fans connected by a single drive belt hang motionless from the moldy, paint-chipped ceiling. Maps of the nearby forest obscure whitewashed walls. Large black grease-penciled grids sketched on overlaying acetate indicate de-forested areas.

He creeps across the room, trying to minimize his creaking footfalls on the scuffed wooden floor. Suddenly, headlights pierce the shuttered front windows, casting vivid yellow lines across the wall that sweep like a grappling hand across the room. He drops instantly to the floor and remains deathly still, his heart pounding as sweat forms a puddle beneath him. The noise of the vehicle fades into the distance and he resumes breathing. As he rises to his knees he spots a worn plastic telephone balanced precariously atop a pile of files on the cluttered desk opposite him. He grasps the handset desperately. Bringing it slowly to his ear, he breathes a sigh of relief as he discovers a dial tone.

"We can't just accept this provocation," snarls Singapore's Minister of Defense.

"What provocation?" asks the Minister of Home Affairs.

"What provocation...?" stammers the Defense Minister. "The sinking of Dominion of course!"

"Yes, we all understand *that*," intervenes the Prime Minister. "But I believe the learned minister is referring to protecting our 'sources and methods'."

He receives a respectful nod of concurrence from the minister responsible for internal security. "Yes Sir. If we accuse the Indonesians of the attack, they'll recognize we've been de-encrypting their communications. And if we accuse and President Megawati's government makes denials, international opinion will demand we justify our accusations."

"So... let's provide evidence," stammers the Defense Minister. "We'll claim we received a distress call – we can even manufacture one if necessary to satisfy *international opinion*," he seethes.

"But the Indonesians would know better," adds the interior minister.

The Defense Minister's mouth moves absently, a vein throbbing dangerously in his forehead. "Surely you don't propose we ignore this... this... *provocation*!"

"No, certainly not," replies the Minister of Home Affairs. "But as long as the crew and passengers of the...," he hesitates and peers over the tops of his glasses at the notation on his report, "... 'Prince Hidayat' is ashore, we risk international embarrassment. Once the crew is back in our hands – or otherwise 'neutralized' – we can make accusations without being forced to respond to allegations of espionage."

"What would you do if you were President Megawati?" asks the Prime Minister gloomily.

The Minister for Home Affairs reflects for a moment before responding, the other ministers leaning forward in anticipation of his assessment.

"Assuming she's even aware the attack occurred, I'd remain silent."

The remaining ministers shift uncomfortably in their seats.

"So you counsel patience?" asks the Prime Minister.

"If we are patient in one moment of anger, we will escape a hundred days of sorrow," announces the minister.

"So, you take refuge in proverbs?" scoffs the Defense Minister.

"No. I take refuge in time," replies the interior minister serenely. "And fate..."

Jessica enters her apartment, tossing her keys on the counter and glancing at the message light blinking on her answering machine. As she reaches to press rewind, the phone begins to ring.

"Yes?" she answers briskly, trying to sound alert in case she's required at the Ministry.

"Jessica," rasps a voice in a loud whisper. "It's Tran."

"Who?"

"Major Minh!"

She nearly drops the phone. "My God! Where are you?" she demands, nudging the apartment door closed with her foot.

"Sukamara."

"Are you alone?" she asks warily.

"No. Lover boy and Jon are with me."

Lover boy? Oh you bastard! She performs a quick mental count.

"Just the three of you?"

"Yes. Mr. Soo is dead. The others are laid up outside of town. This place is crawling with POLRI. What are your instructions?"

She deliberates desperately for a moment. "Can I call you back?" she asks, fishing for time.

"Hell no, you can't call me back!" Tran rasps. "This isn't a public fucking phone!"

"All right, all right," she replies hastily. Closing her eyes she places the map of Kalimantan in her mind's eye. "Get to Pangkalanbun. Copy this number and call me when you get there. We'll bring you in."

"Okay," replies Tran as he jots down the new phone number she provides. "By the way, lover boy wants to know if you've heard anything from his agents," Tran whispers.

Stop calling him that! "No. Nothing yet," she snaps. "I'll see what I can find out and will fill you in when you call me back."

The line is silent for a long moment. "You know about Dominion?" asks Tran.

"Yes. We know."

"I'm sorry, Jessica."

"Just get to Pangkalanbun," she insists.

"Right. Out." The line goes dead.

Jessica reflects for a few moments and dials Colonel Mok on his cell phone.

"Yes?" answers the imperturbable voice.

"They've made contact!" she blurts, oblivious to the fact she is now on a non-secure line. "They're in Sukamara!"

The colonel's usually measured tone quickens. "What shape are they in?"

"Soo is dead. They're on the run. I told them to get to Pangkalanbun and call me back for further instructions. I told them we'd bring them in."

Colonel Mok curses softly.

"What's wrong?" asks Jessica.

"I'm not sure we're going to be authorized to act," he replies.

"WHAT?" gasps Jessica. "No! No…!"

"Jessica," he replies, trying to calm her. "International implications must be considered."

"Stuff the international considerations!" sneers she. "We've got agents out there…"

"Captain Ling!" interrupts Colonel Mok fiercely.

She realizes he's angry when he addresses her by her military rank.

"Get a hold of yourself!" A pause ensues. "I'll call you back shortly," he announces finally.

The phone goes dead in her hand.

A bright morning sun filters through the rubber trees as Chris nudges Jon carefully. The Ghurka's eyes pop open. He remains motionless, appraising his surroundings before rolling onto his back and glancing up at Chris.

"You look like shit," he observes cheerfully.

Chris runs his hand over his face and examines his clothes. It has been three mornings since he last shaved. His new black shirt and khaki pants are caked with mud. Despite a reprieve from rain during the night, his stomach is wet from lying in the damp, decaying leaves; his back is damp with morning dew. He runs his hands through his short, graying hair, trying to shake loose the insects that nested there during the night.

"God, I could use a cup of coffee and a shower," he groans. He detects the look of amusement on Jon's face. "Quit grinning at me," he snaps irritably.

Jon rises and stretches luxuriously as though having just spent the night in a four-star hotel. He glance at his watch, reaches into his pocket, and tosses what is left of the dried fruit to Chris. "It's been twelve hours," he announces.

"Yeah. Yeah. I know," snorts Chris, annoyed the decision is now upon him. He shoves a handful of unidentifiable dried fruit into his mouth and gnaws.

"We don't know what happened to Tran. So we can't just walk down the same road like a couple of lost tourists," he mumbles. He unfolds the map Tran left behind and examines it. "I think our best bet is to hijack a vehicle."

Jon nods his agreement and peers intently at the map. "This curve would be a good ambush position," he announces after a quick evaluation of the terrain. "I can probably get the vehicle to stop and you can close in from the blind spot."

"How will you stop them?" asks Chris.

"This isn't New York City," shrugs Jon. "People are more trusting here. I'll just step out in the road and wave them down."

"And if they don't stop?"

"I'll move."

"Well you'd better move quickly."

It doesn't take long to locate the ambush site. Jon squats at the edge of the road, waiting for an appropriate target. As the sun rises, traffic increases. Water buffalo drawn carts, motorcycles, bicycles and the occasional bus rattle past sporadically.

Chris selects a position across the road on the blind side of the curve just inside the jungle. He has Jon's assault rifle slung over his back, his own weapon resting in sweating hands. Through a small clearing, he observes the Ghurka surveying the light traffic.

Jon suddenly springs to his feet and steps into the road, waving meekly at an oncoming vehicle. Chris edges closer and detects the hum of an approaching motor. He slips his weapon to "Fire" and adjusts Jon's assault rifle to a more comfortable position on his back. The plan is to hijack the driver and force him to take them where they want to go. They don't want to hurt anyone. But he must be prepared to look deadly and to act ruthlessly if threatened.

The vehicle slows and rolls to a stop about ten feet away. Jon walks around to the driver's side to find a pistol thrust into his face. Chris spots the weapon in the driver's hand and explodes from the bushes, plunging the muzzle of his rifle through the open passenger window.

"Lass das!" he hisses loudly in German. "Keine bewegung!"

"*Lass das*?" asks the driver as he turns to Chris. "What the *hell* does that mean?"

"You son-of-a-bitch!" snarls Chris in a shaking voice. "I nearly killed you."

"But you didn't," Tran smiles.

Chris lowers his weapon. "Not yet, but I'll sure as shit keep a watch for the opportunity."

"You guys are shitty hijackers," announces Tran as he glances in the rearview mirror. "Now get in before someone comes along. Chris, get in back, paleface. And keep your head down." Chris drops his and Tran's assault rifles onto the floorboard and flops into the back seat. Jon climbs into the passenger seat beside Tran.

"Nice truck," comments Chris as Tran works the Land Rover around on the rutted road and speeds off to the east. "Where'd you get it?"

"I borrowed it from the company motor pool," replies Tran.

"Cool. We can add larceny and grand theft auto to your 201 File," chuckles Chris. "Did you contact Jessica?"

"Yeah."

"So?"

"You're in deep shit," he replies.

Chris takes a deep breath – he was afraid something like this might happen.

"Why?" he asks apprehensively.

"She's pregnant."

"*What?*"

Tran bursts out laughing and the tension immediately subsides.

"You ass," replies Chris.

CHAPTER 8

Jessica awakes with a start, gazing around in bewilderment. The morning sun cuts a brilliant gash across her living room floor. It slowly dawns on her she's fallen asleep in front of the television. Rising in a stupor, she knocks over a partial glass of Shiraz left sitting on the floor beside the chair. She stares at it dumbly, watching helplessly as the blood red blotch seeps across the carpet. With a sudden groan of annoyance, she snatches up the glass, places it on the bar, and drops a dish towel over the stain.

Wandering into the bathroom, she leaves a trail of discarded clothes. As she starts the shower and adjusts the water's temperature, the events of the previous 24 hours billow through her mind. *Maybe it's just a nightmare*, she attempts to convince herself as steam embraces her naked body. She drags a hand across the fogging mirror and stares at her reflection. The stress is apparent in worry lines and streaks of red shot through the whites of her eyes. "Oh, God!" she gasps and sinks to the floor sobbing. After several minutes, she stops crying, pulls herself resolutely to her feet, and wipes her eyes.

Fifteen minutes later she's in a taxi on her way to Changi Airport. Her hair is still damp from her cursory shower as she places the cell phone to her ear and speaks with the ticket agent at SilkAir.

"I need a one-way ticket on your earliest flight to Pangkalanbun today," she announces briskly.

"One moment," replies the agent and places Jessica on hold.

It takes an agonizingly long time for the agent to return with the flight information. "Ma'am," announces the agent, "the first flight departs within the hour. May I schedule you for a later departure?"

"No, I want *this* flight," snaps Jessica, glancing at her watch. "I'm on my way to the airport now." She provides her alias and credit card information to the still dubious agent.

"All right, Ma'am. I have you on SilkAir flight MI847 departing Singapore at 07:55 and arriving at Pangkalanbun at 10:15. Is there anyth...?" she asks.

"Thank you," replies Jessica and ends the call. She dials the SID operations center.

"Watch Officer. Non-secure line," responds a voice.

"I understand. Do you recognize my voice?"

"Yes Ma'am," replies the watch officer.

"Have we had any contact from our friends?"

"Only what you reported last night."

"What about the passengers they were to pick up?"

There is a pause. "Um. Yes Ma'am."

"Where are they?"

"Stop 32," he replies using the well-worn codename for a particular town in Kalimantan.

"Did they leave a contact number?"

There is an extended pause. "Ma'am. I... we shouldn't be discussing this on a non-secure line. Can you call from...?"

Jessica sighs. She has a reputation as an explosive temper. It's probably time to use it to her advantage. "I obviously don't have access to a secure line right now," she snaps. "Do you know where I was yesterday afternoon?" she asks, aware rumor of her meeting with the Prime Minister and his cabinet has made the rounds at SID.

"Yes Ma'am. I believe so."

"Well I'm on my way back there *now*," she announces. "I don't have time to argue. *Now, give me the number!*" There's a tense silence on the other end of the line, followed by a phone number.

"Thank you," she replies sweetly and, much to the desk officer's relief changes the topic.

"Is the Colonel there yet?"

"No Ma'am."

"When he arrives, please tell him I'm at the Ministry."

"Yes Ma'am."

The taxi screeches to a halt in front of Changi Airport's Terminal A. Jessica grabs her soft-sided overnight bag and slips from the back seat. She hands the driver a wad of cash to cover the taxi and airport fees. To her surprise, as he takes the money, the elderly driver closes his hands over hers and peers intently into her eyes.

"What you are now is what you have been; what you will be is what you do now," he announces. Before she can ask what he's talking about, he turns to usher another passenger into his taxi. She shakes her head in bewilderment and walks briskly through the automatic doors into the terminal.

At the SilkAir counter she uses a Thai passport under her alias name for identification. After SID first recruited her in undergraduate school, she had been sent as an exchange student to obtain her MBA at Bangkok University. Her spoken Thai is nearly flawless and she spent enough time in the region to pass herself off as a native. She travels frequently on her Thai passport and feels most comfortable with it.

As she sweeps to the front of the security checkpoint, ticket in-hand, the security agent waves her down. "Ma'am?

The queue begins..." He halts abruptly when she flashes her laminated SID identity card. "Yes Ma'am," he snaps obediently and passes her through the checkpoint. Before reaching the departure gate, she shoves her real identification and credit cards into an airport locker and drops the key into a waste bin.

The "Now Boarding" sign is flashing when she enters the empty departure lounge. She slides her boarding pass through the electronic reader and trots down the empty jet way. Settling into her seat, she notices the Airbus A320 is startlingly empty. For a moment she wonders if news of the military clash between Singapore and Indonesia has become public. But a quick scan of the Jakarta Post suggests nothing more than a diplomatic protest over Singapore's purchase of Indonesian sand for reclamation projects. It seems the national government wants to skim its share of the profits from the local authorities.

As the aircraft lifts into the air, Jessica breathes a sigh of relief.

"I just left the Prime Minister's office," growls Colonel Mok to the watch officer. "She wasn't there."

"I'm sorry, Sir. That's where she said she was going."

Colonel Mok rubs his balding pate distractedly. "When did she tell you that?"

"About an hour ago... Sir."

Is something going on I'm not supposed to know about? Colonel Mok wonders. *Why would the Prime Minister hide such a meeting from me?* He departs the operations center and walks briskly toward his office.

"Ms. Luan," he announces to his secretary as he passes her desk, "Please get the Prime Minister's Chief of Staff on a secure line." He stalks into his office and nudges the door closed, drops into the chair behind his Teak desk and stares at the phone. A voice suddenly erupts from the innocuous black box.

"Sir, I have the Chief of Staff on the line."

He leans forward and snatches the receiver. "Good morning Sir!" he announces in a forced, cheerful voice. "I was wondering if you are through with Captain Ling. I'd like to speak with her."

"Captain Ling?" replies the gruff voice. "She's not here."

"I'm sorry Sir," Colonel Mok responds smoothly. "I understood the Prime Minister wanted to see her again this morning."

"Mok," snorts the chief of staff. "The PM's meeting with Senior Minister Lee. Captain Ling is not on his agenda."

"My mistake, Sir. I thought perhaps she'd been called back in," explains Colonel Mok.

"You know no one sees the PM without going through me."

"Of course, Sir. Good day." Colonel Mok disconnect the call and presses the button on his speaker box. "Ms. Luan. Locate Captain Ling *immediately*!"

"Looks like they're expecting someone," reports Tran, passing his binoculars to Chris.

"Do you think they're looking for us?" asks Chris. He watches as POLRI cops in tan shirts and blue berets patrol either end of the bridge, halting and checking passing traffic.

"Hard to tell," replies Tran with a distracted glance across the rain-swollen river. Large tree limbs and trash pitch and roll downstream, the brown water tripping over itself as it claws the banks seeking a wider avenue.

"There's no crossing *that*," he grunts. "We're gonna have to cross the bridge if we're going into Pangkalanbun."

"So we attack the bridge with three people?" asks Chris dubiously.

"I'm open to suggestions."

Chris reflects for a few moments. He spots the dome of a large mosque on the other side of the river. "Look. Panga-whatever-you-call-it is right over there. Why don't we ditch the truck and split up. We can take turns crossing the bridge one at a time on foot. They don't seem to be paying much attention to pedestrian traffic."

Tran retrieves the binoculars and surveys the bridge. "You're right," he reports. "It looks like they're searching for a vehicle – probably this one." He motions vaguely over his shoulder toward their stolen Land Rover.

He lowers the binoculars and fingers them absently in his hands, deliberating. "Jon and I could probably get across without too much trouble," he concludes. "There may be no need for you to cross at all. Why don't we find a place to stash you on this side of the river while we make contact with our control?"

Chris shakes his head. "I disagree. They sank Dominion, so they apparently think this is a Singaporean operation. They're probably looking for Asians, not a big white guy like me. If some beastly German comes lumbering across the bridge they'll react just because it's out of the ordinary, not necessarily because they're looking for me."

"No. No. We must cross together," insists Jon.

"Jon, if we go across together, they'll have a better chance of rolling up the whole team," Chris reminds him. "This is not one of those situations where there is safety in numbers."

"But *Sir*," persists Jon.

Chris shakes his head and smiles. "Jon. I appreciate your loyalty. But it'll be safer this way. Trust me." Realizing Jon is unconvinced, Chris passes him an assault rifle.

"Major Minh is going to cross the bridge first," he explains, pointing toward the expanse of concrete spanning the river. "*If* he's successful, I'm going next. You can cover me as I cross. If something goes wrong, kill the bastards."

Burrowed inside a thick bamboo stand screening them from the road, Chris and Jon watch anxiously from a rise near the bend in the river. Chris spots Tran loitering casually beside the road waiting for a group of lumber workers to pass. He falls-in behind them and approaches the bridge at a relaxed pace. As expected, the POLRI focus on vehicles, apparently on the irrational assumption spies don't walk. He waits patiently in line as a single POLRI cop reviews his fellow traveler's credentials.

When his turn arrives, Tran hands his passport to the POLRI guard, bowing and scraping and chattering away in Mandarin as the guard attempts unsuccessfully to interrogate him in Javanese.

Finally, Tran reaches into his shirt pocket and bows, presenting the officer a business card with both hands. The officer accepts the card and turns it over inquisitively, his eyes widening. He glances around anxiously before slipping the card quickly inside his pocket and returning Tran's passport.

"I think Tran just slipped the cop a bribe," chuckles Chris. "He's going across."

Unmolested, Tran saunters across the bridge and proceeds toward Pangkalanbun.

Jon turns to Chris. "So how are you going to get past them?"

"I've got to come up with a plausible story," replies Chris. "What would a German professor be doing walking around near Pangkalanbun?"

"Orangutans," replies Jon simply.

"What?"

"Orangutans," he repeats with a shrug. "Kalimantan is the world's last great Orangutan sanctuary. There are many Western tourists here."

Chris reflects on the news for a moment. "Okay. That makes sense. But why am I walking?"

"Maybe your car broke down? Or you got separated from your tour?" offers Jon, warming to the topic.

"Hmm," hums Chris. "Or maybe I was mugged." A broad smile spreads across his face. "How about I send these clowns on a wild goose chase?"

"A *goose chase*?" asks Jon uncertainly.

"It means 'an attempt to catch the uncatchable,'" explains Chris. He rises to his feet and approaches a tall tree overhanging the river. Without forewarning, he slams his face into the trunk.

"Fuck," he curses as he staggers backward before charging the tree a second time. He drops to his knees; Jon grabs his arm and hauls Chris to his feet.

"What are you *doing*?" he asks incredulously.

Chris turns to the Gurkha, a bloody wound on his forehead and blood oozing from his split lip.

"So, what do you think?" asks Chris. "Do I look like a monkey-lover who just got mugged?"

Jon shakes his head in wonder. "You're crazy, Captain," he announces.

"You're just figuring that out, are you?" chuckles Chris, pulling his arm from Jon's grasp. Licking the blood from his lip, he slaps the Ghurka on the shoulder. "I'd better cross now before I come to my senses... or stop bleeding... or pass out." He climbs from the hiding place and staggers into the jungle.

Moments later, he emerges onto the road and drops to his knees, crawling melodramatically toward guards.

"Können Sie mir helfen?" he gasps, his hand over the bloody gash on his forehead, blood spattering from his lip as he speaks. Since he is speaking German, the guards have no idea what he's saying, but it's clear something tragic has occurred. *Good! They look concerned, not suspicious*, Chris realizes with relief.

Two cops lift him by his arms and help him to a dark blue police Land Rover parked on the bridge abutment. He collapses onto the open tailgate, babbling and making wild gestures. One of the POLRI retrieves a first aid kit and dabs at Chris' wound with a piece of gauze while the other nods sympathetically, urging him to drink from a proffered canteen.

A sergeant approaches, pulling the bloody gauze away from Chris' head. He grimaces and places it back against the injury, grasping Chris' hand and slapping it over the wound to hold the gauze in place. He demands Chris' identification. Chris stares at him dumbly and points toward the road, trying to explain – still in German – he's been mugged. The sergeant becomes anxious.

"Ahhh," gasps Chris finally, *"Der Reisepass."* He reaches into his back pocket and withdraws his German passport. The relieved sergeant takes the document and thumbs through the well-worn pages.

"Rinhart New-bower?" he asks, trying admirably to pronounce Chris' German alias.

"Ja! Reinhardt Neubauer," replies Chris emphatically, motioning to himself.

The sergeant eyes him strangely. "Rumah sakit," he snaps, handing Chris' passport to one of the POLRI guards. The cops seize Chris' arms and haul him to his feet.

"Nein! Nein!" insists Chris as they led him around to the passenger seat. "Ich bin…"

The guard who treated his injuries smiles and announces reassuringly in English, "Hospital. Hospital," and hands him back his passport.

"Das krankenhaus?" asks Chris with relief.

The POLRI shrugs and nods uncertainly.

"Ja! Ja!" roars Chris as he shrugs off the guards' assistance and climbs willingly into the Land Rover.

Jon shoulders his weapon and releases the safety, his finger tightening steadily on the trigger as Chris attempts to tug from the POLRI's grasp. When Chris suddenly reaches out and shakes the sergeant's hand, Jon realizes what's happening and laughs silently to himself. He lowers the weapon and watches the Land Rover pull away, the big German waving to the guards as he crosses the bridge and rolls toward town.

Jon places his rifle in the shallow hole alongside the bag of ammunition and weapons Tran and Chris left behind. He wraps them in canvas and scoops dirt over the top of the hole. After camouflaging the bare spot with leaves and branches, he abandons the bamboo stand and prepares to cross the bridge.

As he starts toward the bridge, he's amused to see the sergeant of the guard has apparently decided to investigate the German's claims – whatever they are – that something occurred on the road. As he walks along the rutted shoulder, a Land Rover speeds down the road on Chris' "wild goose chase."

Tran intercepts him on the opposite side of the bridge. "What the hell's going on?" he demands. "Son-of-a-bitch waved at me from a POLRI Land Rover!"

Chris emerges into the evening breeze. Jon lies stretched out on a bench beside the hospital entrance appearing to read a local newspaper; Tran is lolling atop a short cinderblock wall across the street. Jon lays aside his newspaper and strides up behind Chris.

"Have a nice rest?" he chides. Chris turns slightly and grins at the Gurkha as they continue up the street, just two strangers engaged in casual conversation.

"What's wrong? Didn't you get a chauffeured limo into town too?"

"*We* walked," grunts Jon.

"Where's Tran?" asks Chris as he glances casually around at the pedestrians milling around a nearby coffee shop.

"The Major is covering us. He'll meet us at the safe house once he's sure we aren't being followed." Chris nods and keeps walking, subtly letting Jon take the lead.

They continue several blocks, cutting back and reversing several times to provide the elusive Tran an opportunity to identify anyone who might be tailing them.

CHAPTER 9

SilkAir flight MI847 arrives in Pangkalanbun more-or-less on schedule. Jessica's agent, Irwan, was provided a satellite phone by SID several years before. With guarded reluctance, she withdraws her satellite phone from its case and powers it up, hoping SID hasn't discovered her duplicity and disconnected her service. To her relief, she receives a connection. She dials the number the watch officer provided. The phone rings twice. She disconnects and redials.

A timid female voice replies.

"Sri? It's Yada," announces Jessica using her Thai alias. She hears a gasp, then silence. "How are you?" continues Jessica. "It's been a long time."

"Yes. Yes, it has," replies a strained voice.

"Might you be available for dinner this evening?"

"You're *here*?" asks Sri, incredulous. She has never actually met Yada, her husband's SID handler.

"I will be for dinner. Why don't you pick the restaurant?"

"Um. Of... of course," she replies, a hint of confusion in her voice. "How about Dunia Laut?"

"Certainly! I remember it well." lies Jessica. "I'll see you there at 18:30 if it's convenient."

"Yes. Yes, of course," replies Sri meekly.

Rain falls steadily as Jessica departs her hotel for the rendezvous. The concierge offers to hail a taxi, but she declines, seeking instead the anonymity of the public taxi stand across the rain-swept street. In the phone book, had located the restaurant where the meeting is to take place. As her taxi rolls down Sutan Syahril Road past the restaurant, she asks the driver to turn onto a side street and let her out.

The rain finally relents, leaving puddles of cool standing water and small rivers of mud coagulating on the uneven sidewalk. She backtracks two blocks to the restaurant.

In a Muslim nation, it is hardly proper for a woman to dine alone, much less enter the bar, so Jessica locates a spot on a bench outside the restaurant and relaxes in the damp evening air. Not long after settling in, she spots a tall, darkly dressed woman walking briskly from the alley beside the restaurant, a traditional Muslim hijab framing her haggard face. As she approaches the restaurant, Jessica rises and smiles.

"Sri?" she asks casually as the woman nears. The woman balks, examining the stranger cautiously.

"I... I didn't see you, Yada," Sri responds apprehensively as she leans forward and kisses the stranger on either cheek.

"It's all right," replies Jessica as she seizes Sri's hand. "It *has* been a long time." She glances around exaggeratedly. "Where's Irwan?"

Sri's head snaps up in alarm. "He's very sick," she announces desperately.

"I'll need to see him."

"No!" blurts Sri. "I... I mean he shouldn't have visitors yet."

A couple walk past, glancing inquiringly at the two women.

"Well, then why don't we girls just have a little chat?" She leads Sri inside the restaurant.

The golden hour fades rapidly to deep blue, then black. The interior of the restaurant is aglow with flickering light from candles and oil lamps. Under different circumstances the scene would be quite pleasant, even romantic - in the right company. But as she peers across the table into the eyes of her agent, Jessica realizes they're in grave danger. Sri's quiet reserve is like glass, ready to shatter at the slightest impact.

"You're attracting attention," scolds Jessica disapprovingly. "I spotted you a block away. You looked incredibly uneasy."

"I *am* uneasy," rasps Sri. "You don't know what it's like..."

Jessica leans back in her seat. "Don't I?" she interrupts. "Then why am I here?"

Sri appears confused. "I... I don't mean to imply..."

"No. Of course you don't," interrupts Jessica.

Sri's head droops; Jessica's afraid she's going to cry. "How's Irwan?" she asks.

"I...I told you," stammers Sri. "He's quite ill..."

It suddenly occurs to Jessica Sri doesn't realize why she's here.

"Sri," explains Jessica patiently as she touches Sri's calloused hand. "We know Irwan is wounded. The boat the Americans sent to rescue you came under attack," she explains. "The crew has come ashore and is hiding here in Pangkalanbun. I'm here to bring all of you in."

"You know about Greg?" asks Sri. The expression on Jessica's face betrays nothing. "The American," adds Sri.

Ah, So that's his alias.

"Yes. Greg is working with us."

Sri's anxiety recedes as she realizes Yada is aware she and Irwan have been playing a double-game with Singapore and the Americans.

"We have known for a long time," admits Jessica.

"Now what?" asks Sri anxiously.

"We'll collect Irwan and get out of here."

"Yes. Yes, of course. We're staying in a small house near the river. I can take you there." Sri begins to rise. Jessica gently but firmly grasps her wrist and pulls her back to her seat.

"We have ordered *dinner*," she announces in a steely voice. "It would be inappropriate to leave *before* it gets here."

"How about that one," asks Tran with a nod toward a dilapidated three-story motel, dim lights filtering from between crooked shutters.

Chris wrinkles his nose. The best that can be said is the hotel is so seedy it seems the last place anyone would look for them. "Looks like the Bates Hotel," scoffs Chris, "Anthony Perkins: night manager." Tran laughs; Jon stares at them queerly. "Inside joke," explains Chris.

"You guys case the neighborhood," recommends Tran. "I'll see if I can get us a room." He shoves his hands in his pockets, walks nonchalantly across the street, and disappears into the lobby.

"Let's split-up," Chris whispers to Jon. "I'll head around back. You take the other side. I'll meet you back here in five minutes." Jon's trained eyes have already begun scanning the neighborhood, searching for anything out of the ordinary. On Chris' order, he nods and disappears into the darkness.

The streets have begun to clear as the Muezzin calls the faithful to prayer from speakers atop a mosque's minaret several blocks away. The streets are lit at intervals by the occasional security light or storefront, interior lights remaining extinguished until families return from evening prayers. As the last echoes of the Muezzin's call fade, Chris finds himself alone in the deserted street. He circles the hotel, heading into an alley between the buildings and nearly stepping into the open sewer that frame each street.

A beam of light sweeps the road. He ducks into the shadows as a POLRI Land Rover rolls past. It proceeds down the street and evaporates around a corner. The occasional dog barks in the distance; otherwise, Pangkalanbun's streets are deserted.

He returns to the front of the hotel as Tran emerges from the office with a single key. He leads them up the stairs onto the second floor balcony. "Wait here," he cautions as he steps inside and quickly sweep the room for threats. "Okay," he announces. Chris and Jon enter the room.

"Oh, man I have a headache," Chris groans as he collapses onto one of the two rickety beds. Jon pulls aside the curtain and peers out the window into the blackness.

"You shouldn't have hit yourself with that tree," he comments.

Chris grunts in response.

"You look like shit," announces Tran as he examines Chris' wound.

"Well, looks ain't deceiving," mutters Chris. He shoves a lumpy pillow beneath his head, his forearm resting over his eyes to block the invading light.

"Jon told me what you did," grunts Tran, withdrawing the .45 from behind his back and setting it on the nightstand. "I always said you were a natural spook."

"He's crazy," adds Jon.

"Screw both of you," snorts Chris. He drags himself agonizingly upright. "Now let's call our control."

"You ready to call your *girlfriend*?" chides Tran.

"Don't ever say that in front of her," warns Chris. "She'll cut your nuts off and stir fry them."

"Too late," chuckles Tran.

Chris glances at him sharply before snatching the receiver and dialing the number Jessica provided. Cradling the receiver in his sweaty palm his heart races. He feels strangely like a high school kid calling to ask a girl out on a first date.

Jessica is strolling down the street alongside Sri when the satellite phone chirps inside her purse. She reaches inside her oversized bag and gropes for the phone, retrieving it on the third ring. She extends the awkward satellite antenna and stares at the phone in her hand as if it's some strange oracle. She takes a deep breath.

"Hello?" she answers with forced casualness.

There is breathing, but no response.

"Hello?" she asks again, insistently.

"Jess," croaks Chris, then clears his throat. "Jess, it's me."

Her hand trembles as she responds.

"You idiot! You scared the shit out of me!" she blurts.

"Where are you?" he asks.

"Here," she responds, immediately realizing it's too vague a response. "In Pangkalanbun."

"*Here?*" he gasps. "What the hell are you doing *here?*"

"I'm going to get you off the island," she replies sternly. She glances quickly around at the darkened street and lowers her voice. "Who did you expect, Arnold Schwarzenegger?"

"No. I... Okay. Okay," he stammers. "Have you made contact with our friends?"

"Yes, as a matter of fact."

"When can we hook-up?"

She consults her watch. "Not tonight, it's too late. We might raise suspicions. Tell me where you are."

"Wait one. Where the hell are we?" he asks Tran, who reads the hotel name, address and phone number from the back of a matchbook.

"Got it. Get some sleep," she orders. "I'll call you in the morning."

Having made contact, Jessica's mood lightens as she follows Sri toward the rental house. They walk several blocks before veering off the road and proceeding down a boardwalk toward the river.

The house at the end of the walkway is typical of the dwellings on the mud flats bordering the river. Built on six-foot stilts, the first three feet of wall are constructed of wood slats, the upper section comprised of a series of wide slatted shutters, the roof of corrugated tin. With long shutters to allow air – and words – to pass freely, it's hardly an ideal place for a covert meeting, but it is at least secluded by distance from the other houses.

They climb the notched log stairs and enter the dingy structure. It takes a moment for Jessica's vision to adjust in the dim light, but when her eyes adjust she is horrified at the image before her. In the middle of the floor lay Irwan in a pool of bloody bandages, flies buzzing hungrily around him.

"My God," she breathes as she approaches her agent. She drops to one knee and grasps his wrist, feeling for a pulse. Placing her hand on Irwan's burning forehead, she turns to Sri. "How long has he been like this?" she demands.

"Since yesterday," chokes Sri. "When we heard the gunfire on the beach we came straight to Pangkalanbun. He is sure he'll die here."

Jessica removes the oil lamp from its hook on the ceiling and suspends it above Irwan's head. She forces open his eyelids and examines his dilating pupils. Reluctantly, she pulls the bandages aside; the smell is overwhelming. For Sri's sake, she conceals her wretch with a fake cough and re-covers the festering wound. A wave of nausea nearly overwhelms her. She breathes heavily through her mouth, trying vainly to elude the stench.

"When did you last clean this wound?" she asks, attempting to mask the accusation in her voice.

"It was before the boat," stammers Sri. "Two... three days ago."

Jessica shakes her head sadly. What she smells is infection. There's no doubt, without immediate treatment, Irwan will die. She also realizes no treatment is forthcoming.

Her mind races. The nascent plan does not anticipate evacuating a critically injured patient. She peers at Sri's anxious face in the dim light.

"Sri," she announces softly. "Irwan was right. He won't live through the night."

Sri emits a stifled sob, forcing her fist into her mouth. Jessica rises to her feet and gently grasps Sri's hand, pulling the scraped knuckles from between her teeth. "You knew, didn't you?" she asks gently. Sri nods and buries her face in Jessica's shoulder. Jessica wraps her arms around the weeping woman and strokes her hair.

"Sri," she announces after a few minutes. "Did Irwan tell you what he knew about Khalid?"

Sri stops gasping and pulls away slowly. Wiping the tears from her eyes, she nods quietly. Jessica's anxiety eases as she again embraces her agent.

Through the remainder of the night Jessica sits on the floor, her back against the wall with Sri's head in her lap as they watch the dying man's chest rise and fall with each breath. Near dawn, after Sri has finally slipped into an exhausted sleep, Jessica hears Irwan's last, long rattling exhale.

A tear slides slowly down Jessica's cheek and drips onto Sri's hijab as she lets the new widow continue to sleep.

Chris awakes first. He rises quietly and moves to the window, squinting into the glaring light. Maybe it's the good night's rest, or perhaps having heard the sound of Jessica's voice last night, but this morning he feels a wave of optimism. He steps into the bathroom and splashes tepid water on his face, deciding to leave his growing beard. He thumbs through his money, picks up a hotel matchbook and slips it into his pocket before heading to the restaurant on the corner to scrounge a decent breakfast for his sleeping team.

On the street, people go about business as usual. Merchants roll-open garage-style doors to open-front shops and chat idly with neighboring merchants over strong morning tea and coffee. The grate of un-muffled engines and stench of gasoline fumes fill the air. He waits for a break in the traffic and scurries across the street, dodging between motor scooters and microbuses weaving carelessly through the village.

In front of a restaurant he finds a half-dozen small round-topped plastic tables scattered haphazardly on the crumbling sidewalk. He orders nasi goring, a local dish consisting of a fried egg over rice, and a cup of strong, sweet coffee before settling into a creaky plastic chair. As he enjoys his first real meal in three days, something draws his attention to a non-descript Nissan rolling to a stop in front of the hotel. One of the two men in the vehicle raises a walkie-talkie to his lips, studying the hotel as he speaks. The passenger's hand rests on what was clearly the barrel of a submachine gun.

Chris glances around in panic and spots a phone on the wall behind the counter of the clothing store beside the café. He dashes inside and points at the phone, mimicking making a telephone call. The storeowner shakes his head, wagging his finger. Chris reaches into his pocket and withdraws a 25,000 Rupia note. He can tell by the expression on the man's face he is about to be denied a second time. Fortunately the man's wife waddles over and shoos her husband away. Without comment she rips the bill from Chris' grasp and hands him the receiver.

"Danke," announces Chris earnestly. With shaking hands, he retrieves the matchbook from his pocket, reads the hotel's phone number, and dials the room. The line is busy! He glances anxiously across the street and sees a POLRI Land Rover pull up on the east side of the hotel. He disconnects the call and, before the owner's wife can stop him, dials the number a second time. Mercifully the phone rings. He waves and nods to the woman, who snorts and leaves to serve other customers.

"Ya?" answers Tran.

"Tran! Get out of there. NOW!" hisses Chris.

"Where the hell are you?"

"I'm across the street. The POLRI are closing in on the hotel. There's an unmarked car in front and a Land Rover on the east side: looks like they're waiting for backup. Go down the stairs on the west end of the building and head south down the alley. I'll meet you at the other end!"

Tran slams the phone onto the receiver and growls to Jon, "The cops are surrounding the place. Chris says we have to get out." There's a flurry of activity as they finish getting dressed and rapidly "sanitize" the room to ensure they leave nothing to allow the POLRI to track them. Tran folds a local newspaper over the .45 in his hand and cracks open the door.

"Follow me," he rasps to Jon and slips from the room. They move quickly along the second floor walkway and turn down the stairwell at the west end of the building.

At the bottom of the landing Tran spots a man in civilian clothes holding a walkie-talkie. He realizes by the startled expression it is one of the cops. Flinging the newspaper aside, he trains his pistol on the cop, who freezes in horror.

Tran and Jon rumble down the stairs, reaching the cop as he regains his courage and keys the walkie-talkie. Jon swings the blade of his Khukuri backhanded across the man's neck, severing the vocal cords and arteries in one powerful stroke. The walkie-talkie clatters to the pavement as the man slumps, gurgling, against the wall, blood gushing from between his fingers as his hands grope at the gaping wound.

Without breaking stride, Tran leaps over the dying man and sprints down the alley, slipping the .45 behind his belt and pulling his shirttail over it. Jon stoops momentarily and wipes the blood from the Khukuri onto the dying man's pants. He tucks away his knife and dashes down the alley in pursuit of Tran.

Tran slows to a walk, glancing over his shoulder to see Jon jogging after him. He smiles with relief. Abruptly, his attention is drawn to the end of the alley where a Land Rover appears in front of him. Jon is fifteen meters behind Tran when the officer in the Land Rover's front passenger seat points and yells. One of the POLRI in the back of the vehicle raises his assault rifle.

Time slows to an unnatural half-speed as Tran draws his pistol and opens fire. The first two "double-tapped" bullets hit the armed cop in the chest, flipping him off the back of the Land Rover as is passes nearly parallel with him. The third shot strikes the officer in the side of the head, splattering brain matter on the driver, who releases the steering wheel and flings his arms over his face to protect himself. Several bullets strike the man behind the driver, the remainder ricocheting harmlessly down the alley.

The Land Rover swerves toward Jon who leaps from the vehicle's path as it careens out of control and smashes into a building's rear wall. The driver and officer are crushed between the dashboard and seats as the bullet-ridden body of the man in the rear bounces from the vehicle to impact with a sickening "splat" against the cinderblock wall.

Chris emerges from the stampeding crowd onto the street. "Tran!" he yells over their terrified screams.

Tran glances around in confusion, unable to locate the direction from which the voice has come. Jon grabs Tran's shirtsleeve and spins him around, motioning toward where Chris is standing against the building across the street. Over the heads of the crowd, Chris motions west, raises two fingers, then motions south and raises three fingers. Tran acknowledges the signal and he and Jon join the fleeing melee.

The team gathers fifteen minutes later at a small park three blocks from the hotel.

"It's a damned good thing you woke up hungry or we'd be in a world of hurt," confesses Tran.

"Yeah, well. I want to know how the hell they knew we were there," replies Chris bitterly. "I *figured* the attack on Dominion might be a fluke. But there's no question that someone tipped them off about the hotel."

"We had to take out a cop at the bottom of the stairwell," adds Tran. "They were definitely heading for our room."

"Maybe the hotel clerk got suspicious," offers Chris.

"Naw, he didn't seem the least bit suspicious," grumbles Tran. "Besides, if that was the case the POLRI could have easily rolled us up last night." The three men lapse into a gloomy silence, realizing now that blood had been spilled, the POLRI will pursue them with renewed vengeance.

"The story doesn't get any better," announces Tran. "Jessica called while you were out: looks like your guy died of his wounds last night."

"Damn!" swears Chris. "Did she find out anything about Khalid before he died?"

Tran shrugs. "She didn't say. But now she wants us to perform some sort of Muslim burial rites."

Chris smiles grimly. "So Sri knows," he murmurs.

"Who?" asks Tran.

"Sri," Chris repeats, "Irwan's wife. He must've told her where Khalid is."

"What makes you think that?"

"Jessica doesn't have a sentimental bone in her body," admits Chris. "The only reason she'd go to the trouble to have us perform burial rites is because Sri has the information we need."

"Manipulative bitch, isn't she?"

Chris ignores the jibe. "What are Muslim death rites, anyway," he asks. Tran and Jon shrug. After all, Tran is Buddhist and Jon is Hindu. "Fine," sighs Chris. "So where do we meet her?"

"At a floating market down on the river," replies Tran. "She gave me directions from the mosque downtown." He peers into the distance toward a weathered gold dome and four minarets peeking above the buildings. "It's probably it over there," he adds.

"How're we getting there?" asks Chris.

"On foot. Plan for a movement to contact," replies Tran. "The only cops who can ID Jon and I are splattered against the alley wall now, so if someone approaches any of us, he's just guessing. If that happens, keep your cool and wait for the cavalry."

Chris surveys the surrounding street; there are no POLRI in sight, though sirens continue to wail several blocks away.

"Are you still packin' heat?" he asks as Tran brushes past.

"Yeah, but I'm out of ammo," mumbles Tran.

"Oh, *that's* helpful," snorts Chris.

"All right," announces Tran, his eyes fixing each man in succession. "I'm taking point on the left side of the street. Chris, you cross over and keep a twenty meter interval. Jon, you're rearguard: stay behind Chris. *Everyone*, keep in periodic eye contact. We're almost home."

CHAPTER 10

Dozens of small wooden boats and sampans swarm the riverbank. Merchants drift from boat to boat trading melons for fish, tea for exotic spices.

As they near the market, Tran suggests the team spread out and search for Jessica, recommending they rendezvous at the small shaved ice stand on the street once they made contact. The team splits and fans-out through the riverside market thumping melons and behaving like local shoppers. Chris finds it beneficial to stop at the occasional booth and pretend to sample the merchandise, using the casual pace to sweep the area for signs of Jessica.

Tran is sampling a pungent slice of durian when he notices Chris walk past, trailed discreetly by a small swarthy man with a gimp leg. He sets aside the fruit and follows the man so fixated on the big Anglo the he fails to spot Tran, and now Jon, joining-in the counter-surveillance.

During one of his frequent stops, Chris glances over his shoulder and notes with amusement that Tran and Jon are shadowing him. He was going to wave them away, but suddenly realizes what they're doing when he inadvertently catches the eye of the man with the limp. The man turns on his heel and gropes carelessly through a stack of limp vegetables.

Gaining Chris' attention, Tran nods toward a narrow passage between the merchants' stalls. Chris discreetly returns the nod, sets aside the vegetables he's examining and strides casually between the stalls into the alley.

Jon suddenly notices another man making his way rapidly toward the opposite end of the alley.

Unable to warn Tran about the second man, Jon breaks off his surveillance and takes-off in pursuit of what he suspects may be the man's partner.

Chris slides into the alley with the gimp trailing ten feet behind. His pace slows as he works his way between piles of produce crates scattered around the alley. As the man closes on Chris, Tran slips silently up behind him and seizes his shoulder, shoving the barrel of the unloaded .45 against the man's spine. His silent diplomacy has the desired effect; the man raises his arms resignedly as Chris rounds and punches him squarely in the face. The man's knees buckle and Tran lowers him slowly to the ground.

"So who are you, my friend?" Chris sneers as he rummages through the stunned man's pockets. "Are you just a *really* unlucky mugger..." He detects something in the back of the man's waistband and withdraws a 9mm Browning automatic pistol. "Or are you something else?"

The stalker's associate enters the other end of the alley, halting abruptly when he realizes his partner had been caught. A sneering grin creases his face. As he turns to flee the alley, the grin slides to a grimace as Jon cuts-off his retreat. The man gropes impulsively inside his robe and Jon slashes at him with the Khukuri. Blood spews across the pavement as Jon springs backward, allowing the man to sink to his knees and collapse face-down into a puddle of filthy water. The body still twitching, Jon rolls the man onto his back and feels inside his robe. Tucked in his belt is a Swiss-made SIG-Sauer P220 9mm automatic pistol. Jon jerks the weapon free and stuffs it into his waistband before continuing to check the body for identification. He finds nothing.

Realizing Jon is in control at the other end of the alley way, Chris continues his search of the Indonesian, discovering documents identifying him as a POLRI sergeant. He passes the pistol to Tran who deposits his empty .45 into a dumpster and holds the 9mm on the trembling sergeant.

"Do you speak English?" growls Chris. The terrified cop shakes his head vigorously. "Then how do you know what I just asked you, asshole?" grunts Chris in amusement.

"I don't! I..." The man's voice trails off hopelessly.

"How many of you are there?" demands Chris.

"Many. Many," insists the sergeant.

"Bullshit!" sneers Chris.

At Jon's approach, the POLRI sergeant's eyes widen in horror. Chris detects the splash of Jon's sandals in the soggy alleyway and realizes why the sergeant is so scared, fixated as he is on the bloody Khukuri. "Get us out of here safely or you die. Understand?"

The sergeant utters a pathetic moan, nodding emphatically.

"Which way?" hisses Chris. The sergeant motions vaguely toward the river. Chris seizes his shoulder, spins him around, and shoves him forward. The four men emerge from the alley and start toward the riverbank when Tran suddenly spots Jessica.

"There she is," mumbles Tran, "third sampan to the right."

Chris nudges the sergeant toward the boat. The men wade through knee-deep water and climb into the waiting sampan. The narrow, shallow-draught boat is 20-feet long with a rounded cloth shelter over the middle-third of its length. At one of the identical ends is mounted a small gasoline-powered outboard motor.

Chris winks when he notices the shocked look on Jessica's face.

"Who the hell is this?" she snaps when he shoves the sergeant into the boat.

"A new friend," replies Chris sarcastically.

"A....," her question interrupted by a scream from the nearby alley.

"Time to go!" announces Tran as he pushes the boat from the bank and leaps aboard. He passes the sergeant's pistol to Chris. "Get him under cover," he whispers. Tran and Jon use long poles to drive the boat away from shore before Tran yanks the starter cord and the motor sputters to life.

"Which way?" Tran asks Jessica, who points wordlessly to the north, still uncertain what has transpired.

As they proceed steadily upriver, Jessica slips beneath the shelter. Chris sits impatiently, his pistol trained on the stranger as Sri stares sullenly at the sergeant. "I asked what the hell *he's* doing here," Jessica snaps. "You didn't cause any trouble back there did you?"

Chris' initial euphoria over seeing Jessica fades rapidly. "Yeah," he snorts. "Jon hacked this guy's partner in half. What should we have done, surrender?"

"No. Of course not," she replies. "It's just... well... they're going to be after us now."

Chris shakes his head sadly. "You have *no idea*, do you?" he replies under his breath. Reclining against a crate of rotting vegetables, he glares at the POLRI sergeant. "Why don't you ask him what they know about us?"

"They? They...who?" asks Jessica uncertainly.

"The POLRI. The terrorists. Ask him how they knew we were at the hotel," insists Chris. "Ask him how he knew to look for us at the floating market," he continues with mounting anger. "Ask him who the Arab was! Then ask him why I shouldn't blow his fuckin' head off right now!" he sneers, jamming the barrel of his pistol against the man's jaw.

The sergeant topples backwards off the crate onto the deck, whimpering, hands over his face as if by so doing he can deflect bullets.

"What are you talking about?" demands Jessica.

"The POLRI ambushed us at the hotel this morning," explains Chris. "We had to shoot our way out, leaving six or seven dead behind us."

"How...?"

"Wait! It gets better," he sneers. "Then this guy and his partner were tailing me at the floating market. That's *no* coincidence!"

She shakes her head in disbelief. "No one knows I'm here except us," she insists. "Who could have tipped them off?"

"There's only one answer I can think of," snarls Chris. "You've got a leak at SID."

Expecting an outburst at the accusation, he's surprised at her muted response. "No. I don't think so," she sighs.

Chris stares at her. Shame overcoming anger, he turns away, flinching as if noticing the other woman for the first time. He gives a wan smile. "Hi. You must be Sri," he announces softly, switching the pistol to his left hand and taking her hand in his right. "I'm Greg... well...," he corrects, glancing up at Jessica apologetically, "Chris, actually. I'm so sorry about Irwan." He leans forward and kisses her lightly on the cheek.

"Thank you," replies Sri meekly, still glaring at the POLRI sergeant.

Chris returns his attention to the sergeant. "*Well?*" he snaps, shifting the pistol toward the man. "Are you going to tell me how you found us?"

The sergeant is petrified. "I... I...," he stutters.

"Yeah," replies Chris testily. "You said that before."

"Jon!" he shouts over his shoulder. When the Gurkha enters, the sergeant shrinks even more deeply into the bottom of the boat.

"Have a talk with this guy. Find out what he knows and see if you can determine just how deep in shit we are," orders Chris. He stands to leave. "Jessica? Sri? You'd better come with me," he advises.

"You're not...?" Jessica asks in disbelief.

"No," Chris interrupts icily. "*Jon* is." He herds the women into the bright sunshine.

Jon draws his Khukuri and wipes the Arab's coagulated blood from the blade onto the sergeant's pants.

"No! No! Please," pleads the sergeant in passable English. "It was a phone call – I don't know who it was! We were just told you were at the hotel!"

At the entrance to the shelter, Chris breathes a sigh of relief. He didn't know what Jon would have done to the man and, as angry as he is, he's not certain how far he would permit Jon to go. But the sergeant saw the Gurkha shed blood remorselessly moments before and the continuing horror seems enough to loosen his tongue.

Chris spins back toward the sergeant. "When did you find out we were at the hotel?" he demands.

"This morning," replies the trembling man. "My... my lieutenant received a call. We sent a team to the hotel, but..."

"But they fucked up didn't they?"

He nods meekly.

Chris drops to his knee and leans into the sergeant's face. *Once they start, keep 'em talking*, he reminds himself. "Who were they looking for?" he demands.

"A... an American assassin," replies the sergeant hollowly, for surely he is speaking to the assassin himself. Chris cocks his head and glances knowingly at Jessica who is standing beside him, a steadying hand against the shelter's frame.

He returns his attention to the sergeant, slapping the man suddenly, angry he's let the flow of the interrogation lapse.

"Why is the POLRI doing Khalid's bidding?" he demands. He slaps the cowering man again. "Where is he?"

"I... I don't know," he squeals. "I'm just a lowly sergeant."

"Bullshit!" sneers Chris maniacally. "Jon! Cut off any extraneous body parts until this asshole starts telling the truth!" Jon raises the shimmering blade and steps forward, a cruel sneer on his scarred face.

"Nooooo! I swear by my father's eyes. I DON'T KNOW!!" screeches the sergeant as he balls up into the fetal position, sobbing hysterically.

Jessica grasps Chris' arm tightly. His head snaps toward her; she shakes her head morosely. The sergeant has told them all he can - or will - rather than risk his soul in Paradise.

Colonel Mok is in a blind rage. His people searched Jessica's condo and found evidence of a hasty departure. It doesn't take long to examine departing flight manifests and discover his key agent used her alias to book herself on a one-way flight to Kalimantan.

"Shall I notify Internal Affairs?" ventures one of his officers. "That would be... *standard* procedure," he announces, his voice trailing off as he anxiously awaits the colonel's rebuke.

"No." mumbles Colonel Mok with a miserable shake of his head. "This isn't a defection. She's gone to recover her 'assets,'" he confesses. *I knew I should have pulled her off this operation when I learned about her relationship with the American*, he admonishes himself.

"What are we hearing from our sources in Kalimantan?" he asks tiredly.

The officers glance around uncomfortably, each waiting for the other to speak first. "Sir," replies one officer as he clears his throat. "There has been some unusual activity in the vicinity of Pangkalanbun." He reaches into a folder and places a report gingerly on the colonel's desk. "POLRI district command claims several of its officers have been ambushed and killed by local separatists. We have reason to believe these events may be related to the... uh... recovery effort," he explains elliptically.

"Do you mean to tell me our little band of renegades is taking on the entire district POLRI?" snorts Colonel Mok disbelievingly.

"Well... Yes, Sir. And apparently they're winning."

Colonel Mok falls silent, his bony fingers massaging his throbbing temples. "Please leave me," he sighs.

The four senior officers stand and depart the room quickly. As the door clicks shut, the colonel reaches for the secure phone and dials a private number from memory - a number known to but a few, trustworthy members within Singapore's government. The phone rings several times before a crisp, elderly voice answers.

"Senior Minister," announces Colonel Mok respectfully. "I need your guidance."

Twenty minutes after leaving the floating market, the sampan slides slowly beneath the house on stilts. The passengers clamber from the boat and mount the notched log leading to the front door. Jessica enters first, followed by Sri, Tran and Jon. Chris shoves the cringing POLRI sergeant inside behind them and enters the dank dwelling last.

The stench is appalling. In the center of the room lay Irwan's sheet-covered corpse, flies buzzing hungrily around it. Sri dashes over and shoos away the flies, stifling the sobs that continue to surface despite her heroic efforts.

"So how do we do this?" asks Chris apprehensively, staring at the decaying corpse.

"It is traditional that the body be washed three times by people of the same gender as the deceased," explains Sri timidly. "It must then be covered with sweet smelling spices and perfumes and wrapped in three sheets of white linen." She lamely indicates a sack on the floor in the corner. "Everything you need is there," she mumbles, then adds uneasily, "Are you sure you want to do this?"

The collective group nods in unison. "Yes. Sri," replies Chris solemnly, placing his hand gently on her shoulder. "Irwan was our friend. It's the least we can do." Sri stares back in disbelief. Jessica wraps her arm around the widow's shoulder and escorts her from the house.

"Wh... What are you doing?" asks the sergeant anxiously.

"We are giving this man a proper Muslim burial," replies Tran.

"But... you are not Muslim," gasps the sergeant.

"No," replies Chris over his shoulder. "But a man deserves to be buried according to his faith." With a sigh, he kneels before Irwan's body and pulls aside the filthy sheet. He retches and turns away.

Jon departs the shack with two buckets and heads down to the river to retrieve water for the bath. The women watch silently as he fills the buckets and struggles up the notched log to reenter the house.

Using wet rags, the men wash down Irwan's body, taking care to rinse it the requisite three times. It's sobering, tedious work, compounded by the smell of the putrefying infection and insistent invasion of flies.

The POLRI sergeant clears his throat.

"Sir," he announces anxiously. "I have performed these rites before. May I offer my assistance?"

Tran glares at him. "You understand you will dishonor your faith if we let you assist and you try to escape," he explains.

"Yes, Sir," replies the sergeant. "You are doing what is right and so will I," he promises.

"Jon," orders Tran, nodding toward the sergeant. "Cut him loose."

After an hour, Tran steps onto the porch running a damp rag over his sweating face. He locates the women sitting in the shade beneath the shack, their bare feet submerged in the river in search of relief from the stifling heat.

"It's done," he announces tiredly. "You can come back inside."

Sri glances apprehensively at Jessica who smiles reassuringly and draws the widow to her feet. They follow Tran up the log ladder and into the house. Sri stands in a daze as four men place Irwan's wrapped body on a board and tie it in place. She is shocked to discover the POLRI sergeant is one of the men raising Irwan's body to his shoulder. She watches sullenly as the men carry the body down the notched log and place it in the waiting sampan beneath the house.

An eerie silence accompanies the boat upriver in the afternoon sun. "You choose the place," Jessica murmurs to Sri as they stand on the bow, the warm breeze brushing their cheeks.

Soon, Sri spots a small rise at the bend in the river and announces firmly, "There."

Tran maneuvers the boat toward the bank and runs it aground, the supple mud embracing the bow as the boat slides to a stop. Sri and Jessica step gingerly from the vessel and head for the high ground while the men raise Irwan's body to their shoulders and shuffle up the muddy embankment behind them.

They place the body in a small clearing.

"He should be buried facing toward Mecca," announces the sergeant quietly. Tran fishes the compass from his pocket and orients it to the west. "That should be about right," he announces, dragging the toe of his sandal through the mud in a rough outline of the grave. Chris retrieves a pick and hacks away at the sodden ground. One by one, each man silently selects a tool and joins him as they scraped a hole in the black earth.

Light is fading rapidly as the party set their tools aside and untie Irwan's body from the plank. Jessica holds aloft a small oil lamp to illuminate the funeral. Leaving the ropes beneath the board the men lower the body into its shallow, muddy tomb. The body properly settled on its side, face directed toward Mecca, they whip the ropes from beneath the plank and stand silently, uncertain how to proceed. The sergeant speaks again.

"Before a Muslim dies," he explains. "He hopes to recite the Shahadah: 'There is no God but Allah and Muhammad is his prophet.' After his death, those who mourn repeat these words from the Qur'an: 'We have come from God and unto him we shall return.'"

After an awkward pause, the unlikely mourners murmur the unfamiliar phrase as Sri stands numbly at Jessica's side. Heads bowed solemnly, they listen to the sergeant recite in sing-song Arabic what he recalls of the traditional Dua, the Muslim prayer for the dead. None but Sri recognize the words, or know even if the words he used were correct. But the dignified tones apparently have the desired effect, for Sri regains her composure and quietly follows along with the prayer. As the sergeant's voice trails off, he glimpses movement out of the corner of his eye as the tall Anglo silently crosses himself in the traditional Catholic Christian fashion. Sri notices also, peering at him strangely from beneath her hijab.

Burial rites complete, the men retrieve their spades and begin to shovel earth into the grave. The sergeant takes a place beside Chris.

"You are the infidel," the sergeant whispers. "Why do you pray for the soul of your enemy?"

Chris pauses, a scoopful of dirt hanging in the air. He shakes his head and resumes shoveling. "He was not my enemy, sergeant. And neither are you."

"But you are non-believers," insists the sergeant.

"Sergeant," replies Chris with a sigh as he sinks his blade into the ground and leans exhaustedly on the handle. "Look around," he demands with a wave of his hand toward the others gathered around. "We are all God's children – none better or more pure than the other."

The sergeant peers around sheepishly. "What is their faith?" he asks conspiratorially.

"I don't know and I don't care," replies Chris in exasperation. "A man's faith is between him and God!"

"But you come here to Crusade against Islam," demands the sergeant indignantly.

"No! I came here to find the man who would kill my countrymen simply because we worship God differently!"

"But my partner. The man in the market...?"

"... Was trying to stop me from finding the murderer I seek," interrupts Chris. "Surely Islam does not deny the right of self-defense!" He jerks his spade from the damp earth and resumes flinging dirt into the grave.

The sergeant lapses into silence and resumes shoveling dirt into the hole. After several minutes, he speaks again. "I think it is right you honor this man's faith," he announces.

"*Thanks*," snorts Chris. The grave complete, he shoulders his shovel and stalks silently back to the boat.

Darkness is complete by the time the mourners shove off from the burial site. Jon lights kerosene lanterns fore and aft as Tran pilots the boat down the black river toward the safe house. Chris rests on the bow watching the glistening lights of oil lamps and bare electric lights filtering through the open windows of houses bordering the river, casting shimmering golden light on the rippling wakes as the boat's bow slices through the water.

Sri remains beneath the shelter, staring blankly as the shadows of overhanging limbs form grotesque caricatures that float dissonantly across the canvas cover. Jessica ducks beneath the shelter and takes a seat on a box opposite Sri. She seizes the widow's hand.

"I know it's hard," she announces quietly. "But Irwan believed in what he was doing..."

"No," interrupts Sri. "Irwan believed in money, not causes," she insists in a soft, cold voice.

Jessica tenses. "I can't speak to Irwan's motivation," she admits cautiously. "But he provided information that served the common good."

Sri rips her hand from Jessica's grip. "Don't patronize me!" she rasps. "Irwan was a traitor! He sold his loyalty for money."

"He was paid, yes." Admits Jessica tersely. "Everyone has a role to play: even those with less-than-honorable intentions."

Sri withdraws into a long silence. "Why did you go to such trouble for him?" she asks finally.

"Chris told you. Every man has a right to be buried according to his own faith," replies Jessica.

"But you – *the infidel* – risked your lives for the soul of your enemy," demands Sri. "*Why?*"

Jessica's stomach clenches. *That's why it bothers her. It conflicts with her image of us – of the infidel!* Lunging across the narrow aisle, she rips the cloth bag from Sri's grasp and grapples through it until she discovers what she is seeking. As she withdraws Irwan's satellite phone from the purse, Sri lunges at her. Jessica shoves her onto the deck, where Sri remains, cowering and staring apprehensively as Jessica powers-up the phone.

There is a "beep" and she raises the greenish back-lit screen, setting her face aglow. Scrolling through the "outgoing calls," she discovers an unfamiliar phone number dialed that morning at 06:41.

"Sri?" she asks, her voice trembling with mounting rage. "Who did you call this morning?"

The POLRI sergeant suddenly bolts past Jessica, knocking her aside as he sprints onto the deck.

"Chris!" shrieks Jessica. "Stop him!"

Shaken from his relaxed daze, Chris turns to see a shadowy form dive into the river, water sloshing over the low beam of the shallow-draught boat. He draws the 9mm pistol from behind his belt, eyes scanning the inky blackness.

"Tran! The sergeant went overboard!"

Cursing, Tran swings the boat into a sharp U-turn. "Kill him!" he rasps.

"I can't tell where he is. Kill the engine!" shouts Chris. The engine sputters to silence. A hundred meters off Pangkalanbun, the boat drifts silently, the sing-song appeal of the Muezzin calling the faithful to prayer echoes dissonantly across the tranquil water.

"Where is...?" asks Jessica, emerging from the cabin.

"Shhh!" hisses Chris. He leans out over the water, listening intently for a sound, a splash, an unnatural disturbance on the ancient river. Jon, poised near the stern, holds a pistol in his steady hand as his eyes sweep the river.

Unable to hold his breath any longer, the sergeant suddenly breaks the surface and splashes loudly toward shore. Chris searches for the telltale foam. "I've got him," he announces and snaps-off several rapid shots at the apex of a white-capped wake. The eruption echoes off the water's glassy surface and fades slowly into the trees. Silence falls; the splashing ceases.

"Get the poles!" rasps Tran. He and Jon carefully maneuver the boat to the foaming spot where Chris' bullets struck the river. From beneath the water, bubbles float upward and pop on the surface. A greasy film spreads across the still water.

"Well, that solves one problem," announces Tran.

Lights previously doused for the evening blink to life in homes bordering the river as curious onlookers explore the sound of gunfire. "We'd better get out of here before someone comes to investigate" he declares. Resuming his seat at the stern, he wraps the starter chord around the shaft and yanks. The motor coughs to life.

Chris turns back toward the cabin and spots Jessica staring at him.

"What the hell?" he asks.

She motions for him to join her inside the makeshift cabin where Sri sits, pale and trembling. "That's why," she announces, nodding toward Sri. "I found our leak."

"What...?" Chris asks disbelievingly. Sri hides her face in her hands and he realizes at once Jessica is right. Sri knew where the pickup was going to be. She knew where the hotel was. She knew they would be at the market.

"Dear God," he mumbles. "*Why?*"

Sri nods miserably. "I had to make recompense for Irwan's treachery," she mumbles.

"*Irwan's treachery?*" seethes Chris. "What about yours? You've been feeding us information for years. What the fuck changed to turn it into *treachery?*" he curses, shoving a crate off the teetering pile and stepping threateningly toward her.

"The Fatwa," she sneers defensively, standing her ground before his hulking form. "Those events occurred before the jihad..."

"Dammit, Sri! We are *not your enemy just because some pissed-off Imam says so!*"

Sri lapses into an uneasy silence.

"So are they waiting for us back at the safe house?" demands Chris.

"I... I don't know," she mumbles miserably. "I haven't spoken with him since this morning."

Jessica's face snaps toward Chris then back to Sri. "You haven't spoken with *whom?*"

Sri's eyes widen.

"Khalid's here. Isn't he?" concludes Jessica. "In Pangkalanbun!"

Sri covers her mouth and nods.

"Where was he when you spoke to him?" demands Chris.

"I don't know," replies Sri.

"No problem," replies Jessica with a nastiness immediately endearing her to Chris. "You called from Irwan's satellite phone, remember?"

Chris straightens and glances at Jessica. She nods a silent acknowledgement.

"NO...!" Screams Sri.

Jon's hand closes over her mouth, her arms pinned within his bear-hug. She struggles as Chris rips a long strip of canvas and knots it several times to create a large ball. Jon forces Sri face-down on the deck as Jessica helps hog-tie her hands and feet together. Then Chris forces the knotted gag into Sri's mouth and ties the ends of the cloth behind her head.

With Sri subdued, Chris emerges onto the stern and plops-down beside to Tran at the helm where he is unaware of the events inside.

"Tran, my friend," announces Chris, placing his arm around his comrade's shoulder. "How would you like to quit being the hunted and become the hunter?"

CHAPTER 11

A manservant ushers Colonel Mok through the marble-floored foyer into an atrium drawing room. Decorated in a tasteful mixture of plush modern furnishings and ancient Asian artifacts, the elegant home is smaller than he expects, though more than ample for a wealthy elderly couple in semi-retirement.

Since retiring as prime minister, Lee Kuan Yew lives in a temperature-controlled 70-degrees Fahrenheit; an environment chilling to many of his colleagues more comfortable with – or at least accustomed to – Singapore's Equatorial temperatures.

"Senior Minister," greets Colonel Mok, bowing deeply as he is presented to the elder statesman. "I appreciate your willingness to speak with me about this delicate matter."

The aging icon of Southeast Asian politics smiles benignly. As founder of modern Singapore, Lee Kuan Yew served as prime minister for 30 years before stepping down to assume the specially-created mantle of Senior Minister. Now in his 80th year, he continues to exercise considerable influence, albeit unofficially, throughout Asia.

Mr. Lee motions for his old colleague to be seated before sinking into his own overstuffed leather chair. "It has been a long time, Mok," he smiles. "I sleep well knowing you continue to protect the Republic."

"Thank you Sir," responds the colonel, uncomfortable being praised for doing what he does so naturally.

"How may I be of assistance to SID?" asks the Senior Minister brightly, his hands folded serenely in his lap.

"Sir. It's about Operation Gold Leaf," admits the colonel, knowing Mr. Lee had discussed the mission with the Prime Minister. "There are 'complications' of which you might not be aware."

"I have spoken to the Prime Minister and he is not pleased our involvement with the Americans has placed us at odds with our neighbors," announcing Mr. Lee softly.

Colonel Mok winces. *It's just like the senior minister to approach the topic from the perspective of another. It permits him to remain aloof from the controversy while at the same time asserting a position. But is this his position?*

"But Sir," replies Colonel Mok. "You have spoken of the threat of Muslim extremism in the region for years. We stand in their way. This has nothing to do with the Americans."

The Senior Minister nods. Long before the events of September 11, 2001, he had been warning of the threat posed by Muslim extremists in Southeast Asia pursuing the fantasy of "Daulah Islamiyah," a unified Muslim caliphate consisting of the Southern Philippines, Indonesia, Singapore, Malaysia, and southern Thailand. This is the dream Al Qa'ida promises to deliver in exchange for the Jihad. This is the ultimate goal of Jemmah Islamiya.

"Yes," concedes Mr. Lee. "But our struggle becomes much more difficult when we are identified with the Americans. They are like a lightning rod to the extremists. And – I hesitate to say – the Americans can be undependable allies," he reminds the colonel delicately. "With every election their foreign policies are subject to extreme reversals. If we openly side with them now, we may stir the dragon only to be left to fight it alone."

"Of course, I understand Senior Minister," admits Colonel Mok. "But only the Americans have the power to fight extremism on a global scale. But as you say, they have a short attention span. If they realize success, they'll continue. If not, they'll lose interest and those who fought alongside them will be much the worse off. Therefore we must help them achieve the progress they crave; it's why we agreed to support Operation Gold Leaf. In this matter, our interests are as one," insists Colonel Mok.

"But we risk war with Indonesia," Mr. Lee reminds the colonel. "Our people have already died..."

"Exactly!" interrupts Colonel Mok, his passion overwhelming his manners. "They *cannot* have died in vain," he insists.

The Senior Minister smiles kindly. "Colonel," he replies softly. "I laud your enthusiasm. But do you truly have Singapore's interests at heart?"

The colonel winces. "Sir?"

Mr. Lee changes his approach. "I realize the tragic loss of several of your officers to the terrorist Kastari bin Ali was a tremendous shock," he announces. "But anger cannot color your response to the incident. The important thing is, thanks to your noble efforts, the Jihadists no longer operate in Singapore."

"As far as we know," replies the colonel stiffly. "But be assured: if we fail..."

"And," interrupts Mr. Lee in an even tone, "I understand Ms. Ling has gone to Kalimantan without your authorization."

"Yes, Sir," replies Colonel Mok, tight-lipped.

"I appreciate your interest in her career, colonel. You have been a most effective and compassionate mentor. But I am concerned your objectivity may be at risk in this particular matter."

Colonel Mok springs to his feet, rage building in his usually rational mind. "Sir! You have no cause to question my commitment to the Republic!" he replies angrily. "I was there when..."

"Sit *down*, colonel," interrupts Mr. Lee firmly. Colonel Mok freezes, suddenly aware his passions have gotten the better of him. Realizing this weakness shames him. But he knows the Senior Minister is a decent man, not one to make others grovel. So he withholds his apology and contritely regains his seat.

"I believe the attack on Dominion was ordered by 'opposition' members within Indonesia's government in order to embarrass President Megawati," declares Mr. Lee. "She is a secular... female... leader. The extremists despise her."

"But who would have such authority?" asks Colonel Mok.

The Senior Minister smiles grimly. "It is a peculiar aspect of Indonesia's fledgling democracy," he observes, "that he who loses the election is appointed vice president. It certainly doesn't make for a particularly unified government, does it?"

"You mean...?"

"Perhaps," interrupts the senior minister. "Or those within the military who support the extremist cause."

His mind made up, Senior Minister Lee rises, indicating the meeting is at its end. "I am an old acquaintance with the Sukarno family. I knew President Megawati when she was a child," he announces. "Perhaps it is time I made a social call."

Certain that returning to the safe house will result in immediate arrest; Tran carries the team down river past the glowing lights of Pangkalanbun. They lay-up for the night in one of numerous small tributaries extending into the banks of the Arut.

Despite their exhaustion, Jessica insists everyone bathe and rinse their clothes in the river. "We're going into town tomorrow and we can't look like we just crawled from the jungle," she explains.

"I'm not sitting around naked waiting for the POLRI to pick us up," complains Tran.

"Then go run a patrol or something," she replies dismissively. "Do whatever you need to feel safe. But *we're* getting cleaned up," she announces, motioning to herself and Chris.

Chris grins and tosses Tran his pistol. "Only twelve rounds left. Try not to waste 'em," he advises cheerfully.

"Yeah, well," grumbles Tran. "Don't get distracted and forget about 'Miss Jihad'," he snorts with a glance toward the boat where Sri remains bound and gagged in the cabin. He and Jon strike out into the darkness, pistols drawn as they disappear into the unknown.

"I thought they'd *never* leave," declares Chris. Noting the strained look on Jessica's face, he realizes something's wrong.

"What's the matter, Jess?" he asks tenderly, stepping toward her.

She backs away, her hand raised. "No. I'm not here as your plaything. Just go jump in the river and get cleaned up. I'll rinse out these clothes."

"I never said you were," he insists, but she waves him off anyway. "Fine," he snorts, too exhausted to argue with her in any case.

After a refreshing swim through the lagoon he hauls himself aboard the boat and towels off using rags he discovers coiled in a wicker basket. Peering ashore, he sees Jessica has scraped out a hollow and begun a low fire on the bank of the river. His and Jessica's freshly rinsed clothes are draped over a line strung around four sides of the glowing coals.

As he reclines against the bow, a rippling sound in the water nearby draws his attention to Jessica wading gracefully into the river. He rolls onto his side and watches in rapt silence. Hip-deep in the river, she stands naked, her lithe, wet body glistening in the flickering firelight. She bends forward and submerges her head in the water, then rises and arches her back, running her fingers through her hair as she wrings the water from her shimmering black tresses. She repeats the graceful movement several more times, water trickling in rivulets down her back and flowing over her pert, round backside.

He stares transfixed as she dips a rag into the water and stretches one arm above her head to wash beneath her armpit, her hip cocked, one knee slightly bent, like a cat stretching after a long nap. Water from the rag streams down her ribcage to cascade off her narrow hip before flowing down her thigh back to the river. She exchanges hands and repeats the performance on her other side. Her small, round breasts sway as she rinses her stomach and scrubs between her taut thighs. Small drops of water drip from the ends of her nipples as she leans forward and runs the wet rag over her partially submerged legs.

Gradually becoming aware of his presence, her almond eyes turn languidly toward him. Her hand slides to her side as she lowers the rag into the water, releasing it beneath the surface. She wades to where he lay, watching raptly from the bow of the boat.

"God, you're beautiful," he murmurs as she draws near. She raises a hand and places it gently on his scabbed forehead.

"Did that happen when the Prince Hidayat ran ashore?" she asks.

"No," he responds simply, unwilling to lose the moment among explanations.

She leans forward and kisses him gently on the lips. He responds eagerly.

"Come," she whispers as they part, taking his hand and drawing him gently toward the water. His makeshift towel drops to the deck as he climbs over the edge of the boat and slides naked into the river.

As they stand facing each other, she rests her head against his chest, wrapping her arms around his waist.

"Don't ever leave me again," she sighs, her voice cracking.

"I won't," he responds.

Dawn breaks over the river as Jon wanders from the jungle where he'd spent the night on guard duty. Moments later, Tran emerges down a path they hadn't discovered the night before whistling lightly and carrying a net sack filled with food.

"Breakfast," announces Tran loudly, lowering his voice when Jon cringes and glances anxiously toward the boat. "Are the honeymooners awake yet?" whispers Tran.

As if on cue, Chris' head pops-up over the side of the boat, his eyes glancing around in comic bewilderment. His brow furrows as he spots the two men grinning at him from the riverbank. He slips self-consciously from the boat.

"Ahem," he clears his throat as he approaches. "So what's for breakfast?" he asks as he attempts discretely to retrieve his and Jessica's clothes from the line.

"I picked up some melons, bread and rice at a little stand down the road," announces Tran, stooping to poke the glowing charcoal with a stick. Satisfied the coals are sufficiently hot, he suspends a small pot of water from three sticks forming a teepee above the fire. "You... uh... sleep all right?" he asks with a knowing smirk.

Stepping into his pants, Chris halts and shoots Tran a sour expression. "Yeah. I slept *fine*. How about *you*?" he asks acerbically.

"Fine thanks," shrugs Tran.

Chris hears a muffled chuckle and fires a warning glance at Jon, who suddenly discovers unusual interest examining a melon.

Finally dressed, Chris carries Jessica's clothes to the boat, where he discovers her awake, staring vacantly into the overhanging trees. Sunlight filters between the branches onto the delicate face that turns reluctantly toward him.

"You want to go after Khalid, don't you?" she asks.

"Yeah, Jess. I do," he admits.

"We would be exceeding our authority, you know," she sighs and begins to dress.

"I imagine so," he shrugs. "We'll find out once we contact your people to arrange support. What are your procedures anyway? Satellite phone?"

As Chris steps aboard the boat, he hears Sri stir in the cabin and senses a sudden pang of guilt for having left her hogtied all night. Then he recalls Irwan's fly-covered corpse and his regret all but evaporates.

Jessica continues to dress, evading his eyes and his question. He watches her, waiting for an answer.

"Jess? You can tell *me*," he adds testily.

She reaches out and takes his hands gently in hers.

"Please," she pleads, her grip tightening. "Don't be angry with me. But..." Her voice trails away as tears well-up in her eyes.

"But what?" he implores. "Jess, what's wrong?"

"My presence here is... unsanctioned," she murmurs.

He stares at her blankly. "*Unsanctioned*? What's that mean?" he asks warily.

"It means 'unauthorized'," she sighs, regaining her composure and withdrawing her hands from his. "I'm not supposed to be here."

"*What?*" he blurts before lowering his voice to a low rasp. "How the hell were they planning to bring us in?"

She shakes her head miserably. "They weren't," she mumbles. "No. That's not true," she admits. "When I left, they were still trying to figure *what* to do."

"So, what the hell are *you* doing here?"

Her liquid brown eyes seek his; she remains mute.

"You came for *me?*" he whispers.

"Why should it be such a surprise?" she asks sullenly, arms wrapped around herself defensively as if chilled by a bitter wind.

Before he can respond, Tran approaches the boat, two bowls of rice in-hand.

"Hey. You guys hungry?" he calls. His smiling face freezes. "What's the matter?"

Chris places his hand gently on Jessica's shoulder. "Jess, you need to tell Tran about your instructions," he announces, inviting a lie.

She glances at Chris, who nods encouragingly. Taking several deep breaths, she composes her story and announces: "we're on our own. I'm all the assistance you're going to get. Our orders are to rent or steal a boat and get off this island."

"But... what about Khalid?" demands Tran.

"Tran, if we don't go with her now," affirms Chris, "we're out in the cold," he explains, using the Cold War lexicon for an agent denied by his own people.

Tran gapes; his face reddening. He flings the rice bowls into the dirt. "So... *what?* We cut and run?" he seethes. "We finally have a chance to make something of this fucked-up mission and *you* want to turn tail?" Chris rounds, ready to defend his honor before realizing the accusation is directed at Jessica.

"Major," she hisses. "We have no sanction to kidnap Khalid. This mission has been compromised and we must limit collateral damage. There are... international implications!" She winces as the hated phrase slides so effortlessly from her own lips.

"Well, I'm in command here and I say we go get the son-of-a-bitch!" Tran fumes.

"No. I-am-your-control!" she reminds him fiercely. "You'll do as you're damned-well ordered!"

The two of them glare at each other, Chris standing to one side staring at them in confusion. "Wait a minute. Wait a minute," he cautions as he steps between them. "Let's talk this thing through, all right?" He sees from Jon's expression that he has overheard if not the substance of the conversation, then at least the tone. Chris motions him to join them at the boat.

"Jessica is right about one thing," admits Chris once the four gather. "Our mission was to recover our agent. Now Irwan is dead and Sri isn't of much use. So our original mission isn't just compromised. It's irrelevant."

There are murmurs of agreement all around.

Chris continues. "But the *reason* for the mission was to find Khalid..."

"And we have found him," interrupts Tran. "And SHE knows where he is!" he insists, pointing insistently toward the cabin.

"But we seem to have located Khalid because he's looking for us. And if he thinks we've left Kalimantan – or learns Irwan is dead – he'll disappear again."

"And we'll be back where we started," admits Jessica.

"Right. So I don't see we have any other option but to go after the guy."

Jessica gawks at him in horror. "But we have no *sanction* for such action," she insists.

"Look, Jessica," replies Tran testily. "If you're afraid, why don't you just sit this one out...?"

Jessica reaches around Chris, grasping for Tran's throat; Tran recoils.

"*Afraid*?" she asks in a high-pitched tone. "How dare you use such an idiotic word with me!" she seethes. "Where do you think we are, on the playground?"

Tran immediately backpedals. "I wasn't implying..."

"Oh, yes you were! I've got news for you *Major*," she announces, sidestepping Chris and getting uncomfortably in Tran's face. "I was serving my country when you were still begging for handouts on the streets of Ho Chi Minh City! Don't you ever accuse me of being a coward!"

"All right, killer," grins Tran. "So you're not afraid; but you *are* wrong."

"Major..."

"Tran," interrupts Chris. "Would you and Jon please leave us for a moment?"

Tran stares at Chris then glances at Jessica. "Sure. I'll go take care of 'Princess Jihad'," he shrugs indifferently and ducks sullenly beneath the tarp to enter the boat's cabin. Jon returns wordlessly to the fire and resumes preparing breakfast.

Chris motions for Jessica to leave the boat and join him for a walk along the riverbank. Once they're a discreet distance from the others, he stops walking and peers down at her. She stares across the mist-shrouded river, stubbornly avoiding his eyes.

"Jess," he announces softly. "You're here against orders. What happens to you if we go back now?"

"I'll likely be charged with treason and sent to prison," she admits.

"But what happens if we bring back Khalid?" he pursues.

"I would probably be hailed a heroine," she confesses.

"So?" he replies. "I really don't see we have much choice."

Without further discussion, she removes Irwan's satellite phone from her purse and hands it to Chris. He kissed her on the side of her head, slips the phone from her grasp, raises the antenna, and selects a callback number.

"Istana Pangkalanbun," answers a soft female voice. "How may I direct your call?"

CHAPTER 12

Shrouded by the early morning fog, the sampan sputters upriver toward Pangkalanbun. As it approaches the floating market, Tran steers toward a public pier, disembarking Chris and Jessica with the task of establishing an observation post in the vicinity of Khalid's hotel.

Tran and Jon continue upstream in search of a secluded location to stash Sri. Jon had released her from the ropes binding her through the night. Sri sits sullenly on the bow of the boat, massaging the circulation back into her numb hands and feet.

"Here," announces Jon, presenting a bowl of rice and part of a melon. Sri peers up at him through tragic eyes and turns away, staring forlornly across the river. He can't decide whether to resent or pity her. Here is a woman on the edge of collapse: a widow, exposed as conspirator in the death of her own husband.

A dozen miles north of town, on the shore of a lonely branch of the Arut, they discover an abandoned lumber mill. The forest upstream had been denuded of trees the previous year and the facility had fallen into decay. Tran cuts the engine and steers the coasting boat silently into a dilapidated slip alongside what had once been a loading dock. The air is glutinous, a low fog clinging stubbornly to the ramshackle facility as if trying to conceal the shame it represents.

"Jon," whispers Tran. "Go check it out." Jon draws the pistol from behind his belt and scrambles onto the dock to be swallowed-up by the mist.

Walking through the abandoned mill, he notices most of the mill's salvageable equipment has been hauled away, leaving bare slabs and rusting steel girders too heavy or awkward to be scavenged by the desolate locals. Nature has begun to reclaim the derelict site; jungle plants struggle between cracks appearing in the foundations of sinister-looking skeletal structures.

Moving cautiously through the site, he examines the facility for signs of recent use. But it's soon clear both man and God have forsaken this desolate patch of dead forest. Even the birds avoid the barren landscape and leftover corpse of the defiler.

He returns to the boat.

"Found a place," he announces, dropping from the dock onto the sampan's deck. "About 100 meters north." Tran tosses him a tarp and some rope, then picks up a six-foot chain and flings it over his shoulder.

"Okay, let's go," he snaps to Sri.

"So," spits Sri bitterly as she struggles to her feet. "Irwan receives a proper burial, but all I warrant is this... this..."

"No one's going to hurt you," snaps Tran. "But we can hardly have you wondering around Pangkalanbun until we've cleared the area." With a tug, he and Jon lift Sri onto the dock and usher her into the arms of the dilapidated mill.

They ascend to the high ground where a large section of slab remains intact. Sri collapses onto the concrete, sulking dejectedly as Tran and Jon string a large waterproof tarp between some collapsed girders to create a makeshift lean-to shelter.

Tran wraps the chain snugly around Sri's ankle and places several steel pins through the converging links, using a large rock to bend the pins back over themselves to create a crude but effective lock. He drapes the other end of the chain over a girder and affixes it in place, giving several sharp tugs.

"When we're safely out of here, we'll notify the POLRI where to find you," assures Tran. She ignores him as he speaks and makes no move to recover the food and water left on the ground beside her.

Tran grasps her chin in his hand and twists her face toward his. "Do you understand?" he growls.

She spits in his face. "Kill me!" she blurts. "End my misery now!"

Tran rises and stares down at her in disgust, dragging his sleeve across his face. "No. I think you should live with what you did, you bitch." He tugs on the chain dangling from the I-beam. "Why don't you do the world a favor and end it yourself. It'd only take a few minutes..."

Amid Sri's shrieked curses, the two men return to the boat, her voice fading into the distance.

Chris and Jessica stroll hand-in-hand past the old Ironwood Palace toward the ornate colonial-era hotel, Istana Pangkalanbun. Across from the ornate Istana, they enter a small run down twelve-room inn. The innkeeper eyes the couple suspiciously as the big German attempts to obtain a room.

"Sir," the innkeeper explains crossly, "we do not rent rooms to *unmarried* couples."

"But we *are* married," Chris insists in his affected German accent. The owner leans across the counter and exaggeratedly surveys the ground at their feet.

"I see no luggage," he declares, as if a lack of luggage settles the issue. Clearly the implication is the brash German is trying to exploit his hotel for an illicit tryst with the young, beautiful young woman with the Thai passport.

"Sir. My husband is a visiting professor at the Goethe Institut in Jakarta," explains Jessica innocently as Chris fumbles though his wallet and presents his forged business card. "Our luggage is on the Orangutan Foundation Tour bus," she explains. "I became ill this morning and we were unable to continue the tour." She glances lovingly at Chris. "My husband felt I should have some rest before we proceed."

The old man grudgingly accepts their story and provides a key. Chris and Jessica climb three flights of creaky stairs and locate the small, seedy suite. Jessica stalks immediately across the room and flings open the rickety shuttered balcony doors, revealing an unobstructed view of the grand hotel across the street.

"It occurs to me - darling," she purrs as she wraps her arms around Chris' neck, "we might not recognize our quarry." He kisses her neck, sliding his fingers down her spine and spreading his hands to rest on her narrow hips; he pulls himself against her.

"You've seen the CIA drawings of what Khalid might look like after nearly a year on the run," he replies to cover his arousal. "We'll just have to use our... *imagination*."

"Imagination is *not* one of your shortcomings," she teases.

"I have 'shortcomings'?"

"Yes," she snorts, "timing." She pulls from his grasp. "But we need a reason to be on the balcony all-hours."

"Ahhhh!" Chris laughs as he picks up the receiver and dials the front desk, to which the innkeeper's crackling voice responds.

"Good afternoon, Sir," announces Chris. "I was wondering if you could tell me where I might obtain a bottle or two of white wine."

There is a resigned sigh on the extension. "I thought your 'wife' was ill?"

Chris glances at Jessica's tawny, shapely legs propped casually on the balcony railing as she leans back elegantly in the ramshackle wicker chair. "Yes. But I, on the other hand, am quite well," he reports.

"I will send my son," the innkeeper sighs finally. "You may pay him upon delivery."

Chris and Jessica relax on the balcony, conversing in low tones while watching the comings and goings from the large colonial-style hotel across the street. Nearly an hour later comes a discreet knock at the door. A young boy no older than ten delivers two bottles of unremarkable, room temperature Australian Chardonnay. As Chris fumbles through his wad of Rupiah, the boy peers hopefully into the room only to be disappointed no sins are apparently being committed. His father will be disappointed to hear he is wrong about the couple.

"Something from New South Wales?" asks Jessica hopefully as Chris pushes the door closed with his elbow.

"Hardly," guffaws Chris as he fumbles through the shoddy dresser drawers. "Damn. I didn't ask if he had a corkscrew."

He's in the process of using a chopstick to drive the cork into the bottle when Jessica suddenly leans into the room and rasps, "*It's him.*" Chris slams the bottle onto the counter and stalks across the room, slowing as he strolls casually onto the balcony.

"Where?" He spots a small caravan of Japanese SUVs parked in front of the hotel. A large black-bearded man in a flowing white dishdasha and rimless white cap emerges from one of the vehicles. He's speaking animatedly with what appears to be a uniformed POLRI officer - a fairly senior one by the look of the gold braid.

"Quite the entourage," Chris mumbles. "I count at least four bodyguards besides the POLRI. "

"At least," she confirms.

"We need a better look," he announces finally. "I'm going across."

"Whoa!" laughs Jessica, taken aback at his audacity. "*I'll* go."

"But..."

She smiles endearingly and pats his cheek. "You'd be too conspicuous, *Reinhardt*," she announces sweetly. Before he can argue, she slips from the room and disappears down the stairs. He returns to the balcony.

It takes several moments before he spots her walking casually across the street. *For a beautiful woman*, he realizes, *she has an uncanny ability to appear inconspicuous.*

As Jessica approaches, Khalid is engaged in an animated conversation with another man on the street. His bodyguards fan-out, blocking the sidewalk and forcing pedestrians onto the hotel's manicured lawn. Following the crowd, she turns up the hotel walkway and strides into the large high-ceilinged lobby.

Despite the hotel's age, the nineteenth-century colonial building is as clean and reasonably stylish as an open-air facility can be in the tropics. The elegant colonial Dutch and traditional native furnishings are tastefully arranged in clusters providing comfortable meeting places for hotel guests beneath slowly-rotating ceiling fans.

She retrieves a brochure from the concierge' desk and pretends to study it, eyes focused on the wide front door. Shadows lengthen in the doorway and she leans forward in anticipation. From her right, a man shoves his way brusquely past and stalks to the front desk. He snaps orders to the clerk, who withdraws three keys from the third pigeonhole on the second row of key boxes. He raises the key ring and motions to another of Khalid's bodyguards who meet him at the elevator to hold open the door, directing remaining hotel guests aside.

While Khalid's other bodyguards fan-out through the lobby, Jessica moves closer to the desk and peers at the marking below the pigeonhole from which the keys were withdrawn. It reads 23. She smiles and turns to leave.

A bodyguard steps in front of her, his hand outstretched. Her first instinct is to grasp his palm and twist it behind his back, using his own body weight to force him to the ground before snapping his neck with her knee. Fortunately she takes another second to realize he is merely clearing a path for Khalid, strides regally into the lobby surrounded by a knot of bowing and scraping cronies.

In an inexcusable act of hubris defying all her training, Jessica looks Khalid straight in the eye as he passes. He returns her glance with a gleam she quickly recognizes as lust. Braking eye-contact, she stalks away disinterestedly, hips swaying as she taunts the self-professed holy man.

A thrill shivers down her spine as the terrorist's wandering eyes follow her out the door.

"I've got his room number," Jessica announces breathlessly, bursting into their room.

"Excellent," replies Chris enthusiastically. "Do you think he saw you?"

"No. Of course not," she lies. "He's got a suite, room 23, second floor. None of the POLRI followed him inside. They must be providing perimeter security," she observes professionally. "But you were right. He's got four associates who stay pretty close."

"Are they armed?"

"It's hard to tell. They all dress in baggy dishdashas, like their master. But I think we should assume they're *well-*

armed. What did you see from out here?" she asks as they return to the balcony. He hands her a plastic cup of wine and leans casually on the railing beside her. "I've been watching the POLRI," he reports. "I see no indication they hold him in any great awe. It all seems pretty routine."

Jessica studies him appraisingly. "Go on."

"Well, for one thing," he begins, hesitating to take a sip of wine. "Not one of them left his vehicle when Khalid was on the move - not much they could do to protect him sitting on their asses," he snorts. "But most interestingly, there was not a single glance his direction; they just seemed wholly disinterested."

"Hmmm," replies Jessica, humming as she does when considering the analysis of others. "That would tend to indicate they're merely following orders. So who's got that kind of clout?"

"Dunno," shrugs Chris. "But for the snatch, we can effectively rule out the POLRI in the immediate vicinity. That just leaves the four bodyguards to deal with."

The setting sun casts an orange glimmer framing the low-hanging clouds. An hour earlier, Jessica returned from shopping, the innkeeper smiling approvingly as she strolled through the lobby with several suitcases. Now, as she and Chris step-out for what appears to be an evening on the town, Jessica wears a sleeveless copper colored cheongsam and high-heeled sandals. Chris is dressed in a dark blue Polo shirt and white linen slacks. To onlookers they appear to be merely a couple of well-dressed tourists.

They stroll down the street across from the Ironwood Palace and loiter beneath a wide, overhanging shade tree. As they chat idly, Chris spots Tran and Jon approaching. He mutters to Jessica, "Our friends are here."

Smiling indulgently as if he's just said something witty, she glances casually toward Tran and Jon. "Thank God they've bought some new clothes," she murmurs, taking Chris' arm. "Now let's see how well they can maintain a tail." The couple proceeds casually up the block toward the nightclub about which the innkeeper told them.

Club Bali Hai, is the kind of place popular with Western tourists and young, "hip" Indonesians. The mind-numbing throb of 1970s American disco music and modern Indonesian "dang-dut" boom from 5-foot tall speakers stacked astride the teeming dance floor. A tiny Asian hostess with bleached red hair, halter, 6-inch heels and fake leather mini-skirt leads them to a cramped table for four near the open balcony. Chris feels Jessica tighten her grip on his arm as young women eye him covetously from around the bar - foreign men are assumed to be wealthy and are therefore attractive by default.

By the time Tran and Jon work their way past the bouncer and locate Chris and Jessica, no fewer than a dozen giggling girls have approached them. Tran finds one that doesn't speak English and takes her into tow. Jessica eyes him irritably as the couple approaches the table.

"Heeey. I've gotta fit in man," announces Tran as he drops into a chair and invites the girl to take the seat on his lap. Jon, on the other hand, appears horror-stricken. Apparently the Gurkha Brigade training that taught him to hack a man in half with a two-foot blade doesn't extend to dealing with scantily clad young women. He takes a seat opposite Jessica with his back to the wall and remains resolutely silent.

"Is everything taken care of?" asks Jessica loudly over the pulsating music.

Tran nods. "Yeah. We dumped her near an old lumber mill upriver; I'd say we have about 24 hours before we need to be concerned."

Chris passes Tran a slip of paper. "There's our hotel phone and room number. If you call us, expect the switchboard operator to be listening. The owner's a pretty suspicious guy." He leans back in his chair and studies the room.

The club has a distinct "disco-era" atmosphere, with rotating lights, moonflower lamps and strobes flashing to the beat of the music. Abstract neon designs border the black painted walls and small circular tables crowd around the flashing multi-colored acrylic disco floor. He catches the waitress' attention and waves her to their table.

"Drei... nein. Vier San Miguel, bitte," he shouts in German, pointing to the San Miguel Pale Pilsner beer sign on the wall and holding up four fingers. Then he switches to English. "Jon? What about you?"

Jon smiles gratefully, appreciating his friend respects that, as a Hindu, he does not drink alcohol but will not be offended by the rest of them drinking beer. He orders a bottle of fruit juice.

The sweating waitress flashes a pleasant smile and pirouettes back through the crowd, empty bottles tottering on her tray as she returns to the bar. Tran resumes the conversation. "If the owner is suspicious, shouldn't you find another place to stay?"

Chris laughs. "It's not the *illegal* activity he's suspicious about; it's the immoral goings-on that concern him."

"Of course," replies Tran dryly. He turns to the girl and smiles into her wide, innocent eyes. "Let's dance!" he proclaims, pulling the giggling girl to her feet. The couple approaches the dance floor to be swallowed-up by the gyrating crowd.

When the drinks arrive, Chris grabs his bottle and takes a long, thirsty pull, surveying Jessica from the corner of his eye. Despite the danger – or perhaps because of it – he desires her now more than ever. Her copper silk dress reflects a glowing light along her elegant jaw line, highlighting her beautiful upturned face. *There's a mystical quality about her*, he muses: *hardened case officer; quiet intellectual; passionate lover*. They've been together long enough for him to appreciate that she loves and hates with equal intensity. Here they are in a foreign land, under fire, on the run, and as likely as not to die before the next sunrise. Yet she seems wholly at ease, watching the younger women "drill" to the music of Indonesian disco diva Inul Daratista.

"Drilling," is Indonesia's version of "dirty dancing." It drives Muslim clerics crazy and for that reason as much as any other its popularity has been sweeping through Indonesian youth in recent years.

She notes his bemused expression. "Whaaat?" she asks, like a teenager caught in a lie.

"Go ahead," he urges, motioning toward the dance floor. "Give it a try."

"Ah!" she laughs in her controlled manner. "I couldn't do *that!*"

Chris examines the gyrating girls on the dance floor, his gaze returning to Jessica. His hand slides lightly down her exposed arm. "Oh, but you *have*," he murmurs. She lets-out an girlish squeal and kicks him beneath the table. Jon glances at them sheepishly, not privy to Chris' comment, but clearly suspecting he is the reason for the outburst. Jessica flushes and glances down self-consciously, a smirk on her face as she examines the half-empty beer bottle in her hands.

A few minutes later, Tran and his "date" bump and grind their way back to the table. Tran drops exhaustedly into his chair, the girl plopping onto his lap and giving him a long, wet kiss. "This is a *great* club," he announces.

"All right, Tran. Break her heart and let's get down to business," announces Chris.

Tran rises and the giggling girl slips from his lap. He kisses her hand, presents her with a second beer and sends her on her way. "You're killin' me, Chris," he announces in mock indignation as he drops back into his chair.

"I know. I know," laughs Chris. "Your country appreciates your sacrifice. Take two purple hearts and call me in the morning. Now, have you guys found a safe house yet?"

"Yeah," replies Tran, pulling a hand drawn map from his shirt pocket and unfolding it on the table. He flattens it with the palm of his hand. "We found a small one-room house in the business district. It's located near the outskirts of town not too far from the river. There are lots of foreigners in the area so we should be able to come and go without attracting too much attention."

"Good. Good," adds Jessica eagerly. "We have an observation post across from the hotel and have already located our subject." She recounts the events of the day, omitting the embarrassing breach of tradecraft she committed by initiating eye-to-eye contact with Khalid.

"Four bodyguards?" repeats Tran warily as she finishes describing the target.

"Plus POLRI," adds Chris grimly. He examines the dour faces around him. "Of course there is an alternative..." His voice trails off. He fiddles with his now empty beer bottle as the team eyes him closely.

"And that is?" asks Tran.

Chris rolls his head back and stares at the ceiling before slowly lowering his gaze to his fellow team members. "We could just cap this guy and be done with it. It'd be a hell of a lot less complicated than snatching him – safer, too."

Jessica jerks erect and shoots a glance at Tran and Jon. To her relief, the others appear as ill at ease with Chris' suggestion as she. "Hey, I'm just throwing out ideas," protests Chris.

"Well whatever we do," announces Tran, sidestepping the tricky question of assassination. "We have to move soon. Sri's not gonna remain on ice very long."

"Our key problem is that we don't have time to develop the target," explains Jessica analytically. "We don't know his daily routine or habits..."

Tran shakes his head impatiently. "You're thinking like a case officer," he interrupts. "This isn't a recruitment. It's a snatch. We'll have to force events, not wait for 'opportunities.'"

Jessica stiffens.

"Tran's right," agrees Chris and Jon nods his agreement. "We know the target and we know the current situation. We'll have to launch this operation from a standing start."

In Jessica's experience, gathering intelligence is a long, painstaking process. It's difficult to adjust to such an aggressive shift in her paradigm.

"That's *suicide*," she hisses.

"No. It's *not*," insists Chris. "You said yourself time is against us. What we need to do now is plan how we're going to separate Khalid from his bodyguards and get him off the island."

"And what about the bodyguards we *can't* separate him from?" she asks sharply.

Tran's eyes cut to Chris and Jon, then back to Jessica. "We'll have to take 'em out," he explains reasonably.

"Just... *'take them out,'* will we?" she squeals in a pitch higher than her usual, well-modulated tone.

"Jess, all he's saying is..."

"I know what he's saying!" she fumes. A rush of despair washes over her; events have taken control. But she reminds herself the decision she made in her quiet apartment in Singapore a mere two days ago have foreclosed all but the action they are proposing. She lets out a long sigh.

"Yes," she agrees simply. "You're right."

CHAPTER 13

Early the next morning, Jessica and Chris hop the bus to Kumai, a small port city on the inlet from the Java Sea five kilometers south of Pangkalanbun.

It's a fresh, sunny, humid morning; the kind one should expect after a night of heavy rain. The bus bumps down the dirt road toward the port, swaying and lurching erratically as the driver struggles to maintain control on the crumbling, potholed road. Their fellow passengers are local fishermen and their families heading down to the village for the day. Chris and Jessica keep their conversation to a minimum to avoid arousing undue attention. Though by the poorly concealed glances of admiration from the male passengers, it is obvious Jessica has drawn more than just a passing interest.

When the bus draws up across from the inlet, Chris and Jessica disembark. Surveying the port, Chris is visibly disappointed. Jessica notes the expression on his face and chuckles warmly.

"What did you expect?" she mutters as she slips her arm through his and urges him forward, "the Port of Singapore?" The port town of Kumai is little more than a run-down fishing village. They walk arm-in-arm together across the river road and down to the docks.

Too late, they catch a glimpse of an armed POLRI cop standing near the entrance to the docks. He's rummaging through a villager's backpack and waves impatiently for them to halt. "Keep walking," Chris mumbles and chats animatedly in English with his heavy, comical German accent. Moments later they hear a shout.

"Keep moving; look casual," Chris repeats. They continue nonchalantly along the makeshift boardwalk. A clomp of boots on wood warn the cop is fast approaching. Suddenly a hand seizes Chris' shoulder and spins him around. The red-faced cop shouts at him in some unrecognizable Indonesian dialect.

"Womit kann ich ihnen dienen?" responds Chris, sweeping the cop's hand indignantly from his shoulder.

"Pengenalan," the insists cop, then switches to English. "Identification," he demands, a hand resting threateningly on his holstered pistol. Jessica and Chris glance at each other and shrug indifferently. They each hand over their passports and wait patiently as the cop thumbs roughly through the documents, scarcely knowing what he's looking at.

He glances sharply at Chris and raises the passport. "American?" he accuses.

"Nein. Ich bin Deutsch," scoffs Chris indignantly. "G-E-R-M-A-N," he repeats slowly.

The cop grunts his understanding not that Chris is German, but he is at least *not* American. He glances disinterestedly at Jessica's passport, hands both documents back to Chris, and points insistently at the sign beside the entrance. He attempts to explain something Chris assumes means, "Next time stop at the damned sign."

"Ja. Ja," Chris answers jovially and waves to the cop as the officer stalks away. "Prick," he mutters from the corner of his mouth as the cop returns to his post.

He takes Jessica's hand. "Shall we?" They continue down the boardwalk toward a decaying wooden hut with several dilapidated fiberglass hulled boats rocking alongside its small pier.

"Good Lord," mumbles Chris as they near the door. "Are these things even seaworthy?"

"They'd better be," snorts Jessica. "This is the only place in town to rent boats."

Entering the office, it takes a few moments for their eyes to focus in the dim light. An elderly woman glances up from her newspaper, rises agonizingly behind the wooden desk, and asks them something in the local dialect Jessica assumes means, "May I help you?"

"Yes," replies Jessica. "Do you speak English?"

The woman grumbles something that probably would have been unintelligible even if they *had* spoken the language and waddles into a back room. She reappears moments later with a young girl in tow. The girl examines the couple strangely and averts her eyes.

"My name is Ani. May I assist you?" she asks timidly.

Chris bows awkwardly. "Guten morgen, fraulein. My wife and I want to rent a boat for a few days trip along the coast. Might you have something available?"

"Certainly," she replies, still avoiding his gaze. "Please follow me." The old lady plops down at the desk and rattles her paper, disappearing between the yellowing folds. The girl leads Chris and Jessica onto the creaking dock.

"How many passengers will you have," she inquires.

"Just us, fraulein," lies Chris, motioning toward himself and Jessica. "But I don't like small boats. So, please, something big enough so I don't get sea sick."

"This way," replies the girl and leads them around behind the hut.

"I've seen her before," whispers Jessica to Chris. "She was at the Bali Hai last night. I think she's afraid we might have recognized her."

"Why?" asks Chris.

Jessica rolls her eyes. "Well, if you were a nice little Indonesian girl would you want your strict Muslim grandmother to know you were 'drilling' at a night club all night?"

Chris relaxes somewhat. "No," he chuckles. "I guess not. But that could be helpful."

"My thoughts exactly," she smiles. "Why don't you let me deal with her? You just look around. Go 'kick the tires' or something."

"Perhaps this is acceptable," announces the girl, motioning to a wooden hulled, 1960s-era, 30' diesel cabin cruiser tied up alongside the back pier.

"Ja, Ja. This looks good," responds Chris and immediately separates from the women, jumping aboard and poking around the cabin while Jessica remains on the pier with the girl.

"You look familiar," announces Jessica. The girl goes rigid. "Didn't I see you last night at the Bali Hai?" Jessica asks.

The girl's eyes widen. "Um. No. I... I live here..." she insists in a panicky voice. Jessica places her hand reassuringly on the girl's arm.

"Don't worry dear," she whispers conspiratorially. "I won't mention it if you don't tell anyone Reinhardt and I aren't *really* married."

The girl smiles and sighs. "Yes. I saw you too," she admits. "You were the most attractive couple in the club," she confesses.

Jessica blushes unexpectedly.

No longer feeling threatened, the girl perks-up accordingly. "It's a very good boat," she announces brightly, ushering Jessica aboard. "The engine was overhauled just last year." As they tour the boat, it appears despite that, the weathered exterior, below decks is surprisingly clean and well maintained.

Chris starts the motor and steers the boat on a short spin up river, gaining a feel for its seaworthiness. While he plays coxswain, weaving between incoming fishing boats, the two women chat animatedly out on the bow. By the time he steers them back toward the pier, the women return to the cabin, apparently having become the best of friends.

"So is it acceptable?" asks Ani.

Chris nods. "Ja! We'll take it."

"Well, there are a couple of things you should be aware of then," Ani announces. "While you're at sea, you should stay within sight of shore at all times."

"Why?' asks Chris. "Is something wrong mit die boat?"

"No. No. It's just...," she leans in close and whispers. "There have been reports of pirates operating off the coast."

"*Really*?" asks Jessica in mock alarm. She turns to Chris. "Perhaps we shouldn't go. It doesn't sound safe."

"Oh, it is!" the girl insists. "The Navy caught some pirates several nights ago. Now they have two boats patrolling the coast."

Chris scratches his beard, thinking. "I don't know," he mumbles. "This is a big island for just two boats to patrol."

"Oh, no," giggles Ani. "They operate from a base over there," she explains, pointing vaguely in the direction of the south end of town. "They just go down to Kuala Kapuas and back."

"Darling," announces Jessica as though she's just had an inspiration. "Perhaps we could go up the coast at the same time! That would ward off any pirates in the area..."

"Ja! That would be good." He turns to the girl. "What time do the patrols leave?"

"About six in the morning," she reports. "I know some of the sailors. I could arrange..."

"Ah!" laughs Jessica, interrupting the girl's offer. "That's too early in the morning for me. But thank you Ani.

I'm sure the pirates have been chased off after the other night."

They agree to rent the boat for a week. "But we need to return to Pangkalanbun and check out of our hotel," explains Jessica. "Is there someplace we can berth the boat upriver?"

"Yes," replies Ani eagerly. "My family has a house on the Arut," she explains. Grasping a piece of paper, she begins to sketch a crude map. "It's a small house," she confesses. "But it's bright blue and really easy to find."

"Oh, Ani," Jessica protests lightly. "We don't want to inconvenience your family..."

"No. It's all right. Father and mother are in Banjarmasin for the month," she reports. "Our renters pick up and drop off our boats at the house all the time. It's more convenient for our Pangkalanbun renters than coming down here to Kumai."

After renting the boat, it's early afternoon by the time Chris and Jessica set off down the inlet into the coastal waters of the Java Sea. Ominous clouds are beginning to roll in and Chris experiences a sense of déjà vu as the boat – forty-five critical feet smaller than the Prince Hidayat – trudges through the heaving swells.

Jessica clings tightly to his arm. "My God, is this what it was like the other night?" she asks.

Chris guffaws. "You have *no* idea."

"Will it be like this all the way back to Singapore?"

Chris doesn't respond immediately. "I hope not," he replies finally. "If we do this right, we'll only have to go a few hundred miles in this thing."

She glances at him quizzically. "Why only a few hundred?"

"Because you're going to call Colonel Mok and arrange to have the RSN meet us in the Strait of Karimata."

Jessica's jaw drops. "*What*?"

"Look, when we snatch Khalid, all hell's going to break loose," explains Chris. "We'll be damned lucky to get off the island. Then there's the patrol boats back in Matua. The longer we're at sea, the less our odds of survival. So unless…"

"You're out of your mind!" she interrupts. Feigning a call to Colonel Mok, she holds her hand to her ear in the shape of a phone. "Oh, hi colonel," she mocks. "We've violated orders, murdered Indonesian police officers, created a major international incident, and – by the way – may have started a war between Singapore and Indonesia. Could you please pick us up in the Strait of Karihoochi…"

"Karimata," corrects Chris.

"…we promise not to kill anyone else," she continues.

"Dammit, Jessica! You're already *at* war!" he bursts, slamming his fist into the helm. "So is Indonesia, Malaysia, Thailand… Why the hell don't *any of you* understand that?"

"Any of *you*?" She rages. "You mean we *poor, ignorant Asians?*"

Chris grits his teeth. "You know damned well that's *not* what I mean. For God's sake, Kastari blew himself up right in your faces! Suddenly there are JI cells popping-up like weeds all over Southeast Asia. Where the hell did *they* come from? The rest of the world might not be at war, but the extremists are," he snorts. "And as far as I can tell *they're* winning!"

"Don't lecture me you pompous ass!" She hisses. "In six months, you'll be out of uniform and all of this will have been just a quick thrill; another big adventure to brag about at cocktail parties with your lawyer friends!"

"That's not fair."

"Yes it is!" she shrieks. "You'll be safe at home and the rest of us have to clean up your fucking mess!"

"Right! WE might abandon you, so you'd better not defend yourselves," he scoffs. "*That's* a winning attitude!"

"Ohhhh... fuck you!" she shrieks and stomps out onto the deck, cursing that there's is nowhere else to go.

Nearly an hour after departing Kumai, Chris steers the boat into the mouth of the Arut. Jessica had taken a seat on the deck, her back resting against the front of the paint-chipped pilothouse. Water taxis and small fishing skiffs slide past them heading downriver. Beneath massive, overhanging trees, the boat proceeds upstream, silent but for the rumbling diesel engine. Rounding a bend, Chris suddenly throttles-back.

"Jess. I need your help," he calls gently. "If you're still refusing to speak to me, you can just nod."

She glances over her shoulder and, noting his impish grin, momentarily forgets her anger.

"Are we there?" she asks.

"No. But I recognize t bridge up ahead," he insists excitedly. "We left some supplies buried on the left bank of the river. I'm going to see if I can recover them." The boat keels over slightly as he runs the bow aground.

"So what do you want me to do?"

"The current is pretty swift," explains Chris, stepping aside so she can take the helm. "You'll need to keep pressure on the throttle so you don't get dragged downriver." She grasps the throttle, feeling the engines battling the current.

"How long will this take?"

"Shouldn't be more than a few minutes," he announces and darts onto the deck before she can ask anything else. Grabbing the bowline, he drops onto the muddy embankment, ties the rope to a large tree and gives a quick wave before disappearing into the dark jungle.

Nearly twenty minutes later, he returns to the boat smudged with mud and carrying a dirty, canvas-wrapped bundle. As Jessica spurs the boat forward, he tosses the bundle onto the deck, releases the bowline, and rinses his hands in the river before clambering aboard.

"I've got it," he announces as he returns to the cabin and regains the controls.

"You've got what?" asks Jessica.

"A little something to improve our odds."

Within the hour they locate Ani's house on a tributary off the Arut. Unlike most homes along the riverbank, Ani's place is fairly secluded, separated from neighbors by a thick stand of trees and overgrown jungle. It's bright blue, decorated with an intricate repetitive pattern of white. A plank boardwalk extends along one side of the house, protruding over the water as a pier. Framing the pier is a tall, ornately carved ceremonial gateway.

Securing the boat to one of the sturdier pilings, Chris leads Jessica cautiously up the walkway. They pass the house and head down the long driveway to the road with Chris cradling the canvas-wrapped bundle in his arms.

"How the hell do we tell them where to find us," groans Chris, glancing up and down the hopelessly unmarked road.

"According to Ani's map, Pangkalanbun is that way," announces Jessica pointing northeast. "Tell Tran to head south down the river road. We can watch for them from here."

"Sounds good. Better make the call," suggests Chris as he dumps the bundle into a nearby bush. Jessica pulls the satellite phone from her bag and dials Sri's number. Tran answers immediately.

"It's me," she announces without introduction.

"Hello, you!" responds Tran brightly.

"We've got a boat and are docked at a private home on the outskirts of town. Did you get a car?"

"Yeah. We're all set. How do we locate you?"

Jessica explains the general route to the house. "What are you driving?"

"A silver Toyota Kijang LGX," he announces. "It's sort of a cross between a station wagon and a SUV."

"Fine. We'll watch for you."

By the time Tran locates Chris and Jessica and returns them to the safe house, the weather had broken. Deluged by rain, threatened by lightning, rattled by crashing thunder, the three dart inside.

Jessica disappears into the bathroom to change into dry clothes.

"Are the Sings all set for the pickup?" asks Tran.

"Not quite," responds Chris, pulling the wet shirt over his head and flinging it with a splat onto the concrete floor.

Tran eyes him warily. "What's that supposed to mean? Don't tell me they refused..."

"No," grunts Chris. "They haven't had the opportunity. We didn't contact them yet."

"Why the hell not?" Tran asks testily.

"I don't know," replies Chris, shaking his head miserably. "I just wonder if we're making a mistake."

"You mean the 'snatch?'"

"Yeah. Maybe we should just cut our losses - you know, take the boat and head for home before we make things worse."

Tran leans against the edge of the table and motions for Chris to explain. "What happened? I thought you said everything went fine."

"It did. But it's just... we may be doing the wrong thing," replies Chris dejectedly.

"Is that what Jessica thinks?" asks Tran, perceptively.

"Yeah. Yeah. It is," replies Chris. "She thinks we're dragging her country into a war not of its choosing."

"If they don't believe it's their war, why'd they send her here?"

Chris buries his face in his hands. "Argh!" he groans and shakes his head. "They didn't, Tran. She came on her own."

"*What*?" blurts Tran. "Why the hell would she do that?"

"Apparently for me," shrugs Chris.

Tran stares at Chris for a few moments before realizing what Chris is trying *not* to say. "So its love is it?" he asks sourly.

"Yeah. I suppose so."

"What about you?"

Chris nods silently.

Tran flings his arms in the air. "Well, that's great. That's just fucking great," he swears in exasperation. "We're at war and you're playing the fucking Dating Game."

Chris glowers. "Yeah? Well if she *hadn't* come, we'd be on our own getting out of here!"

"Maybe we'd be better off," growls Tran. "At least you'd be focused on the mission instead of getting into her panties!"

"Dammit, Tran! That's not what this is about!" replies Chris. "Need I remind you she's the one who identified Sri as the leak? If it wasn't for her, we'd be in some shit-hole Indonesian jail – or worse: strung up on meat hooks in some JI camp!"

The bathroom door rattles open and Jessica steps-out, dressed in shorts and a tank top, toweling her hair dry. She freezes when she notices the men glaring at one another. "What?" she asks tentatively.

"Nothing," snorts Tran and stomps from the room.

Jessica stands, silhouetted in the light emanating through the doorway. She suddenly seems so small and young and fragile. Chris feels an anxious tightness in his chest.

"That was about me, wasn't it?" she asks.

"No," grumbles Chris. "It was about priorities." He walks past, kissing her on the cheek as he pulls a dry shirt over his head on his way out the door.

She stands alone in the depressing little one room house, thunder reverberating off the tin roof. From the corner of her eye she catches a glimpse of black metal piled in the middle of the kitchen table. Approaching the table she spots three short-barreled SS1 assault rifles strewn in pieces across the surface, dirty rags scattered about indicating someone has begun to clean the weapons. She lifts a small satchel hanging over the back of the chair and finds it unusually heavy. Inside, she finds a dozen loaded SS1 magazines and several Chinese-made hand grenades.

The rain is torrential; Chris pauses beneath the rickety awning that overhangs the front of the house. Lost in thought, he scarcely notices people walking along the sidewalk either in resigned tolerance of the rain or running defiantly in spite of it, heading to Mosque for evening prayers.

As he turns to go back inside, he spots Tran and Jon dodge between cars as they jog across the street toward the house. Tran holds a newspaper aloft for protection from the deluge. Something in his body-language foretells bad news. He steps beneath the awning, shakes the puddle from the paper and hands it to Chris.

"Take a look at that," he announces.

Chris glances at the Chinese language newspaper and starts to protest before noticing the photo on the front page: shattered remnants of buildings on a street in some unnamed town.

"Where is this?" demands Chris.

"Bali. A bombing at a nightclub killed a couple of hundred tourists two nights ago," he announces. "It's pretty grisly..."

"Do they say who did it?"

"Yep," he replies without further elaboration as he grasps the paper from Chris' hand. "Let's go inside."

Jessica is sitting at the table reassembling one of the rifles when the men enter the house. She glances up.

A long roll of thunder drowns-out Chris' initial words.

As the rumble fades, Tran raises the newspaper and reads, translating the article into English as he speaks:

"(AP) JAKARTA - Oct 12, 2002. At 23:05 local time, bombs ripped through two nightclubs in Bali's Kuta Beach resort area, leaving several hundred dead and wounded.

"Windows throughout the town were shattered. Scenes of horror and panic inside and outside the bars followed. The local hospital, unable to cope with the number of burn victims, has requested Indonesian military and Australian government assistance.

"The bombing is believed to be the work of the Al Qa'ida-linked extremist organization, Jemaah Islamiya..."

Chris retrieves the rain-soaked paper from Tran's grasp and places it gingerly on the table before Jessica, the photo of the carnage face-up. She glances down at the paper, picks it up and silently finishes reading the article in her native Mandarin. When she's through, she quietly sets the paper aside and stares at the floor for what seems an eternity.

"It's not going to end unless we end it," she sighs.

"No, Jess. It's not," replies Chris softly. "They've declared war and we have to do something other than await the next attack."

"Then let's do it," she declares with a certainty that makes Tran grin.

CHAPTER 14

Colonel Mok is in a foul mood. Nothing has been heard from Jessica or her team in three days. Admiral Lang's insistence on updates, while expressing confidence in Singapore's judgment, is becoming annoying. The listening post on Sentosa sends nearly hourly reports of something serious amiss in Pangkalanbun. The POLRI had dispatched elements of BRIMOB – the paramilitary mobile brigade – to the area from Java. The good news is that apparently no one is yet in custody. But the net is closing and prospects for the team's survival are worsening by the hour.

His driver delivers him to his favorite Thai restaurant in Jurong. Madame Pim Kunchai, the restaurant's proprietor and his good friend, welcomes her distinguished guest at the door.

"Jimmy," she croons as she kisses him lightly on the cheek. "You look so tense."

Madame Kunchai is sincerely concerned about the colonel. His wife had been her best friend and confidant until she had died of cancer ten years before. She knew Jimmy Mok as a kind and gentle man. Truth be told, she would like to be more than his friend. But Jimmy needs her friendship at this point in his life. Herself a widow of twelve years, she can afford to wait a little longer.

Colonel Mok smiles for the first time in days. "Pim, would you please join me in a glass of sherry?" he asks with customary formality. He seldom asks her to join him for a drink unless he needs to unburden himself. But because of the classified nature of his work, it's an odd sort of therapy. She listens sympathetically as he talks about everything *except* what's bothering him.

They're seated at a table in the private dining room reserved for "special guests." Their conversation gravitates toward the usual subjects: music and literature. As he sips his second snifter of Majesty, he finally begins to relax, taking solace in Pim's wit and elegance. So engrossed with his host is he that when his cell phone rings, he nearly ignores it.

"Excuse me," he announces, glancing casually at the caller ID. His jaw drops and he stiffens.

"Please forgive me," he blurts and rises, flipping open his phone and pressing it to his ear as he stalks to the side exit and bursts into the alley behind the restaurant.

"Yes?" he replies, hedging against the possibility that someone other than Jessica might be using her phone.

"Sir," a wavering female voice responds. "Do you recognize my voice?"

"Yes! Are you all right?"

"I am fine," she assures him. "Just listen. I'm with our friends. We need your assistance."

"My hands are tied," he growls. "You tied them when you did this... this... irresponsible thing! Now we have to mitigate the damage..."

"We've found him," interrupts Jessica.

"You've found *who*?"

"Khalid. We're bringing him out with us," she declares.

"What do you mean you're 'bringing him out?'" he asks sharply.

"We're kidnapping him tonight," she announces. "We'll be bringing him out by boat."

"Jessica! You can't be serious!"

"We'll be in a thirty foot cabin cruiser, hull number... IDL 36599."

"Jessica, *I order you* to..."

"Have the navy meet us north of Billiton in the Karimata Strait after noon tomorrow," she interrupts loudly over his protests. "Do you have that?"

"No," he snaps. "Just a minute." He gropes through his pockets and withdraws a pad and pen. "Say again."

She repeats the information as he copies it down and repeats it back to her.

"I'm not sure I can make this happen," he admits desperately.

"I trust you," she replies and disconnects.

"Dammit!" he swears and re-dials her number.

She doesn't answer.

The rain ceases for the moment. Chris lays deathly still, listening to the sound of cars splashing down the wet street in front of the hotel. In the distance echoes the occasional rumble of thunder. He inhales the warm, dense air.

"You okay, Jess?" he asks quietly, staring at the slowly rotating ceiling fan to avoid her gaze. She stirs beside him; he turns and notes the melancholy look in her eyes.

"Yes," she smiles faintly. "I'm just ready for it to be over."

"You know," he replies, looking at his watch, "if Khalid doesn't arrive soon, we're going to have to abort the mission."

She responds with a mocking smile; he senses what she's thinking.

"Do you hate me?" he asks.

"No," she murmurs. "I could never do that."

"Are you afraid?" he asks.

She shakes her head. "No. I'm not afraid to die, if that's what you mean," she responds quietly. "I just don't know what happens *next*."

"Jess," he pleads, raising himself to one elbow. "Don't do this for *me*. Do it because it *needs* to be done. Do it because it's the *right thing to do*."

She smiles a slight, pitiful smile and places her hand gently on his cheek. "You Americans," she sighs. "You still believe in right and wrong," she observes tenderly, as if speaking to a child.

Under normal circumstances her condescension would enrage him. But here, with the woman he loves – a woman putting her life in jeopardy for his sake alone – he feels nothing but tenderness. And guilt.

"Yeah, Jess. We do," he admits.

She leans forward and kisses him tenderly. "You're a good man," she purrs.

The tender moment is broken by the noise of slamming car doors. Chris pulls away and turns to stare out the window. Three SUVs disgorge the terrorist and his bodyguards. Chris watches the men disappear into the lobby as the SUVs drive away. He spots a POLRI Land Rover on the west side of the Istana. Tall trees block his view of the east side, where he's certain a second vehicle has taken up position.

"They're inside," he reports to Jessica. "Four bodyguards and Khalid. POLRI are in their usual places. All's quiet."

Jessica dials Tran and passes-on Chris' report, ending the call with a terse, "We're moving out now."

She slips from the bed and adjusts her long dark linen skirt and blouse. Chris stands-by silently and watches her pull a black hijab over her head. He escorts her to the door and opens it. She hesitates momentarily then abruptly pushes the door closed and throws her arms around his neck, kissing him feverishly. Without further comment she turns, opens the door, and disappears into the dark hallway.

Chris remains inside the closed door after she departs. He waits for her to get to the car then crosses the hallway and descends the rear stairs. As he steps into the street, he hears the high-pitched whine of a small-engine vehicle. The Kijang bolts from the alley beside the hotel and sputters down the street. Hands thrust in his pockets, he strolls casually to the end of the block, crossing the street to the southeast corner of the Istana. As expected, a POLRI Land Rover is there, the driver reading a newspaper as his partner dozes peacefully. Skirting the front of the hotel, Chris glances up at Khalid's second floor window and spots a bodyguard leaning on the balcony railing casually smoking a cigarette.

All's quiet as he strolls through the nearly empty lobby and disappears into the elevator. Despite the short trip, it takes the aging elevator an agonizingly long time to reach the second floor. Emerging into the dimly lit hall, he glances down the corridor and spots a man beside the door to Khalid's suite, his chair leaning back on two legs.

Chris raps on the door to Tran's room.

"Did you see the goon guarding Khalid's door?" asks Chris as he enters the room. Tran turns from the balcony.

"No," he admits. "How's he look?"

"Relaxed," reports Chris after some thought. "Leaning back in a chair beside the door."

Tran glances at Jon. "What do you think?"

"I suppose I could come up the fire exit at the other end of the hallway," replies Jon. "I'll be in position to move against him when you're ready."

"Shit," curses Tran, slapping his forehead. "With him in the hallway, how am I going to get to the breaker panel?" The three of them glance at each other awkwardly.

"Oh, well. No plan survives initial contact with the enemy," grunts Chris. "Let's lure the bodyguards down to the lobby and we'll catch them coming back up," he suggests. "Once Jess sets off her diversion they're going to try to get back to Khalid anyway."

"I don't see any other option," replies Tran. "Here's what we'll do. Jon, go ahead and take up your position in the emergency exit. When the bodyguards head downstairs, you take out the guy at the door. Next, Chris and I will take up positions outside Khalid's door and you move to the breaker panel. As soon as you hear the elevator start moving back up from the lobby, kill it. We'll wait as long as we can to see if the POLRI outside scramble, then do the forced entry."

He glances around. "Any questions?"

There are none.

"Good. Jon, you'd better get moving..."

Jessica cruises slowly past the POLRI station, a small, white, paint-chipped, one-story building with steel mesh over the windows and a fenced-in motor pool along its eastern side. Several cops lounge in front of the building, smoking and chatting.

She parks at the back of the block and departs the vehicle on foot. It occurs to her the best angle of attack will be from the rear of the building. But is it unguarded?

After a small group of tourists pass her on the street, she ducks into the dark alley. It takes a few seconds for her eyes to adjust as she picks her way through the darkness.

Reaching the rear of the police station, she cranes her neck to peer through an open window and spots a group of cops playing some sort of card game in the station's back room. Laughter and stale cigarette smoke drift into the alley. She creeps closer and peers inside. Besides the half-dozen cops, she counts four obvious prostitutes. They're laughing uproariously, drinking and partying with the cops.

Suddenly there's a shout. She backs away from the window and spots a cop standing in an open door. Her stunned expression must make him all the more suspicious.

He stalks toward her spouting a torrent of accusations. Unsure what he's saying, she stammers her response in Thai, biding time as she gropes for a cover story. He grasps her arm and drags her into the police station. They burst into the back room with a clatter. The card players glance up from their game, annoyed at the interruption.

The cop speaks rapidly to a fat man with an eye patch; obviously the senior officer. The fat man dumps the hooker from his lap and groans to his feet, his chair toppling over against the wall. Approaching Jessica, he snaps something in the local dialect. She shakes her head and responds in Thai.

He grunts something else she doesn't understand; she stares back at him blankly. When she fails to respond, he reaches for the large cloth bag slung diagonally across her torso. Shoving her against the wall, he rips the bag over her head and dumps the contents onto the concrete floor. He stoops to recover her fake passport, his chubby fingers thumbing roughly through the pages.

"Thailand?" he asks. She nods briskly. He turns to the other cops and mumbles something that elicits a nasty retort. One of the cops rises and leaves the room. The fat cop stands, leering, inspecting her up and down, like a butcher surveying a choice piece of meat. He raises his hand and cups her clothed breast. She recoils, wrapping her arms around her torso and averting her eyes, trying to appear shy and unthreatening. She's reassured her traditional Muslim garb provides an excuse for false modesty.

The prostitutes laugh appreciatively as the fat cop raises Jessica's long skirt to exposes her smooth, shaved legs and polished, pedicured nails that shine between the straps of her locally made sandals. Jessica swats at his hands, knocking the skirt from his grasp as she cowers against the wall in increased apprehension.

He raises his hand again to touch her when the cop who'd left the room reappears with a young man in civilian clothes. The fat cop snarls something to the young man who turns to Jessica and speaks to her in Thai.

"The Major wants to know what you were doing in the alley."

"I... I'm here with a group of nurses from Muslim Medical Association," she lies. "I was looking for my guide. He left to meet someone and didn't return. I... I thought he went down the alley."

The man translates her answer to the Major, who snaps something back at him. The man nods and translates for Jessica's benefit.

"He said you should not be out alone this time of night. It isn't proper. He wants to know where you are staying."

"My hotel is nearby," she replies vaguely, hoping he doesn't ask for details. "Please tell him I thank him for his concern and tell him I'm on my way back to my hotel now."

After the man translates, the major snorts something that makes the other officers laugh irreverently. Then he growls something to the translator, who flushes and turns to Jessica.

"The... a... Major asks that you wait for him in his office," he explains, a trace of wariness in his voice. "Would you please follow me?" He seizes Jessica's arm politely but firmly.

"Why?" she demands, her panic rising. "I have done nothing wrong!"

"Please," the translator implores as he tugs her toward the heavy wooden door. "It is just a formality."

The first thing she notices when they enter the musty office is a large, ornate desk with a large glass ashtray overflowing with cigarette butts. Before the desk is a lonely straight-backed chair showing signs of other-than social use.

A handcuff hangs piteously from one arm. There are dark stains on the seat and floor she rather suspects are dried blood. To her relief, the translator guides her to another, less intimidating seat beside the major's desk.

He bows and turns back toward the door.

"You're not *leaving*," she insists.

"Aaaa, yes," he replies reluctantly. "The major wants to speak with you alone." Before she can respond, he slips from the room. There is a loud "click" as he locks the door behind him.

She glances around frantically, her eyes darting from desktop to bookshelf in search of a weapon. She lunges across his desk and retrieves a long, stainless steel letter opener from the half-open desk drawer. Raising her forearm, she carefully slides the weapon up her sleeve and returns nervously to the chair to await the inevitable.

Moments later, a key rattles in the lock and the door groans open. The major waddles in, closing the door and locking it behind him. He faces her and she immediately averts her gaze, staring demurely at the floor. The "creak" of wooden floorboards announces his approach. The rattling belt buckle and telltale sound of his zipper confirm her suspicions. His pants clatter to the floor.

The shuffle of shoes on the gritty wood surface tells her he is standing before her. He reaches down and cups her chin in his hand, raising her face upward. She spots his semi-erection and glances up hatefully into the pockmarked face, aglow with anticipation. He mumbles something in Indonesian she didn't understand, but the meaning of which is clear.

Her eyes locked with his one good eye, she lets the letter opener slide from within her sleeve into her waiting hand. He reaches to unbutton her blouse and she rises to her feet, grabbing his windpipe with her right hand and squeezing with all her might. His eyes bulge as he sputters in surprise.

Before he can recover from shock, she leans into him and thrusts the steel blade with all her might upward beneath his sternum and into his heart, partly withdrawing then driving it back into him again and again until it seems as if the blade will emerge on the other side of his body.

His face freezes in incomprehension. She stares furiously into his one good eye; fingers buried in his windpipe, watching his pupil dilate as his body sags and collapses. Together, they sink onto their knees as he leans against her, his one good eye rolling back into his skull. The life gone from his miserable body, she withdraws the blade from his chest and shoves him contemptuously onto the filthy floor.

She glares at the dead major, feeling hollow. No pity, no remorse. Nothing.

A howl of laughter rises from the next room and Jessica realizes it's time to leave. She unlatches the painted-over window and opens it.

Oh, shit!

A wide steel mesh screen blocks her escape. She gropes frantically for some sort of release, but finds nothing. *Fine*, she resolves as she wrenches the window shut. *We'll do this the hard way.*

She sweeps clear his desk, leans on the edge on the edge and closes her eyes. His cronies know why he brought her in here, so they're going to get it.

She begins breathing in long, slow deep gasps. After a few moments her breaths become interspersed with moans as she concentrates on the scene framed in her mind's eye. Her hips writhe against the edge of the desk as her hand slides along the cool cotton embracing her dampening crotch. A loud moan escapes her lips, surprising in its intensity. The desk creaks rhythmically as the next moan comes louder, longer. Her supporting hand slips from the desk, sending the overflowing ashtray clattering to the floor. She lets out a yell. Not a cry for help, but one of ecstasy. Her groans become louder, longer; more demanding as she rocks back and forth on the desk, the vibrations shaking the remaining files onto the floor. Finally a long, loud, shivering moan hang suspended in the air, echoing through the stuffy room before receding into a loud pant that subsides into shallow moan.

Laughter erupts in the next room; several men clapping as they pay tribute to their virile major, unseen but clearly in conquest. Jessica sits up, horrified at the pleasure she's just given herself in the midst of the danger. She stares at the pathetic figure on the floor and feels nothing. It's a carpet, a discarded pile of trash unworthy of regret.

She wrinkles her hijab, musses her hair, and slaps her cheeks for color. After a decent interval, she takes a deep breath and unlocks the door. With a mighty tug, she jerks it open and backs meekly into the hallway, closing the door behind her.

"Thank you. Thank you," she purrs to the dead major unseen on the floor as she bows her way out of the office. In the hall, several cops grins at her lecherously. The young interpreter glances up from behind his desk.

"Have you finished your... interview?" he asks in surprise.

"Yes," she replies bashfully. "The major is... tidying up."

The young man leads her from the building. As they emerge into the damp night, she bows to the civilian.

"You have been most kind," she announces timidly.

He smiles indulgently. "May I escort you back to your hotel?" he asks.

Jessica giggles girlishly. "No, Sir. Thank you. assalamu alaikum," she murmurs. He smiles brightly as she turns and departs down the street.

Passing the motor pool, she catches sight of a gasoline storage tank on stilts just inside the compound. She returns to her car and collapses in the front seat, hands trembling as she reaches beneath the seat and withdraws her satellite phone and two hand grenades.

CHAPTER 15

Chris flinches when the phone on the nightstand springs to life. Tran nods for him to answer it.

"Ja?" he answers.

"I'm in position," responds Jessica tersely.

"She's ready," he reports to Tran.

"Ask her if we can have fifteen minutes," asks Tran.

"Can we get fifteen minutes?" he asks Jessica.

"No. I just killed a POLRI major," she replies urgently. "We have to move before they discover the body..."

"Shit," he mumbles. "What happened?"

"It doesn't matter!" she snaps; he immediately feels foolish wasting time with unnecessary questions.

"You're right. You're right," he replies quickly. "Are you still in a position to provide the diversion?"

"Yes. But get moving!" She insists.

"Okay. Five minutes," he agrees, holding up and examining his watch, "from... now."

"Right!" she replies then the line goes dead.

When Chris glances up, Tran is staring at him in disbelief. "What the hell? *Five minutes?*"

"She had to kill a cop," explains Chris. "She's in deep shit. We have to move now or she won't be able to help us."

He tosses the receiver to Tran. "Make it sound good," he advises.

Tran dials the front desk and asks to be connected with Room 23. The phone rings several times before a gruff Arabic voice replies.

"Sir? This is the concierge. I am sorry to bother you so late in the evening," announces Tran in ingratiating, stilted English. "There is a police officer down here with a package for the guest in room 23."

The man responds in English. "Who is the package from?"

Tran covers the phone and mumbles. "Sir? He says it is from the POLRI commander, Colonel Shihab."

"All right. Bring it up," growls the man.

"One moment Sir," replies Tran. He places his hand over the mouthpiece and winks at Chris before returning to the phone. "I'm sorry Sir, but he says his orders are to wait in the lobby."

Tran hears a muffled conversation in the background, then "all right. Someone will be down shortly."

Tran hangs up the phone and nods tersely to Chris. "Let's go!" he rasps.

Chris grabs the assault rifles from the bed and tosses one to Tran. He leans into the door, his eye screwed tightly to the peephole. From down the corridor comes the clatter of a door being unlocked and opened; a light appears at the opposite end of the hall and disappears as the door closes again. There is a muffled conversation with the man on guard followed by the sound of footsteps on the antique wooden floor echoing through the hallway. The elevator doors creak open and the men disappear inside.

"Two men," reports Chris with relief. He tenses and reached for the doorknob.

Jon squats in the stairwell of the emergency exit; he hears the bodyguards emerge from Khalid's room. Heart pounding, he slides the Khukuri from its concealed scabbard, its reassuring heft in his sweating palm. Carefully cracking open the door, he peers into the hallway. The door guard stands with his back to him, facing down the hall toward the two men that just disappeared into the elevator. As the elevator doors begin to rumble closed, Jon takes advantage of the racket. He pulls the door open in one smooth motion and steps silently into the hall.

Jessica leaves the car and walks two blocks past the police station before doubling back along the dimly lit street beside the motor pool. Her eyes sweep her watch. She reaches into her pocket and grasps the first cold, egg-shaped grenade.

From within the police station comes woman's scream, followed by frantic shouts. Realizing she's out of time, she retrieves the grenade from her pocket, slips her finger through the ring and pulls with increasing intensity. As she glances down to see why the ring hasn't budged, it suddenly pops loose with a loud "click." She heaves the grenade over the fence. It collides with the steel fuel tank with a loud *"clunk"* drawing the attention of the cops spilling from the building. There is a shout behind her as she sprints down the street toward the car. *Why hasn't it gone off?* Rounding the corner, she pulls the second grenade from her pocket and jerks loose the safety pin. *Oh, God. Please tell me it wasn't a dud...*

An explosion erupts from the motor pool; streams of liquid fire arching dramatically through the air and falling back toward earth, grappling for fleeing victims. She grins maniacally and heaves the second grenade into the alley, where it strikes the rear of the police building and clatters onto the cobblestone pavement.

Finally she reaches the Kijang, jerking frantically on the door handle before realizing the car is locked. She reaches into her pocket and grabs the key. As she inserts it into the lock, an earsplitting *"CRUMP"* erupts over her right shoulder. A shockwave knocks her to the ground; a section of fence protecting her from the blast lands on top of her, pinning her to the pavement. She panics, kicking and clawing violently as flames licks the shattered wood.

As the elevator door closes, the guard at the door reaches absently for his chair. A sudden rumble in the distance catches his attention and he turns away at the critical moment. Jon's hand closes over the guard's mouth; he jerks back the man's head to expose the front of his neck. The blade slices effortlessly across his victim's throat, the coppery smell of blood filling Jon's nostrils.

From a distorted view through the peephole Chris sees Jon make his move on the ill-fated door guard.

"Now!" he rasps, rips open the door and sprints down the hall toward Khalid's suite. As Chris and Tran approach, Jon is lowering the guard's twitching body to the floor, hand still firmly over the man's mouth to stifle any dying cry.

As they pass the elevator, it begins to hum. "I've got it," Tran rasps and disappears into the electrical closet. Chris takes-up a position with his assault rifle covering the door to Khalid's suite as Jon drags the bodyguard's corpse down the hallway and dumps it into the fire escape. There comes a series of loud clicks as Tran flips the breakers. The lights at the far end of the hall blink off; the elevator groans to a halt, powerless.

Tran emerges from the electrical closet and stops momentarily at the elevator door, pressing his ear against the cold metal. Inside he hears the sound of panicked voices. He nods enthusiastically.

"Got 'em!" he hisses and joins Chris at Khalid's door. He tosses his assault rifle to Jon and pulls the SIG SAUER 9mm from his belt, taking his favored two-handed grip.

With a mighty shove, Jessica heaves the section of fence off her and glances around in a daze. What's left of the motor pool and police station is a mass of flame.

Struggling to her feet, she realizes the blast has temporarily deafened her. People are fleeing from the flames in a surreal silence, uncertain of what has just occurred. She takes advantage of the confusion to staggers to the Kijang where she discovers the keys laying on the ground amidst the shattered glass. Her eyes swim as she attempts to focus on the door lock. After several failed attempts to unlock the car, she realizes the driver's side window has been shattered by the blast. She reaches through the opening and unlocks the door, sweeping shards of glass from the seat before dropping behind the wheel. Miraculously, she locates the ignition on her first attempt and twists the key; the car hums to life. She slips it into gear and pops the clutch. The car jerks forward and slams into the row of the parked motor scooters in front of her. They clatter to the ground like so many dominoes. She curses, restarts the engine, and backs-up, struggling to maintain control as she cranks the car into a U-turn and speeds toward the Istana.

Several more explosions follow in her wake. *Probably stored munitions*, she realizes, glancing back over her shoulder. Eyes returning to her front, on-coming headlights blind her. She swerves toward the curb, narrowly avoiding a collision with the several POLRI Land Rovers speeding away from the Istana toward the police station.

Tran holds up three fingers and counts down quietly, "three...two...one...NOW!" he finishes with a shout. Chris rears back and raises his foot. With a mighty yell he concentrates all his weight against a point just above the door handle. The slatted door splinters under the impact and caves into the room with a crash. Chris senses, rather than sees, Tran explode past him into the room shouting, "down! Down! Get down!"

The bodyguard spins toward Tran from the balcony where he'd been staring toward the blaze in the distance. Whether or not he understood Tran's order, he makes the mistake of grappling for a weapon dangling from a sling over his shoulder. Tran snaps-off two rapid shots. The bullets enter the guard's forehead and explode from the back of his skull. A small submachine gun clatters to the floor as the bodyguard staggers backwards, topples off the balcony and crashes into the bushes below.

Chris bursts into the room behind Tran, the assault rifle raised, both eyes fixed over the top of the weapon as he sweeps the right side of the room, searching for movement. *There!* Khalid is on the sofa, some sort of hookah pipe in-hand, eyes wide in horror as Chris shuffles toward him, weapon at the ready. He slaps the pipe from Khalid's hand and grabs his hair, dragging him from the sofa and heaving him face down on the floor.

"What... what do you want?" rasps Khalid as Chris plants his knee in his back.

"Shut up," growls Chris as he runs his hands down the prostrate man's sides, frisking for hidden weapons.

Tran disappears into the bedroom and emerges seconds later.

"Clear!" he announces. "So far, so good..."

Gunfire erupts down the hallway.

"Stay with Khalid!" shouts Tran over the roar. With raised pistol, he shuffles cautiously toward the shattered doorway. Shoulder against the doorjamb, he glances quickly around the doorframe into the hall. Withdrawing, he closes his eyes and replays the scene in the corridor in his mind's eye. Jon is advancing toward him, smoking weapon in hand. It's safe. Tran steps cautiously into the hall.

"What happened?"

Jon motions vaguely toward the dark end of the hallway. "The bodyguards. They weren't in the elevator," he gasps, adrenaline still surging through his body. "They came up the west stairwell."

"Did you get them both?"

Jon nods and walks past him into the room. "Yeah. Are we ready to move?" he asks, eyes still wild with agitation.

"Just finishing-up," announces Chris. He places duct tape over Khalid's mouth, wrapping it several times around his head. Then he wraps heavy tape around the hands and wrists behind Khalid's back.

"Gimme' a hand with this asshole," Chris growls as he tugs on Khalid's arm. Jon grabs Khalid's other arm and helps Chris drag the petrified figure to its feet. Weapons dangling from their free hands, they follow Tran out the door and down the dark corridor, dragging Khalid between them.

The wall and doorway at the end of the hall are riddled with bullet holes, the floor littered with splinters of shattered wood. They step over the bloody, twisted corpses of the two bodyguards. As they enter the stairwell, Khalid drags his feet, slowing them as they lope down the stairs into the service hallway on the first floor.

"Start walking or I'll blow your fucking head off," hisses Chris. Either too scared or too stupid to cooperate, Khalid collapses completely, making Chris and Jon drag his dead weight.

"Shit!" curses Chris. He spots a laundry cart sticking out of a utility room. "There," he growls, pointing to the cart. They heft Khalid to his feet and dump him head-first among the soiled sheets and towels. "That's better," snorts Chris and he and Jon race the cart along the corridor in pursuit of Tran.

Nearing a set of double doors at the loading dock, Tran spots several hotel employees emerge from an intersecting hallway. He raises his pistol and yells something in Mandarin. The panicked employees scatter, most retreating down the hallway in the direction from which they'd come. One bolts through the double doors.

"Dammit!" curses Tran and sprints after him.

Lights snap-on all around the hotel as guests recover from their initial shock and begin searching for the source of the gunfire. Jessica is parked in the Kijang beneath a huge spreading tree by the loading dock at the rear of the hotel. She's using her torn hijab to wipe the blood from her face when she spots a hotel employee burst through the double doors onto the loading dock, glancing around rabidly. Spotting her car, he runs toward her, yelling something unintelligible.

Leaning out the window to respond, she spots Tran burst from the double doors in pursuit. As the employee's head snaps toward Tran, Jessica thrusts-open the car door, striking the man in the stomach. With an agonized gasp, he doubles over and staggers backwards. She twists in her seat, plants her left foot on the ground, grabs the doorframe and heaves herself from the seat, driving her knee into the man's face. His head snaps backwards and he collapses unconscious into the bushes bordering the driveway.

"Do you have him?" shouts Jessica as she rushes to the rear of the SUV and raises the tailgate. Before Tran can respond, Chris and Jon erupt through the loading dock doors pushing the wicker laundry cart with Khalid's bare feet sticking out of the top of it. Reaching the edge of the dock, they flip the cart on end, dumping the struggling man off the dock and onto the driveway, where he collapses in a dazed heap.

Jon drops four feet from the dock onto the ground and helps Tran drag Khalid upright. He resists as they attempt to force him into the waiting vehicle; Tran raises his pistol and strikes Khalid across the back of his head, knocking him unconscious. They dump the limp body into the rear of the SUV, throw a tattered blanket over him, and slam the tailgate.

Jessica is already behind the wheel when Tran and Jon dive into the back seat. Chris is about to climb into the front passenger seat when he spots hotel guests peering down at them from the building's rear windows. He lets loose a burst of automatic rifle fire into the air, driving the curious onlookers away from their windows.

He drops into the seat, yelling, "*Go! Go!*"

CHAPTER 16

It's late evening when Senior Minister Lee Kuan Yew's chartered Singapore Airlines 777/200 touches-down at Soekarno-Hatta Airport outside the Indonesian capital of Jakarta. As with most things relating to Mr. Lee, the diplomatic protocol dealing with the "unofficial" state visit of the former prime minister is complicated.

The airliner taxis to a discreet hangar set apart from the main terminal and pulls partway inside the massive open doors. On command, a spit-polished honor guard scrambles to take its place lining the red carpet leading from the stairs into the hangar. At the foot of the stairs, the Minister for Foreign Affairs meets Mr. Lee. The Foreign Minister is effusive in his greetings as he shakes Mr. Lee's hand and leads him quickly to the waiting limousine.

As they speed toward the Presidential Palace, the Foreign Minister finally grows weary of pleasantries and becomes somber. "The events of the past few days have been disturbing," he notes elliptically. "I hope your visit can relieve some of the tension."

Mr. Lee nods benignly. "Perhaps," he responds simply.

Realizing Mr. Lee is going to say no more, the Foreign Minister continues. "President Megawati will meet you immediately," he explains. "As requested, there will be no public announcement of your arrival." Infuriatingly, Mr. Lee merely nods his understanding and remains resolutely silent.

The limousine slides through the entrance of the Presidential Palace, up the curved driveway and stops before floodlit marble front steps. A small presidential honor guard lines the stairs as the Foreign Minister leads Mr. Lee through an arched foyer. Beneath a gold eagle and shield of the Republika Indonesia awaits President Megawati, gold-fringed red drapes framing her squat physique. Several ornately uniformed TNI Indonesian military officers stand alongside her. She steps forward and offers her hand, welcoming Mr. Lee in English.

"Senior Minister," she announces with all apparent reverence. "Welcome to Indonesia."

"It is my pleasure," he responds courteously, his sharp eyes remaining fixed on the scowling officers beside her. "Am I to understand we'll be speaking alone?" he asks pointedly.

President Megawati recoils slightly at his bluntness, so unusual for an Asian, yet so in character for the intrepid Mr. Lee. She quickly regains her composure. "Why... certainly. If you wish." She turns to the two officers. "Gentlemen, if you will please leave us..."

One officer hesitates only momentarily before bowing obediently, deferring to his commander-in-chief. "Yes Ma'am," he snaps. The second officer remains standing rigidly; an admiral in the Tentara Nasional Indonesia Angkatan Laut, or TNI-AL, the Indonesian Navy, he does not by nature defer to elected politicians.

"You're Excellency," he responds through gritted teeth. "I understand this discussion regards *navy* matters."

Senior Minister Lee eyes the officer coldly. "No, *Admiral*," he replies. "This regards relations between nations." Mr. Lee knows the admiral by reputation. He's one of the officers SID has identified as a leader of the "Greens"

- members of the military supporting formation of an Indonesian Muslim state ruled by Shari'a law. It is such officers on whom the JI relies for influence within the military.

The admiral glowers silently at Mr. Lee.

"Admiral," purrs President Megawati. "Perhaps you will hold yourself available for...'consultations' as needed."

The admiral hesitates. "Yes Ma'am", he mumbles and withdraws reluctantly to an antechamber. President Megawati slips her arm endearingly through Mr. Lee's and escorts him toward the reception area as the two leaders exchange polite inquiries about the health of mutual friends and family members.

They arrive in a large, high-ceilinged room, the polished marble floor partly concealed beneath a lush green and gold rug lined with similarly upholstered chairs. On narrow tables lining the walls stand large ornate vases attesting to Indonesia's cultural history. Two chairs, slightly larger and more heavily cushioned than the others, are arranged at angles to each other, a small round-topped coffee table between them. On green-trimmed white wood paneled walls are incongruous floor-to-ceiling murals of the president and various members of the Sukarno family.

Still exchanging benign pleasantries, they take their seats and, after a white clad servant serves tea, are left alone in the room.

"I was wondering when your government might react to the tragic events of late," announces the president finally.

"Yes," replies Mr. Lee. "We are deeply saddened by the horrific attack on the peaceful people of Bali. The Republic sends its warmest condolences and offers whatever assistance you may require to hunt down the animals that perpetrated the act."

"Thank you," replies President Megawati as she primly sips her tea. Leaning forward, she places her cup on the edge of the table beside her. "However I was referring to the tragic loss of one of your naval vessels," she announces, watching him closely for a reaction.

He nods solemnly. *How dare you taunt me*, he seethes inwardly, though his expression betrays nothing of his anger. "We are of course appalled at the actions of your navy. Our vessel was in international waters when it was attacked without provocation. I assume you are ready to offer your apologies and assurance those responsible will be severely punished."

"Senior Minister," replies Mrs. Megawati cautiously, nervously twisting a napkin in her hands. "There is no question as to whether your vessel was in our territorial waters. But before we can discuss... *responsibilities*... we must address the larger question: what was your ship doing within our exclusive economic zone in the first place?"

Mr. Lee smiles tolerantly. *Economic zone versus territorial waters; a nice distinction*, he realizes. "It was not in your waters," he reiterates politely. "And the Republic of Singapore disputes that it must clear its transit through international waters with the Indonesian navy."

President Megawati angrily slaps the arm of her chair. "You were running spies in Indonesia's sovereign territory," she insists. "*That* is an act of war!"

Mr. Lee considers for a moment before responding with a question. "Why is the government of Indonesia harboring an international fugitive?" he asks casually.

Mrs. Megawati stiffens. "I am not aware of any such activity," she scoffs. "The question is of Singapore's interference with Indonesia's internal affairs..."

"Khalid," he interrupts. "He has been indicted in Singapore and the Philippines."

"Yes," she acknowledges tersely.

"Then why do you not arrest him?"

"I have no information to indicate..."

"We provided detailed information to your intelligence services regarding Khalid's presence in Kalimantan," interrupts Mr. Lee. "Of course if they failed to inform you..." His voice trails off, leaving the president a convenient "out" if she wishes to pursue it.

Her eyes wander to a photograph of her late father on the wall, former Indonesian President Sukarno. "There are 'complications' to governing Indonesia of which you cannot conceive," she sighs as if addressing her long deceased father. Her eyes cut icily back to Mr. Lee.

"We are not a single-party state like Singapore. *I* must balance competing interests," she insists.

"I understand," responds Mr. Lee calmly. "But surely the recent events in Bali illustrate..."

"...There are dangerous forces in Indonesia that must be handled delicately," she interrupts. "And I cannot have Singapore - *or the United States* - interfering in our domestic affairs!"

"But you have extremists within your own government," he reminds her. "Their presence poses a great risk to The Republic."

"We are *trying* to build a democracy," she replies crossly. "If extremists are elected, *what am I to do?* You - and the Americans - you want me to crush the extremists. If I do, you accuse me of violating human rights and withdraw your support. Then I am left alone to deal with angry extremists!"

Mr. Lee nods his understanding, his expressive eyes conveying empathy.

"Madam President, if we work together quietly," replies Mr. Lee softly. "Perhaps we can assist each other to avert a war neither of our peoples desire..."

The Mobile Brigade commander picks his way among the smoldering remnants of the shattered police station, sidestepping the twisted remains of a police officer and several scantily-clad women.

"What were so many senior officers doing in such close proximity?" he asks his POLRI escort, nudging a playing card with the toe of his boot. "Weren't they aware of the alert?"

His escort, a young POLRI lieutenant, adjusts his bandaged arm within its makeshift sling, grimacing in pain. "Of-of course, Sir," he stammers. "The major was holding a... a conference to discuss the matter when the incident occurred."

"So I see," observes the colonel sourly as the lieutenant flushes. "What do you believe caused the explosion?" he asks.

An elderly man in civilian clothes standing nearby supplies the answer. "Grenades," he grunts over the cigarette dangling from between his lips. "Set off the petrol tank and ammunition storage room."

The colonel eyes the man distastefully, noting he appears to have just climbed from bed: a pair of baggy pants droop below his protuberant belly; the buttons on his hastily clad shirt are misaligned. "And you know this how?" asks the colonel.

The man reaches into his shirt pocket, withdraws two metal strips, and tosses them to the colonel, who juggles to catch both. He examines the strips, his pulse quickening. "Arming levers," he breathes.

"Mmm hummm," responds the cop. "Chinese Type 86 fragmentary grenades," he confirms.

"Thank you..." the colonel's voice trails off in question.

"Moetojib," the man responds, thrusting his stubby fingers into his shirt pocket and withdrawing another cigarette. "Detective Moetojib."

"So this was clearly sabotage," growls the colonel. "And you were just as clearly unprepared," he snaps to the lieutenant, who remains mute beneath the BRIMOB officer's withering stare.

"He's alive!" shouts one of the firemen..

A dozen feet away, a team of firemen and paramedics are dissecting a heap of rubble. The colonel scrambles over to them and helps the searchers clear away the debris. Beneath the wreckage lay an officer bathed in blood, his right arm twisted awkwardly behind his back; his face splintered with fragments of glass and wood.

The colonel reaches beneath the wounded man and lifts, helping the paramedics drag his shattered body from the rubble. His crushed arm dangling uselessly off the stretcher, the officer gropes for the front of the colonel's fatigue jacket with his one good hand, searching the impassive face desperately. "It was...a...a... woman," he gurgles.

"What do you mean?" snaps the colonel. "How do you know?" The officer releases the colonel's jacket, his shaking hand pointing across the shattered room. "There," he gasps. "Her bag...," he exhales loudly and collapses onto the stretcher.

The colonel sifts through the debris, locating a torn canvas bag near the remnants of the door leading to the alley. Beneath the shredded material, he discovers makeup, a singed wad of Indonesian Rupiah, and the sketch of a neighborhood with an address written on the back of a cocktail napkin.

"Slow down, Jess," Chris cautions. "We don't need to call attention to ourselves." She acknowledges his advice with a curt nod, wiping her sweaty palms on her skirt before renewing a death-grip on the wheel. The west end of town seems eerily quiet as the underpowered Kijang whines down the empty street toward the river road.

"Uh, oh," she mumbles. "Roadblock ahead." The three passengers lean forward and peer intently through the windshield at the makeshift barrier looming a half-mile ahead.

"They must've called-in the bridge patrols to seal off the city," announces Tran. "Turn left up ahead; let's find another route."

Steering the Kijang onto a side street, Jessica glances again into the rearview mirror. "Uh, oh," she groans.

Chris' head snaps over his shoulder; he spots an armed Land Rover closing from behind. Tran and Jon glance back also.

"Punch it, Jessica," orders Tran. "Get some distance between us!" He twists in his seat and gauges the temporarily growing gap as the car lurches forward. He leans forward and examines the road ahead. "Take the next left," he snaps.

The Kijang tilts perilously on two wheels as Jessica jerks the steering wheel right and takes the corner, tires slipping on the damp pavement. At the next block she turns left and left again, doubling back the opposite direction before darting among the parked cars lining the curb in front of a row of ramshackle shops.

"Put it in park; headlights off; foot off the brake. Get down!" Tran hisses as he kicks open the passenger door and rolls out onto the deserted sidewalk. Dashing to the end of the block, he peers around the corner in time to see the Land Rover rumble past. He sprints to the opposite end of the short block and watches the Land Rover proceed several more streets before skidding to a stop in the middle of the wet pavement. After what seems an eternity, the Land Rover turns right and speeds away. Satisfied they've shaken the patrol, he dashes back to the car.

"Looks like we shook 'em for the moment," he pants as he slides into the back seat. "But now they'll be on the lookout for the Kijang," he declares. "We're gonna have to dump Khalid at the safe house and ditch the car. Jon and I will go find another one."

Jessica takes an indirect route to the safe house. Circling the silent block twice, they search for signs of surveillance. Detecting none, she backs the car up the gravel driveway and kills the engine. The three men heft the unconscious Khalid from the rear of the car and drag him inside. They dump him on the cold concrete floor, reinforce the duct tape around his ankles, and blindfold him.

Jessica tosses Tran the car keys and he and Jon head outside. Chris draws aside the tattered curtains and squints through the filthy window. He spots Jon walk to the sidewalk, peer up and down the deserted street and signal toward the house. The Kijang rolls slowly to the edge of the driveway and Jon slips into the passenger seat. The car sputters to life and disappears down the street.

Chris lets the curtains drop closed and turns to Jessica. She's pale and sweating. He suddenly notices the bloody gash on her jaw line.

"Are you all right?" he asks tenderly as he approaches. She raises her hand and runs it lightly over the scabbing wound.

"Yes," she replies quietly. "I think so. I was too close to the second explosion."

"Let's have a look," he replies, guiding her to a chair. He retrieves a bottle of water and soaks his handkerchief. Blotting the wound, he locates several pieces of shattered glass and picks them carefully from the cut. She seizes his hand and holds it to her uninjured cheek, closing her eyes.

"Are we going to make it?" she asks desperately.

"I don't know Jess," he admits, peering across the room at Khalid beginning to stir. "I think so. But I don't know." He returns to quietly cleaning her wound. Finally he has to break the silence.

"That was one hell of a bang you made," he comments.

"I blew up their motor pool," she snorts, grateful to talk about the event. "There must have been ammunition or something stored nearby; there were secondary explosions."

"So I heard," chuckles Chris. "Nice job."

"Thanks."

He rinses the bloody handkerchief and places it on the table. "Do you want to talk about the cop?" he asks.

He's been through this before: the adrenaline rush of combat; the guilty relief of survival; the seeping apprehension it could have ended very differently.

"No. It had to be done. I'm okay with it," she lies. "But, thanks. Maybe later."

Chris nods his understanding and paces from window to window, peering into the darkness.

"I can't help feeling we should have gone straight to the boat," he announces finally. "The longer we wait, the more time they'll have to cut us off from the Java Sea."

"Tran and Jon will be back soon," replies Jessica encouragingly. "We'll be better off in a fresh vehicle. Then we can make our way to the boat."

"Hmph," he grunts. He glances at Jessica and flashed a falsely reassuring smile.

"I can't see a damned thing from in here," he announces. "I'm going outside to have a look around."

CHAPTER 17

Alone in the house with Khalid, Jessica finds herself despising the bound man on the floor. He begins to stir, squirming like a caterpillar on a hot sidewalk as he struggles against the tape. Jessica rises slowly and approaches him. Sensing her approach, he lifts his head and turns blindly toward her. She places the sole of her sandal on his forehead and crushes his head against the floor.

"Not so tough without your bodyguards, are you?" she scoffs. He jerks violently and resumes writhing, straining against the tape. She kicks him in the ribs. A hissing sound escapes through his nostrils.

"Stay still or I'll put a bullet in your head, *pig*," she sneers. He lay shivering, his breath coming in wheezing gusts. Reluctantly, she stoops beside him and picks the hastily-wrapped tape away from his nose. He grunts and nods emphatically, indicating she should continue. She rips the tape from his mouth and he gasps, breathing heavily.

"Thank you," he coughs.

"Yeah," she responds dispassionately.

"May I have water?"

"Sure." She retrieves a half-empty bottle from the table and lifts his head, holding the bottle to his lips. He guzzles thirstily.

"Who are you?" he demands between gulps. "Why are you helping the infidel?"

Her lips curl into a sneer. *Infidel*.

"You are being extradited to Singapore to stand trial for conspiracy to commit murder," she explains tersely. "That's all you need to know."

"No," he replies confidently. "Allah will never permit it."

She laughs nastily. "Allah doesn't protect murderers," she scoffs.

"I have no will, only that of Allah..."

She slaps him across the face.

"No! You're a murderer!" she hisses. "Don't blame your choices on God."

"You are not Muslim," he responds dourly. "You do not understand..."

"Oh, I *understand*," she hisses. "It was your bomb that killed several Singaporean police officials last December, wasn't it?" she asks, slapping him again. "It was your bomb that murdered all those innocents in Bali, wasn't it?" she demands with another slap.

"Casualties of war," he growls. "They were but handmaidens of the Americans."

"The Americans didn't attack you. You attacked them!" she scoffs.

"No! They and the Zionists have been crusading against Islam for centuries!"

"So you murder the people of Asia?"

"We fight all supporters of Zionist..."

"Singapore is not Zionist!" she insists angrily. "Neither is Indonesia! And neither were those innocent people in the nightclub!"

"Infidel! All of them!" he shouts. She stares at him as if he's deranged. "You're crazy," she insists.

He snorts and shakes his head. "You are just a foolish woman. Such things are beyond you," he spits. "Now stop this foolishness and release me!"

She grabs his beard and shakes it angrily. "This *foolish* woman is going to see you hang," she seethes. "I'm going to watch you dangle at the end of a rope until what's left of your rotted soul runs out your arse."

He explodes with a torrent of expletives in muddled Arabic and Javanese. Clapping her hand over his mouth, she sits on his chest, pinning him to the floor. "Shut up! Shut up!" she orders.

He shakes her hand away and continues. "You coward! You don't even have the courage to look me in the eye!" he taunts.

In a fury, she grasps the edge of the tape and rips it from his face. She leans in, her nose inches from his, her hot breath in his face. "Is this close enough?" she asks.

He stares back, blinking rapidly as his eyes adjust to the light. A glint of recognition flutters on his face.

"The whore from the hotel!" he announces with creeping realization.

In a fit of rage, she grabs his sweating bangs and drags him upright. Spinning around behind him, she wraps her arm around his neck and twists.

"I could fucking kill you right now!" she breathes. "It would save my country the trouble."

His eyes bulge as he gasps for air. "I've done nothing to you!"

"Oh, yes you have," she rasps, tears welling in her eyes. "Your bomb killed my husband, Captain Peter Chang..."

The wind rises; a threat of rain hangs heavy in the air. Chris circles the safe house a third time, lurking in the shadows, moving cautiously between the sheltering buildings. He feels safer outside where he can detect an enemy's approach rather than inside conceding the initiative to the enemy. As he slides deftly through the alley and approaches the rear of the safe house, a dog barks steadily in a nearby yard. An occasional un-muffled vehicle sputters in the distance. Otherwise all's quiet. *But is it too quiet?* He asks himself with a nervous chuckle at the cliché.

He collapses tiredly against the back wall of the house, inhaling the fresh, damp air. A drop of cold water strikes his face, followed by another and another as the rain steadily increases. The rumble of thunder and jagged bolt of lightning announce the arrival of the storm. He draws back against the house and slithers around the corner. As he reaches for the doorknob, he hears a "yelp"; the dog stops barking.

His hand drops from the handle and he turns away, squinting toward the abandoned warehouse across the driveway. A gust of wind whips the rain between the buildings, branches creaking, wet leaves rustling in the gale-force wind. Fat rain drops drum on the ubiquitous sheet metal roofs of the buildings nearby. The hair on the back of his neck bristles. He reaches behind his belt, withdraws the Browning 9mm and sinks against the house, disappearing at a crouch into a small cutout beneath the eaves.

There! - the telltale splash of a boot striking a puddle. Amid the menacing thunder, a voice rasps orders. From the corner of his eye, he glimpses movement. A man dashes across the driveway and disappears into the shadows behind the house!

Or is it an animal?

He edges toward the side door, seeking desperately to warn Jessica.

"Clank."

He halts again. *I know that sound – an unsecured buckle striking a weapon's magazine.* Flashbacks of the Salvadoran jungle erupt in his mind; recollections of the sounds of undisciplined guerillas moving down trails in the darkness. He can smell their perspiration; hear the rhythmic breathing of a column of straining men; sense movement through the night. He peers intently through sheets of rain.

Directly across from him, unaware of his presence just thirty feet away, a black-clad assault team of five BRIMOB emerge from the alley alongside the adjacent building, edging along the wall opposite him. Lightning flashes, silhouetting the assault team as they move into position to isolate the safe house.

Chris raises his pistol slowly, fixing its sights on the point man at the head of the squad. The scout raises his fist, signaling a halt; squad members drop to one knee in the tall weeds whipped by the wind. The scout sweeps his weapon's sights left-to-right across the path before him. Discerning nothing, he rises and motions the team forward.

Jessica twists Khalid's head, the vertebrae in his neck crackling she reaches the extent of his range of motion. One violent jerk and Peter's death will be avenge and...

"Crack!"

Her blood runs cold. Springing to her feet, she flings the choking Khalid aside and lunges for her assault rifle.

His strangled laughter pursues her across the dismal room as she searches desperately for the source of gunfire.

"*You see?* Allah will not permit it!" he shrieks.

Blinded by his own pistol's muzzle flash, Chris lunges toward the dazed assault team, firing frantically into the dark mass of men scrambling before him.

A murky figure looms in his peripheral vision. Chris turns and fires blindly into the blackness. Movement to his right; he spins and fires again. Another vague figure surges toward him. Before Chris can fire, there is a collision, a crash of limbs and torsos as the two men land in a tangled heap. The pistol slips from Chris' grasp, clattering into the darkness.

A fist strikes his jaw; a gloved hand closes over his face, grinding the back of his skull against the gravel driveway. In one fluid movement, Chris turns his head, simultaneously bringing his forearm sharply across his attacker's wrist. The hand slips from his face, the body weight shifting off-balance. Chris rolls aside and the man topples sideways into the gravel.

Rolling to his knees, Chris gropes frantically for his lost pistol. A glint of steel flashes past his eyes: a knife! He stumbles to his feet, reeling backwards and glancing around desperately for a weapon – any weapon.

Lightning silhouettes the shadowy figure as it lunges toward him. Chris spins aside, grabbing the man's shoulder and propelling him headfirst into the building's wall.

"Chris! *Down!*" Jessica shrieks.

Chris drops instantly to the ground. As the man staggers to his feet, a sonic snap passes close over Chris' head, Jessica's bullets slamming his attacker against the wall. The man slides to the ground, his dying eyes wide with shock.

"Come on!" insists Jessica. Chris clatters blindly toward the house. As he dives through the open door, she turns and sprays bullets down the driveway before backing into the house, slamming and locking the door.

"How many are there?" she shouts, dropping the empty magazine from her weapon and inserting a fresh one. Chris grabs one of the remaining assault rifles and stumbles toward the window at the front of the house.

"Five in the driveway," he gasps. "They're all down. I think I saw one run behind the house. There're probably more!" He notes the horror in her eyes. "Don't worry," he announces with forced calmness. "Tran and Jon are still out there... somewhere."

"In here!" erupts a strange voice. "Servants of Allah! *In here*!!!!"

Chris turns to see Khalid struggling to his knees and frothing rabidly, fanatical eyes ablaze.

"What the...?" Chris swings the butt of his weapon across the side of Khalid's head. The terrorist topples sideways, collapsing unconscious onto the cold concrete floor. Chris turns angrily to Jessica. "Why the hell...?"

"He needed water," she lies.

Chris raises his hand for silence. "Listen!" he hisses.

Minutes pass in agony as they listen to shouted voices outside the house. The slosh of boots through sticky mud announces a coming assault. Chris drops to one knee and raises his weapon on the door just as it collapses, several BRIMOB spilling into the room. The point man trips over the chairs Jessica scattered around the entrance, rope strung between them in a sort of tangle-foot arrangement. The remainder of the assault team collides with him, cursing as they stumble into each other. An eerie light floods the room as a vehicle's headlights shine through the open door, backlighting the confounded assault team. Chris grits his teeth and opens fire.

As quickly as it began the gunfire ends. Chris and Jessica stare warily at each other; mouths agape at the scope of carnage. Deafened by gunfire, they meet a surreal scene: a gray haze hangs in the air, diffusing the light that filters-in from outside the house into a ghostly glow. BRIMOB in the yard call-out uncertainly to their comrades inside.

A dreadful realization seizes Chris: the paradigm has shifted. A comparatively low risk snatch of a foreign terrorist has escalated to war with the nation in which *he* is now the transgressor. His last hope is to get Khalid out of Indonesia as justification - a rationale - for his actions.

Jessica catches a glimpse of movement in the window over Chris' shoulder. "Chris!" she shrieks as the glass explodes, showering him with splinters. It's as if he'd been struck with a baseball bat. Spinning from the impact, he drops his weapon and corkscrews to the ground in a stunned daze.

Jessica fires again, but he can't see at what. Spotting his weapon on the floor a few feet away, he attempts to reach for it, but his arm won't respond. Its then he notices his left deltoid hanging like a piece of raw meat from his mangled shoulder. It's strange, except for a searing ache, there's surprisingly little pain.

"Chris! *Move!*" screams Jessica.

He glances up, seeing her fumbling to reload her weapon and staring in horror at something behind him. He turns in time to see a man lunge at him through the shattered window. Chris rolls aside and the man lands in a heap on the floor beside him. Beneath his hip Chris discovers his assault rifle. With his right hand he grabs the stock and rolls, swinging the weapon blindly with all his might toward the rising attacker. The front site disappears into his attacker's eye socket, the bloody rifle sliding from Chris' grasp as the man tumbles backwards, hands pawing at his shattered face. Chris lunges frantically for the weapon, managing to get his finger through the trigger guard. He seizes the grip and squeezes the trigger.

The man's head explodes.

"*Where's Tran?!*" shrieks Jessica.

Tran and Jon hijack a Mitsubishi refrigerator truck across town, dumping the unconscious driver in an alley and taking his wallet, hoping the police will assume he's been mugged. They're pleased with themselves as the truck rumbles toward the safe house. Being a common commercial vehicle, the fish truck's presence on the road at night is unlikely to raise suspicions.

As they near the safe house they meet the disheartening sound of gunfire echoing through the neighborhood. Tran's blood runs cold.

"Go! Go!" he shouts, drawing his pistol and peering frantically into the distance. As they near the safe house, Tran spots a BRIMOB Land Rover approaching from the opposite direction and screeching to a halt in front of the house. The doors swing open and men spill from the vehicle.

"Ram 'em!" barks Tran as he braces his heels against the dashboard.

Face etched with rage, Jon downshifts and crushes the accelerator to the floor. Men pouring from the Land Rover glance-up in time to see the 24,000 pound Mitsubishi refrigerator truck slam into them. Those caught between the truck and Land Rover die instantly, crushed by the impact of steel on steel. The remaining BRIMOB are dragged beneath the truck as it propels the Land Rover over them, driving it several yards across the pavement before the mangled frame comes to rest against a telephone pole.

With a shrill war cry, Tran kicks open the passenger door and drops to the pavement, his pistol raised, searching frantically for targets. He snaps shots at BRIMOB scurrying like panicked ants across the yard. A gunner on the Land Rover parked in the middle of the yard swivels his weapon toward Tran and is rewarded with a shot to the chest that sends him sprawling across the vehicle's hood. The body slides slowly off the truck and sinks into the mud. Tran scrambles past the gunner, dropping to one knee in the blood-wet grass as he rips spare pistol magazines from the pouch on the dead man's belt. He ejects the empty magazine from his pistol, slams a loaded one in its place, and continues up the yard, firing at anyone in uniform.

As Tran works his way forward, Jon wrestles the truck into reverse. Cutting the wheels toward the house, he grinds the truck into gear and mashes the gas pedal; the truck lurches across the lawn, colliding with the back of the machine gun-armed Land Rover and propelling it toward the front door.

"Oh, shit!" yells Jessica as she spots the Mitsubishi churning wildly across the muddy lawn toward the house. She flings aside her weapon throws herself on top of Chris as the Land Rover crashes through the wall, collapsing the front of the house before coming to a rest atop the pile of dead and dying BRIMOB.

Amid the dust, Jon thrusts his head through the truck's shattered windshield, peering around rabidly until he spots Jessica dragging Chris across the floor, blood flowing from his mangled shoulder. Jon frowns and emerges zombie-like from the open front of the truck, dropping onto the blood slick pile of BRIMOB bodies. Disentangling an MP-5 submachine gun from an officer's corpse, he draws the charging handle to the rear and peers into the chamber, ensuring the weapon is loaded.

"Jon!" pleads Jessica in a quivering voice. "Chris is wounded. Give me a hand!"

Instead of reaching out for them, Jon raises the submachine gun.

"Move aside, Captain Ling," he announces in a dead voice. "I have my orders..."

Jessica's head jerks toward the Gurkha. "NO!" she screams. "No. No. Jon. No. I... I'm countermanding those orders!"

"Please Captain Ling," replies Jon, his voice cracking. "I take no pleasure in fulfilling my duty."

Chris stares at them dumbly. "What's he talking about?" he mumbles. Jessica ignores Chris' question, focusing instead on the slowly advancing Gurkha.

"I *order* you to lower your weapon, sergeant!" she shivers, wrapping her tiny body around Chris as she tries in vain to protect his life with hers.

"Captain Ling, I..." begins Jon, the clatter of rubble interrupting him.

"What the hell are you *doing*?" demands Tran.

Jon's weapon remains trained on the couple. "This doesn't pertain to you, Major," Jon replies.

"Tran!" Jessica shrieks. "He's trying to kill Chris!"

The SIG 9mm appears in Tran's hand, its sights trained on the back of Jon's head. "Are you out of your fucking mind?"

"I have my orders..."

"NO!" sobs Jessica. "Your job is to protect Chris..."

"And to kill him if it appears he will fall into enemy hands," replies Jon in monotone.

"No one's about to fall into enemy hands," Tran growls.

"The uniforms," responds Jon. "Look at their uniforms."

"So...?"

"BRIMOB. They've sent the mobile brigade here to search for us. Pangkalanbun is surrounded. There's no place left to run." He readjusts his grip on the weapon. "I have my orders."

"Who gave you such a dumb-ass order?" hisses Tran.

Peering over the sights of his submachine gun, Jon mutters simply, "Captain Ling."

Chris' head swivels toward Jessica. "Jess?" he asks, trying to focus on her eyes.

She mops the beading sweat from his brow and hugs his head to her chest. "No. No. It was a standing order," she sobs. "This was *not* supposed to happen!"

"Then countermand it," rasps Tran. "Countermand it now!"

"She can't," announces Jon. "It was anticipated in crisis such an order might be countermanded. It's... irrevocable."

"Then how about I kill you first," announces Tran through gritted teeth.

Jon's grip on the submachine gun loosens. The barrel droops slightly. "Do it. I very much don't want to carry out this order," he admits.

Tran's finger tightens on the trigger.

"Wait," Chris groans. "Do you hear that?"

"I don't hear anything," replies Tran.

"Exactly!" exclaims Jessica. "There's no one else out there!"

The room is silent but for the breathing of four desperate people.

"The mission isn't blown, Jon," insists Jessica' "Do you hear me? It's *not blown!*"

Jon hesitates before slowly lowering his weapon; it slips from his hands and clatters to the ground. Tran shuffles cautiously to the Gurkha's side, maintaining his pistol on him as he retrieves the submachine gun.

"Go pick up Khalid, Jon," he snaps. "You too, *Captain* Ling. Get him in the truck."

"They'll have the town surrounded by now," warns Jon as he and Jessica walk over to the semi-conscious Khalid and drag him to his feet. Injured and disoriented, Khalid wobbles between them as they drag him across the cluttered floor toward the truck.

Chris groans and slumps forward onto the floor.

"Chris!" screeches Jessica, releasing Khalid's arm and springing to Chris' aid. The heavy terrorist sags against Jon's small frame.

"Come, Major," announces Jon. "Let her assist the captain. Help me get Khalid into the truck."

Tran slings the submachine gun over his back and shoves the pistol into his belt. He grasps Khalid's right arm and twists it over his shoulder. The two men drag the disoriented terrorist over the rubble, through the gaping hole in the front of the house, and around to the rear of the truck. Tran seizes Khalid's hair and slams his face against the tailgate.

"Stand still asshole," he sneers. With his free hand, he flips the locking handle and the spring-loaded rear door rolls open with a clatter.

The BRIMOB sniper on the roof across the street did his best to cover his team. But the smoke and haze clinging over the battlefield make his optical sight useless. Preparing to descend from his perch, he spots several men climbing over the rubble. He raises the scope on his Pindad SPR-1 sniper rifle.

He spots one – no, two – men dragging another toward the rear of the truck. At first he thinks the man in the middle is wounded; but he recognizes the dishdasha and realizes the man is bound and bloody. The remaining two men are forcing him into the truck. The sniper's heart races, his breath quickening as he places his crosshairs on the head of one of Khalid's captors. Trying to restrain his excitement, he slowly lets out a breath, his finger tightening on the trigger.

"Crack!"

"Get aboard," Tran orders. He and Jon heft Khalid into the truck's open bay. Khalid's muddy bare foot slips from the bumper and he topples sideways, knocking Tran to the muddy ground. Cursing, Tran struggles to his feet and is about to punch Khalid in the face when he discovers Khalid no longer has one, just a bone and blood gap where his face had been.

He then notices the echo of the gunshot.

"Sniper!" yells Tran. He and Jon dump Khalid's body and dash down either side of the truck, clawing their ways over the rubble to regain the relative safety of the house.

The sniper swears; lowering his rifle and ripping back the bolt to chamber another round. By the time he regains a sight picture, the men are gone, having disappeared into the haze. All that remains in their wake is a twisted, blood-spattered body in a dishdasha splayed in the mud behind the truck.

"A fuckin' sniper," repeats Tran as he and Jon scramble into the house. He scrapes Khalid's brain matter from the side of his face and flings it to the floor in disgust. "He must be on the roof of the building across the street,"

"Well, we don't have time to go chasing after him," announces Jessica. "We've got to get out of here quickly."

Chris peers vaguely at Tran, his eyes not quite focused. "Where's Khalid?" he mumbles.

Tran shakes his head. "Dead."

Tran's expression reveals a familiar reality, tragic, painful, and brutally honest. *Our plan has unraveled*, it reads. Chris lets out a long groan and turns to Jessica. "Let's get the hell out of here," he moans.

Jessica twists his arm over her shoulder and drags him to his feet. She waves Tran aside, struggling to help Chris over the pile of rubble and through the shattered front window of the truck. "Behind the seat," she directs, slipping Chris onto the bench. She climbs aboard and sits next to him on the hump.

"Why Ms. Ling," mumbles Chris as she places her arm protectively around his shoulder, "are you making a pass at me?"

"He'll be fine," she announces with a tense laugh.

Like most vehicles in the former British Southeast Asian colonies, the truck is right-hand drive. Tran climbs into the passenger seat, his pistol trained on Jon.

"You drive," he orders; Jon grinds the truck into reverse and backs it with a lurch from the front of the house. Wood and plaster collapse from the roof as the truck withdraws.

The sniper is in a rage, furious at his ineptitude and incensed at his complicity in the murder of the man he was sent to rescue. When the truck lurches into reverse and claws its way backwards across the lawn, he wipes the tears from his eyes, raises his rifle and searches for a target.

All he can see is the massive white box and cab staggering through the mud toward him. He squeezes off a shot through the roof of the truck. Jacking back the bolt, he chambers another round, tucks the rifle back against his shoulder and fires again.

The truck reaches the street, careens off the curb and spins left. He snaps off three more rapid shots as the truck speeds away, working the bolt frantically until the empty magazine follower locks it open. As the truck disappears into the haze, he lowers his rifle and cries for his own soul, which has surely lost its place in Paradise.

"Man!" groans Tran as he peers into the shattered side mirror. "That was too fuckin' close."

Chris raises his head and grins painfully at his friend, then turns at Jessica, whose arm remains locked around him.

"It's all right," he announces. "We're clear."

She doesn't move.

"Jess?" he repeats. Her arm slides from around him and drops limply to her side. Her body sags against him.

"*Jess?*" he calls, panic rising as she remains motionless. "*Jess!*" he shrieks, grabbing her arm and wrenching her toward him. Her lifeless body slumps into his lap. It's then he notices the bloody wound in her back.

"Oh my God!" he groans in an inhuman shiver. "Oh my God..."

Tran lunges across the back of the seat, placing his fingers against Jessica's carotid artery. They sit in tense silence as he searches in vain for some sign of life. Tran glances up at Chris, who sits, dazed and shaking.

"Chris," he announces softly.

Chris stares blankly, his eyes fixed on the back of Jessica's head. Tran grasps Chris' good shoulder and shakes him. "*Chris*," he repeats insistently.

Chris slowly turns to Tran's tear filled eyes.

"She's gone," Tran croaks.

Chris stares down at Jessica, stroking her hair carefully as if afraid he might wake her. He turns her face gently toward him; her haunting eyes stare back accusingly. With trembling fingers he forces her eyelids shut and turns away with a shudder.

"What have I done?" he asks hollowly.

Tran stares back in silence, too stunned to speak.

Chris hugs Jessica's lifeless body to his chest and weeps unashamedly.

The truck rumbles-on into the night.

CHAPTER 18

With the coming of dawn, an azure horizon slowly backlights the craggy buildings lining the road. Silence reigns aboard the blacked-out truck as it gropes like a blind elephant toward the edge of town.

"Are you sure they were BRIMOB," mumbles Tran.

"Yes Sir," responds Jon in monotone. "They'll have cordoned-off the town by now." He knows their tactics. With BRIMOB on the ground, the POLRI now has the troops available to block every road, patrol every trail, and search every house. Their prospects for survival are rapidly fading.

"So how do we get past them?" asks Tran.

Jon's head swivels toward him, a curious expression on his face. "You don't really think we *can*, do you?"

"We have to try..." announces Tran.

Rolling past the end of the block, a beam of yellow light sweeps the side of the truck. All heads snap simultaneously to the right, eyes glimpsing in passing the gleaming razor wire tangled around the wooden barricades silhouetted in the headlights of a stationary Land Rover at the end of the street.

Jon's foot remains steady on the gas pedal as the truck continues down the road, its bullet-ridden frame mercifully obscured in the hazy dawn. After several blocks, Jon steers the truck into an alley; it grinds to a halt in the sheltering shadows of an abandoned, vine covered warehouse. He kills the engine; the three men remain silent, awaiting the patrol's inevitable approach. When after a few minutes nothing occurs, Tran turns to Chris.

"There was our turn," he whispers. "The boat's about three miles south down the river road."

"So?" asks Chris dejectedly, his hand lightly stroking Jessica's blood-matted hair.

Tran purses his lips. "*So*, we've got to figure out how to slip past these bastards and reach the boat before sun-up."

"What if Jon's right?" mumbles Chris. "What if we're finished?"

Tran seizes Chris' good arm and jerks it to get his attention. "What if?" he hisses, "w*hat if?* Okay, I'll play that game. What if Jessica was still alive? Would you be sitting there feeling sorry for yourself?"

Chris glares sharply at Tran.

"She's dead," continues Tran. "I hate it. I hate it more than you'll ever know. But she died trying to get us all out of here alive. And if that doesn't mean anything to you, I'll leave your sorry ass here with a pistol so you can stick it in your mouth and do the honorable thing."

"Fuck you," snarls Chris.

"No," laughs Tran viciously. "Fuck *you*." He jerks the handle and shoves open the door. Chris lunges across the seat and grabs Tran's shirt. "Come back here you piece of shit," he hisses.

"What?" challenges Tran. "*Now* you want to fight?"

"I...," Chris' eyes fill with tears.

"Let's finish this thing," pleads Tran. "It's what Jessica would have wanted."

As if awaking from a nightmare, Chris drags his sleeve across his eyes. "Okay," he replies weakly. He turns and glances back at Jessica. "Okay," he repeats, stronger and more firmly the second time. "We can probably slip past the roadblock on foot," he advises. "Between us, we can probably carry Jessica."

Tran shakes his head. "No. We've got a couple a miles to go and its getting light. We'd be pretty exposed swinging down the road dragging a corpse..."

Chris winces painfully.

"Sorry Chris," shrugs Tran. "But you know what I'm saying."

"Why don't we fight our way through the roadblock," offers Jon in a low voice. Tran and Chris eye him skeptically.

"*We?*" asks Tran coldly, his pistol clearly directed at Jon. Tran's body language screams the obvious; he no longer trusts Jon.

The Gurkha purses his lips and bows his head dejectedly. His hand slides slowly behind his back, he grasps the hilt of his Khukuri, and carefully withdraws the machete from its sheath. Tran raises the pistol to Jon's face, the cavernous barrel inches from the Gurkha's nose.

Ignoring the silent threat, Jon removes the knife from behind his back, the flat of the blade in the palm of his hand. He presents the handle to Chris, surrendering his weapon.

"Do it silently," he announces, as if ending his life is a simple matter of expediency. At first Chris thinks Jon is merely being melodramatic, but the stone cold gleam in Jon's eyes tell him he's wrong. The man who less than an hour before was ready to kill Chris is now offering-up his own life.

Chris stares at the Gurkha, uncertain how to respond to the bizarre offer. Tran holds no such reluctance. His left hand springs-out and grasps the handle of the Khukuri, ripping the blade from Jon's outstretched hand. The Gurkha barely flinches as blood trickles down his palm and drips onto the seat. Jon's utter lack of resistance is the evidence Tran seeks.

He looks to Chris. "Well?" he asks.

Chris sighs deeply. "Give it back to him," he announces. Tran passes the machete handle-first to Jon, who retrieves it silently in his bloody hand and slides the weapon back into its sheath.

Sergeant Yowono stalks impatiently between the barricades, a caged animal anxious for the kill. His beret is squashed down over his shaved skull, one side dragged arrogantly over his right ear in a poor imitation of a French Foreign Legionnaire. The stub of a cigarette dangles from between his thin, scowling lips. He reaches up, pinches the smoldering butt, and whips it to the ground. His hand reaches absently into his breast pocket for another.

He glowers at the half-dozen members of his squad huddled around their Police Land Rover at the bridge abutment as they listen to the radio, talking in hushed tones. A light rain persists, unnoticed by the men lounging beneath the tarp stretching between the Land Rover and a nearby tree. He glances across the barricade at the patrol's second Land Rover, its front end protruding from an alley between two buildings a few yards ahead of the roadblock, its driver relaxing against the front bumper of the truck trying unsuccessfully to transpose Javanese over the local Katingan newspaper. On the Land Rover's hood rests a MAG-58 machine gun, its bipod perched atop a pile of leaky burlap sandbags strewn atop the folded-down windshield. The gunner lounges in the passenger seat, his feet resting on the hood, half asleep with a rain poncho over his head.

The clatter of a passing vehicle elicits scant interest from the driver; he peers vaguely around the corner the building as the ghostly white truck lumbers past on the cross street. He mumbles something to the gunner who merely shrugs and draws the poncho more tightly around his shoulders in a vain effort to fend-off the water dripping from the overhanging eaves.

"Private Hastuti!" barks the Sergeant. The driver casts aside his newspaper and snaps to attention. "Yes, sergeant."

"Go to the end of the block and see where the truck went that just passed."

"Yes, sergeant," the private responds unenthusiastically, dragging the M-16 rifle off the hood and crushing his jungle cap onto his head. "Ahmad," he announces to the gunner. "Stay awake. You're on your own 'til I get back." He shrugs into his web gear and shuffles down the street.

The sergeant watches with annoyance. *The men are getting sloppy,* he realizes. *I'll tighten-up on discipline when we redeploy to garrison after this mission.*

He watches the slovenly private shamble to the end of the block and glance left and right, peering up and down the deserted street. He turns and shrugs helplessly at his sergeant.

"Allah, give me patience," mumbles the sergeant irritably and motions sharply for Hastuti to continue down the side street in the direction the truck had taken.

The sloshing of boots on the mud road alerts Tran to the man's approach. He leans against the wall, peering around the edge of the building, and spots the soldier wandering aimlessly up the street, kicking a tin can ahead of him. When the soldier nears the building, Tran springs from behind the covering wall and brings the butt stock of his SS1 across the man's face. The soldier staggers slightly and clatters to the ground in a heap. Tran drops to a firing position, directing his automatic rifle down the deserted street. Seeing no one else approaching, he grasps the unconscious soldier's web harness and drags the limp body around the corner.

Sergeant Yowono glances impatiently at his watch. "Malingerer," he hisses when Pvt. Hastuti fails to return. He motions to the cluster of soldiers beside the Land Rover parked at the bridge. "You and you," he barks, selecting his most dependable privates. "Go bring Hastuti back here."

The men spring to their feet obediently, grab their weapons, zigzag between the road block's wire entanglements, and advance up the street toward the end of the block. As they pass the shadows between the buildings, they spot Ahmad sleeping behind his machine gun, his feet resting on the sandbags.

"Stay awake, Ahmad," they chortle.

Ahmad grunts and nods groggily.

As the soldiers pass, Jon rises from behind the Land Rover, wipes the blood from his Khukuri, and slides it back into its sheath. Ahmad's body sags forward over the machine gun's receiver, blood seeping off the green plastic poncho and mixing with the mud beneath the vehicle.

Jon grasps Ahmad's bangs and lifts him gingerly off the weapon, wedging the corpse in an awkward upright position between the seats. He hefts the machine gun from the sandbagged hood and inches his way to the end of the alley, peering into the overgrown field across the street. Seeing nothing, he checks his watch and awaits the signal.

"Shit," hisses Tran as he leaves the protection of the crumbling building and lowers himself onto his belly in the tall weeds. Crawling through the drenched field, he slithers through puddles of brackish water like a poisonous snake closing on unwary prey.

The stench of rotting vegetation reminds him of the decaying back alleys of post-war Ho Chi Minh City - the home he left as a young man to seek freedom in America, only to serve most of his military career in third world toilets like this one. A ball of insects swarms hungrily around his head; he resists the overwhelming temptation to swat at the invading pests. Reaching the edge of the field, he parts the weeds with the muzzle of his weapon and assesses the scene.

Twenty meters away, across the slimy road rests a Land Rover at the bridge abutment. One of the soldiers has opened the oxidized hood and is conversing tersely with the man behind the steering wheel. Apparently the battery is dead, because the sergeant is cursing angrily at the driver as he attempts to crank the unresponsive engine.

One of the on-looking soldiers shakes his head in disgust and wanders away from the dead vehicle. He hesitates in the middle of the road and changes direction, stopping less than ten feet from where Tran lay sweating in the tall grass. Tran's heart throbs in his chest as he attempts to control the roar of his quickening breath. The soldier's wooly eyes are directed vaguely to Tran's right. Suddenly the soldier tenses, un-slings his weapon, raises it, then upends the rifle and presses the butt on the ground as he leans the M-16 against his hip. He unbuttons his fly and urinates into the weeds.

A bitter smell of fermented rice fills Tran's nostrils as he lies still, the sound of water trickling against the weeds as the stream flows downhill to where he lay in a small depression. He closes his eyes and holds his breath, anger throbbing in his temples as he resists the instinct to kill the man right then and there.

The trickle tapers-off and the soldier picks up his weapon and, slinging it over his shoulder, returns to the gaggle of soldiers hovering around the Land Rover.

Tran slips the safety on his weapon to "Fire" and awaits the signal.

"He's a prick, Dian," grumbles Budi as the two soldiers assigned to find Hastuti near the end of the block. "In a 'civilized' society such a rabid animal would be put to death."

Dian laughs appreciatively. "He's still our sergeant," he reminds his friend. "Once we're back in garrison we'll take some leave and get away from the animal for a few days. Maybe go to Jakarta..." He halts abruptly, head cocked curiously to one side. "What was that?"

Budi peers up at the cloudy sky. "Thunder," he replies and the soldiers resume walking.

Slowly a beat-up white truck emerges around the corner coming toward them. They realize immediately by the shattered windshield and bullet-ridden cab this is the vehicle they seek.

On spotting the truck, one of the soldiers shouts and shoves the other aside. But before the soldier can bring his weapon into play, Chris jams the accelerator to the floor. The massive chrome grill catches the soldier mid-chest, the momentum carrying the breathless man forward as the truck rumbles down the street toward the roadblock, the soldier's contorted face gawking back at Chris over the top of the hood.

The soldier that was been knocked to the ground yells and clambers to his feet, cursing as he grapples for his M-16 and raises it toward the escaping truck. He squeezes the trigger, only to be reminded he's forgotten to chamber a round. He lowers the rifle, rips the charging handle to the rear, and lets it fly forward. Shouldering the weapon he squeezes the trigger, emptying the 30-round magazine in a matter of seconds.

Bullets pepper the wooden tailgate, splinters ricocheting through the open bay as bullets pass through the rear of the cab and snap past Chris' ear. As the truck nears the roadblock, he spots the cops scrambling to bring their weapons into play; he heaves himself sideways into the seat, foot jammed against the accelerator as he seeks refuge behind the dashboard.

The Land Rover groans, its engine turning over twice before seizing completely. The sergeant's muttered curses drown-out for the moment the grumble of the truck at the end of the street. At the sound of gunfire, the sergeant springs from behind the wheel, knocking the driver to the ground in his haste. He reaches for the M-4 carbine he'd carelessly tossed into the seat, cursing fiercely as he struggles to untangle the sling from around the gearshift.

He barks orders to the stunned soldiers, some of whom stare in muted shock at the approaching truck; others fumble with their weapons and scatter for cover.

Tran aims at the cluster of confused soldiers and squeezes the trigger. "*CLICK!*" It takes him a few moments to realize the assault rifle has misfired. He grabs the charging handle and jerks it rearward; a live round springs from the ejection port and "pings" over his right ear. He releases the handle and the bolt slams home, chambering another round. He squeezes again. "*CLICK!*"

From the corner of his eye he spots the massive white truck rumble into view. "Shit," he curses, springing to his feet and hurtling forward swinging the malfunctioning assault rifle as a bludgeon.

As the truck roars past, Jon readjusts his grip on the machine gun and emerges from between the buildings, the three-foot-long belt of linked ammunition swinging from the receiver as he closes-in behind the truck for cover, moving forward as the monster claws through the barrier. He works his way between the shattered wood and wire left in the truck's wake, treading carefully over the tangle of debris, and entering the BRIMOB perimeter.

Confused soldiers scatter from the truck's path. Jon steps from behind the truck and leans into his weapon; a throaty "TUT-TUT-TUT-TUT" erupts as the machine gun bucks in his sweaty hands, empty brass casings and disintegrating steel links spewing from the ejection port. Several soldiers are knocked spinning to the ground as the heavy 7.62 mm rounds slam into them.

Jon continues forward, halting occasionally and turning the weapon on a new target, like a machine grinding methodically forward regardless of the human toll. An inhuman shriek draws his attention to Tran swinging his automatic rifle in a violent arc, hammering a struggling soldier to the ground and pouncing atop the man to finish the grisly act.

The Mitsubishi truck collides with the Land Rover and drives it across the abutment. The police vehicle twists off the edge of the bridge, peeling back a section of rail as it rolls down the embankment and splashes into the water below. The momentum of the 24,000-pound truck carries it over the edge of the bridge along with the Land Rover. Instead of sinking into the river, the massive bullet riddled vehicle groans onto its side and collapses against the embankment with an exhausted hiss.

"Major!" yells Jon; Tran's wild eyes jerk toward him. Jon motions frantically toward what he can see of the side of the truck protruding over the edge of the embankment.

"Oh, shit," curses Tran, casting his battered weapon aside and darting to the edge of the river. "C'mon," he yells to Join and the two men slide down the churned earth to the water's edge. Chris emerges, cut and bleeding, but miraculously unhurt from the truck's missing front windshield, dragging Jessica's twisted body one-handed, oblivious to everything around him.

"Get that Land Rover from between the buildings," snaps Tran. Jon turns immediately and disappears at a trot over the rise. Tran steps forward to assists Chris, whose eyes cut hungrily toward him, stunned at his friend's sudden appearance.

"It's okay. It's okay," repeats Tran soothingly as he stoops to lift Jessica's body. Reluctantly, Chris releases Jessica's hand and in a zombie-like trance follows Tran up the embankment.

Jon darts across the road toward the Land Rover parked outside the perimeter. Rounding the corner into the alley, something strikes him in the face; he staggers and falls, the weight of the machine gun crashing against his chest as he collapses onto his back.

A voice above hisses something as he lay, breathless and disoriented in the mud beside the vehicle. Struggling to regain focus, he notices the birdcage flash-hider of an M-16A1 rifle inches from his bleeding nose. The weapon trembles. Jon's foot shifts slightly, brushing the soldier's boot. In a flash, he grasps the rifle barrel with his right hand and rolls sideways, forcing the muzzle toward the wall as he cocks his right leg. A single shot rings-out, exploding a chunk from the brick building as Jon strikes, his foot crashing into the soldier's knee cap, which shatters with a sickly "crack!"

The soldier screams and stumbles forward, landing on top of Jon, pinning the machine gun between them. Using the weapon as a lever, Jon seizes the stock and heaves it off him, sending the soldier tumbling onto the ground beside the Land Rover. Jon continues his roll until he is atop the disoriented soldier, one hand sliding over the man's throat as the other draws the Khukuri from behind his belt. Raising the blade to strike, his eyes lock momentarily with the soldier's tearing, terrified face: a young man of no more than sixteen years.

And he hesitates.

In the boy's eyes he sees reflected a most hideous horror: the last moments of a young life realizing it's about to end.

Breathing heavily, something seizes Jon's chest, an invisible hand grasping his lungs, his heart. His grip loosens on the boy's throat and he lowers his machete, slipping it back into its sheath. He releases his grip and rises to his feet over the boy who lay wallowing in the mud.

Disgusted with his own weakness, he retrieves the machine gun and dumps it into the rear of the Land Rover.

He walks a few paces and recovers the M-16 from the ground. Staring down at the sobbing boy, he pops the rear pin from the receiver and flips the weapon open, withdrawing the bolt, and heaving it onto the roof. With a growl, he swings the weapon against the edge of the building, twisting the aluminum receiver and rendering it inoperable.

He drops the broken M-16 into the boy's lap and climbs into the Land Rover's driver's seat. Glancing grimly at the dead gunner's corpse, he nudges it from the passenger seat and crushes the ignition switch on the floorboard. The starter whirs and the motor catches; he shakes his head in dismay at the battered soldier cowering in the mud, releases the clutch, and drives from the alley.

Headlights sweep the haze as Jon weaves the Land Rover between the shattered barricades and skids to a stop beside Chris and Tran. Jon leaps from behind the wheel and helps Tran gingerly load Jessica's body in the rear of the truck, carefully tucking a poncho around her small form. The three men scramble aboard. As Jon places the truck in-gear, Chris awakens from his trance and gawks at the gruesome scene as if seeing it for the first time.

Amid the shattered remains of Tran's assault rifle are three bodies, bludgeoned to death by the single man's uncontrolled fury.

Several more bodies are strewn across the road in macabre, twisted shapes bearing testimony to sudden, brutal death caused by Jon's machine gun. Where his truck passed through the perimeter, the barricade and razor wire are strewn like burst entrails across the road, slopping lazily over the embankment.

Sirens approaching from the distance lend urgency to their departure. "Wait one!" Tran barks and springs from the vehicle. Hurrying onto the bridge, he tosses aside the untouched barricade and rolls it into the river. He darts back to the Land Rover, stooping momentarily to gather several abandoned M-4 carbines from the road before collapsing into the passenger seat.

"Maybe that'll convince them we escaped across the river," he explains breathlessly as he passes one weapon to Chris and places the other automatic rifle across his lap.

"Okay, Jon" he gasps with a curt nod in the direction of the river road. "Get us the hell out of here!"

CHAPTER 19

A shrill whistle echoes through the open-air galley. Indonesian sailors enjoying breakfast glance up in alarm. It can't be a drill this early in the morning, they realize. Utensils clatter onto metal trays as a mad scramble ensues. The building empties rapidly as men spill out onto the grass, running rowdily for the missile boat swaying at anchor beside the pier.

Admiral Widjaja ambles from the Western Fleet Headquarters building, his aide yapping alongside like a hyperactive Pekinese.

"One vessel, Hartanto. *One vessel*," the admiral growls. "This must be a low-profile mission or we'll have the Americans all over us."

"But Sir, the Singaporeans will be on alert after what happened to Dominion. It's suicide to go out there alone!"

The admiral glares disapprovingly at his subordinate. "Don't be ridiculous," he snorts. "As soon as the RSN sees we are in the area, they'll turn about and run for home. They have no nerve for such things; Singapore is a paper tiger."

"Of course, Sir," Hartanto agrees uncertainly. Having previously conducted joint anti-piracy patrols with the RSN, he suspects the paper tiger at least has teeth. As the admiral enters the rear seat of his staff car, Commander Hartanto braces stiffly in salute.

"You have no backbone, Hartanto," growls the admiral. "That's why you'll never have a combat command." The car pulls away, leaving Commander Hartanto's salute unreturned.

Ten minutes later, the 43-man crew of the South Korean built PSK Mk IV Mandau Class Missile Boat is making preparations to get underway when the admiral strides briskly up the gangplank and returns the officer of the deck's salute.

"Where's the captain?" he barks.

"On the bridge, Sir," confirms the young ensign and scrambles to take the lead up the ladder and announce the admiral's arrival.

The grizzled old captain is a veteran lieutenant commander passed over for flag rank awarded to his more politically astute colleagues. He is none-the-less a competent officer, well-liked by his men and considered "politically dependable" by the "Green" faction of the TNI-AL.

The ensign emerges from below decks. "Sir, may I announce..."

"Chahaya!" interrupts the admiral as he pushes past the young officer and embraces his old comrade.

"Admiral," replies the shocked captain. "To what do we attribute this honor?"

"Infidel, Chahaya. We are going to hunt down and crush the infidel."

"Allah be praised..."

Unrestrained jungle closes in around the Land Rover, branches groping the sides of the truck as it crawls slowly down the decaying one-lane road into the pitch-blackness beyond.

"There," hisses Tran, pointing to a gravel road appearing from the jungle on the right. The vehicle slows, Jon preparing to turn down the darkened path when Tran notices lights flickering between the trees.

"Keep going," rasps Tran; Jon swerves back onto the road, bypassing the turn as he spots a dark blue POLRI patrol boat parked beside the dock. They drive another 50 meters and Jon steers the Land Rover off the road, burying it nose-first inside the dense thicket.

"What now?" asks Chris.

Tran peers into the trees, the light of a false dawn emerging through the canopy. "We're out of options," he announces finally. "We either fight our way to the boat together or disburse and leave each of us to make his own way home."

"No," replies Chris firmly. "We arrived together and we leave together... all of us," he insists. Jon nods his emphatic agreement.

Chris paws feebly at Jessica's tarp-wrapped corpse. "I've got her, Sir," announces Jon. He slides beneath her and raises the body onto his shoulder, arm locked around her legs. The three men filter into the jungle, moving cautiously between the intertwined vines. Reaching the edge of a clearing they spot a single cop walking slowly along the dock, his rubber soled boots thudding on loose planks.

A shout comes from a crewman aboard the patrol boat.

"If we're gonna make the rendezvous, we'd better take the boat away from them," observes Tran.

"What do you have in mind?" asks Chris. Jon adjusts his Khukuri and squats beside them, listening in silence to Tran's plan.

Chris and Tran carry Jessica's body upriver, locating a small skiff they'd passed earlier in the evening. They settle Jessica's stiffening body into the boat and stand in awkward silence. Tran clears his throat and reaches to shake Chris' hand. "See you on the other side," he mumbles; Chris smiles weakly back at him. There is little emotion words can convey at this point.

"Twenty minutes," Tran reminds Chris, who gives a half-hearted thumbs-up, watching warily as Tran fades into the twisted mangrove.

The pain in Chris' shoulder is becoming more persistent. He takes a deep breath, his gaze falling reluctantly on Jessica's corpse. A bead of sweat rolls down his forehead; he intercepts it with the back of his hand.

Suddenly he realizes for the first time his hands are stained with blood – Jessica's blood. He wipes them on his pants, but the stain persists. He rubs harder, more emphatically against the rough cotton, but the stains seem to grow darker, more pronounced. His hands began to burn, as if he has seized hot coals. Clenching and unclenching his fists, his fingers seem to stick together, the sweat-smeared blood coagulating between them.

Unable to withstand the feeling, he flings his leg over the side of the boat and drops into the shallow water. Thrusting his hands beneath the surface, he rubs rabidly, clasping and unclasping them, digging his fingernails into his palms and scratching furiously.

Then he stops.

Raising his hands slowly from the water, he realizes the stains are still there, his raw skin crimson beneath. A sharp pain pierces his gut, twisting relentlessly.

You killed her, you son of a bitch, he scolds himself. *You knew it would happen; it HAD to happen. But you pushed, pushed until someone had to die. Why? Was it worth it?* He gasps, the sound his own exhale wrenching him from his masochistic reverie. *Who'll ever trust you again?*

He stares into the overhanging trees, tears streaming down his face as he reaches deep into his soul and grasps desperately for his last ally – his only ally. His head droops as he crosses himself with a trembling hand.

"In the name of the Father, the Son, and the Holy Spirit..."

Tran creeps from the jungle to the edge of the river and wades silently into the water, his assault rifle suspended above the surface as he moves slowly forward, the muddy riverbed sucking at his sandals.

The patrol craft's stern rides low facing the embankment, its single bow mounted MAG-58 machine gun directed away from shore. He sees the crew's backs, blue tunics stained with sweat as they chat idly, unaware sudden death approaches.

Something clatters onto the deck; a crewman turns to retrieve the fallen object. His gaze sweeps past Tran, who stands rigid, head bowed, barely breathing in the chest-deep water. The crewman gazes vaguely into the darkness, shaking his head before turning and resuming his conversation. Miraculously unseen, Tran continues his journey to within a few meters of the boat.

"Entschuldigung Sie bitte!"

The POLRI shuffle to the port side for a better view of the approaching skiff, its driver waving frantically and yelling.

"Es tut mir leid, aber..."

Tran raises his assault rifle and levels it on the unsuspecting crew, his sights fixed on center mass.

Hearing Chris' voice, Jon slides the Khukuri from its sheath and dodges through the remaining ten feet of jungle. The guard on the dock turns suddenly at the sound of his approach.

"Corporal?" The soldier shouts in a panicked voice as he raises his weapon tentatively toward the shadow flickering toward him. Jon lands with a crash on the wooden pier, the Khukuri slipping from his sweaty palm and clattering across the dock as he stumbles blindly forward. He meets the guard head-on; they collide, tumbling off the pier in a tangle and splashing into the muddy shallows beside the dock.

Fingers clawing frantically at his face, Jon's hands close around the desperate guard's throat as the terrified man flails wildly beneath the surface, a mere foot of water between lifesaving air and suffocating death.

At the guard's desperate cry, the POLRI react in confusion, scrambling for mislaid weapons and cursing in frustration. Noting the confusion on-board, Chris gropes behind his belt and withdraws the SIG 9mm, fixing the nearest crewman in his sights. As his finger tightens on the trigger, he hears Tran's assault rifle erupt.

One crewman, peering over the bow with his back to the attack is struck in the back of the head; his rifle drops into the river, his body toppling forward into the water as if diving in after it. Another is hit in the back just as calls-out orders. He freezes in mid-sentence, slumping over the coxswain's seat. The third crewman turns toward the sound of gunfire and is struck several times, spinning full circle before collapsing in a heap on deck.

Belatedly realizing his skiff is about to collide with the patrol boat, Chris drops his pistol and dives for the rudder handle. Veering hard to port, the boat sideswipes the hull as he kills the engine and seizes one of the fenders dangling over the side of the larger vessel.

Peering around, he spots Jon, drenched and covered with mud, approaching the patrol boat along the pier as he sheaths his recovered Khukuri. He steps cautiously aboard the swaying vessel, his hand waving aside the haze of burnt cordite enveloping the scene and checks the crewmen's bodies. He discovers the man slumped over the helm still alive, his shattered spine leaving him paralyzed from the neck-down. His breathing is labored; death just minutes away. Jon unsheathes his Khukuri and lifts the man's head by his bangs. With one quick movement, he puts the dying man out of his misery.

He's suddenly aware of Chris' presence nearby. "Sir," he mumbles. "Is the other one dead?"

Chris spots a uniformed body bobbing near the river's surface, half its head missing.

"Yeah, Jon. He's a goner," Chris reports.

He struggles, one-armed, to lift Jessica's corpse from the bottom of the skiff. Jon leans over the rail, grappling for a handhold on the rope securing the tarp-wrapped body. Alive, Chris remembers being able to lift Jessica's petit frame effortlessly, her nubile form hungering for his embrace. Now it requires the combined strength of two men merely to lift her unwilling corpse aboard.

Tran drags himself over the stern and drops with a drenched "splat" onto the deck. Glancing at the empty assault rifle, he drops it onto the floor and stoops to help Jon lift Jessica's limp body and carry it below deck.

Chris struggles aboard, angry and trembling. One-handed, he grasps the collar of the man slumped against helm. He jerks the corpse off the wheel and flings it against the side of the boat. Lifting the man's feet, he flips the body into the river. Tran and Jon emerge from below.

"What are you doing?" asks Tran.

"Clearing the deck," grumbles Chris. "Wouldn't you rather head to sea in a fast patrol boat than a rickety-old cabin cruiser?"

Tran and Jon glance at each other and shrug. Without further discussion they lift the last body by its wrists and ankles and heave it over the railing into the river. The body bobs on the surface momentarily before disappearing slowly beneath the surface. Tran starts the engine as Jon cuts the rope securing the boat to a tree onshore.

Chris glances up into the growing light. "We're going to have to run like hell," he announces and thrusts the throttles forward. "Shit!" he swears.

"What's wrong?" asks Tran as he approaches the helm.

"We've got, *conservatively*, two hundred miles of open-ocean to cross and only half of a tank of gas," reports Chris, motioning angrily at the fuel gauge.

Tran frowns. "Looks like we're going to have to steal some fuel," he shrugs.

Chris shakes his head slowly. "Oh, we are so screwed," he groans.

"No we're not," interjects Jon with an impish grin. "Wait one." He disappears below decks, reappearing a few moments later buttoning the tunic of a fresh POLRI uniform. He passes another one to Tran.

"Sorry, Sir. They didn't have your size," he shrugs.

Chris smiles grimly. "Good plan," he laughs sarcastically. "Is there a Javanese dictionary down there, too?"

"We'll wing it, Chris," responds Tran testily. "We've come this far and we're sure as hell not giving up now."

"You're right," replies Chris. "But we can't afford to spend a lot of time foraging for gas." He squints upriver. "When they start discovering bodies, all hell's gonna break loose."

"Right," replies Tran. "If we can't find something along the inlet, we'll try to hijack fuel at sea."

Moments later, the patrol boat emerges from the mouth of the river into a large cove. Along the swampy banks they spot fishing encampments and small clusters of shanty wood homes with thatched roofs. Chris steers the boat along the shoreline while Tran scans the swampy banks for signs of a refueling station.

"I see something," he announces. He lowers the binoculars and points across the cove. Chris cranks the wheel and the boat turns smoothly into the wind, heading toward the opposite shore.

"Where?" asks Chris, reaching for the binoculars. Tran passes them to him.

"The old building between that large stand of trees," he announces, pointing ten degrees off the starboard bow. Chris squints into the binoculars and spots what appears to be an abandoned gas station.

"Is it still *functioning*?" he mumbles, his question answered as a small launch pulls away from the pier and sputters upstream. "Yep," he confirms and steers the boat toward the station.

Approaching the pier, Chris feels suddenly out of place. "I'd better get out of sight. Jon. Take over." He retrieves an M-4 carbine and disappears below deck. "I'll cover you from down here," he calls from within the cabin.

Trying to ignore the presence of Jessica's shrouded body a few feet away, Chris slides open a small window and pulls the sheer curtain over the opening.

As the boat nears shore, the rotting pier becomes more pronounced, a twisted wreck with planks absent at odd intervals, like a prizefighter missing teeth. Halfway along the pier, listing badly, are two dilapidated gas pumps, large Pertamina Oil Company decals peeling from rusting sheet metal encasements. Corroded pipes protrude beneath the pumps and follow the pier to the shore.

At the base of the pier is a small rise capped with a rough wooden plank building. Like many of the dilapidated structures in the region it lists dangerously, a result of endemic tropical storms that ravage the island on a regular basis. Its slanting walls defy laws of physics dictating such a structure cannot stand for the weight of its own roof. But there it stands, as it apparently has for half a Century, still in service, the owner having shored up the walls with long wooden braces showing a similar state of decay.

Jon edges the boat alongside the pier nearest the pump, carefully avoiding any contact that might collapse the teetering structure into the water. An elderly man emerges from the shack's doorway and shuffles down the hill toward them.

"Sir! Please take the helm," Jon rasps then leaps onto the pier, waving the station's owner away with an arrogant flip of his hand. The old man hesitates then turns and walks sullenly back up to the porch, where he squats on his haunches and watches with sneering contempt as the POLRI exercises the privileges of power.

Jon shoves the nozzle into the open tank and immediately began fueling the boat. The pump is agonizingly slow, clunking and wheezing asthmatically as the yellowed digits on the register roll lazily forward.

"Jon," Tran mumbles, unheard by Jon who is shaking and cursing the unresponsive pump handle. "Jon!" Tran repeats insistently.

Jon glances up irritably.

"We have company," reports Tran with a nod toward the shack. Jon rises and stretches, glancing casually over his shoulder and noting a POLRI sergeant approaching unaware that he is not among friends.

Jon's eyes cut anxiously to Chris, who's watching events from behind sheer curtains within the cabin. The muzzle of an M-4 Carbine appears at the edge of the open window. Jon shakes his head slowly. To his relief, the muzzle disappears back inside the cabin.

As the sergeant picks his way carefully along the wobbly pier, Jon continues to pump, ignoring the cop's shouted attempts to gain his attention over the rumble of the idling engine.

"Amateur," Jon scoffs under his breath as he senses the sergeant behind him.

"Apa ini?"

Squatting over the gas tank, Jon nods "Ya," he laughs.

"Permisi?" the sergeant snaps, grasping Jon's shoulder and jerking him to his feet. In one smooth motion, Jon seizes the sergeant's hand and twists his arm behind his back. He grasps a handful of greasy black hair and drives the sergeant's face into a tall piling that supports the pier. The cop's knees buckles and Jon loses his balance. To avoid falling, Jon releases the sergeant and steadies himself on the piling as the dazed sergeant rolls off the dock, sinking into the water between the boat and pier.

A second cop wanders through the station onto the back porch. He is about to ask the owner where his sergeant is when the old man winces. The cop follows the owner's gaze to see his sergeant roll off the pier into the water.

"Apa?" he shouts, unslinging his MP5 submachine gun and racing wildly down the grassy knoll toward the pier.

"Jon! We have company!" yells Tran, ducking beneath the helm and groping for the M-4 at his feet. Jon rips the pump handle from the tank, drops it onto the pier and dives onto the boat just as the cop stops running and raises his submachine gun.

"Chris!" Tran blurts, the words barely leaving his lips when a three-round "tat-tat-tat" rings out. The cop staggers backwards like a drunk stumbling away from the bar and keels over into the grass. Chris withdraws the smoking weapon from the open window and yells, "Go! Go! Go!"

Jon drags himself to his feet, rips the Khukuri from its sheath, and dives for the rope securing the boat to the pier. As the frayed rope parts, Tran wrenches the gearshift into reverse and shoves the throttle forward, the boat shuddering backwards away from the pier. He cranks the wheel to port and jams the boat into drive, pressing the throttle forward as the high-powered engine churns-up muddy water, launching the boat toward the middle of the river.

Within minutes, the patrol boat bursts into open water. Chris emerges from below deck, the black M4 in his hands. Tran turns the wheel over to him and began stripping away his POLRI tunic, flinging it onto the deck as if removing a contaminated garment. Jon follows Tran's lead, unfurling the POLRI tunic into the wind and releasing it. The light cotton shirt dances merrily through the air before floating to the surface of the sea to be swallowed up by the foaming wake.

"I'll take it Sir," Jon announces as he shunts Tran aside to take control of the speeding boat. Tran reclines onto a side bench, nestling the assault rifle between his knees as he reloads.

Chris drops onto the bench opposite, his wounded arm hanging uselessly at his side. He fishes the satellite phone from his pocket and frowns. "We've got one more little problem," he announces. "Jessica's phone is dead and we don't know how to contact Colonel Mok to tell him we'll be aboard an Indonesian police boat. When they see us they may just blast us out of the water."

Tran shrugs and reclines against a pile of life jackets. "We'll jump off that bridge when we come to it," he snorts, draping a wet towel over his face and closing his eyes.

Moments later, the boat bursts from the mouth of the cove into the Java strait, the rising sun pursuing it across an emerald sea.

CHAPTER 20

At sea for hours, it feels as if they're making no progress whatsoever. The boat speeding northwest, the ocean seems to unfold endlessly before them. The weather is depressingly spectacular, though for once Chris was hoping for a little fog or rain to cover their escape. If the Indonesians have aircraft, it won't take them long to locate the fleeing vessel.

Tran lay snoring loudly, the wet towel having slid from his eyes onto the deck. Chris reclines with a POLRI hat drooped over his face to protect him from the blistering sun. He rests, mesmerized by the steady drone of the engines and soothed by the rhythmic bucking of the hull against the choppy sea. He drifts in and out of a fitful sleep. Occasionally the boat slips out of sync with the swells and jolts him awake.

It just happened again.

He struggles upright in his seat, fresh blood oozing from his bandaged shoulder as he adjusts the makeshift sling. Pawing at the crusty black cloth securing his muscle, he attempts to restore the circulation without compounding the damage. The fingers on his left hand tingle as the feeling returns. Satisfied with the result, he squints into the sun, noting its position in the sky before surveying the endless sea ahead of them.

"What time is it?" he shouts over the roar of the wind.

Jon glances at his wristwatch. "Ten-eighteen," he reports precisely.

Chris staggers to the helm; steadying himself against the windshield frame, he examines the acetate-covered map wedged between the instrument panel and compass. "Where do you figure we are?" he asks groggily, comparing the map to the surrounding nothingness. "I don't see land anywhere."

"We should be about two and a-half hours from our rendezvous point," guesses Jon. "We estimated ten hours and it's already been nearly seven and a-half."

"Yeah," agrees Chris tentatively. "But I'd be more comfortable if we had GPS. No telling how far the current has driven us off course. Want me to take the helm for a while?"

"No Sir," replies Jon in his best parade-ground manner. "You're injured. Get some rest."

Chris claps his bodyguard on the shoulder. "Thanks, mom," he replies gratefully and totters back to the bench. He wads-up one of the dead crewman's jackets and is starting to recline when something catches his attention. He sits bolt-upright, rubbing his weary eyes. Uncertain what he sees, he reclines on the bench, head supported by the jacket as he maintains weary watch.

"Guys," he announces finally. "I think we have company."

Tran sits-up, instantly alert. "Where?"

Chris points off the port quarter to a tiny black dot on the horizon.

"That could be *anything*," observes Tran, squinting.

"Yeah. But I've been watching for a while and it seems to be heading the same direction as us." Explains Chris. "I can't tell if it's closing, though."

"Fine," shrugs Tran. "We'll check it again in a little while." He lays back, adjusts the life jacket he's using as a pillow, retrieves the wet towel off the deck, and drops it over his eyes. Chris shakes his head in admiration of his friend's nerves. Propping himself against the railing, he reclines, staring intently at the black dot.

A jolt startles him; he suddenly realizes he's drifted off to sleep. Scanning the sea, he frowns, hauls himself to his feet, and approaches Jon. "Let me take the helm," he insists, reaching for the wheel. "You need to go forward and retrieve the machine gun. We're going to have company soon."

Jon glances at the growing dot on the horizon and nods. Climbing onto the bucking bow, he removes the MAG-58 from its mount and heaves it onto his shoulder. He drops onto the deck and approaches the stern, sliding the machine gun into the rear mount.

Clunk!

Tran jerks upright. "What the hell are you doing?" he asks sleepily. Jon motions silently over the stern, letting the weapon swivel forward, muzzle drooping toward the deck as he returns to the bow to retrieve the ammunition can.

"Shit," curses Tran. "It *is* getting closer." He climbs stiffly to his feet and wobbles unsteadily to the helm. "Where do you think we are?" he asks Chris.

"Oh, hell. I don't know," groans Chris in frustration. He motions angrily toward the map. "We should be about here," he explains, identifying a spot not far from where they suppose the RSN is waiting. "But for all I know we're heading for *Australia*."

Tran nods. "What if the Sings aren't in the Strait when we arrive?" he asks, voicing the question on all their minds. Each man glances around, waiting for the other to be first to respond. Jon finishes loading a belt of ammunition into the machine gun and slams the feed tray. He jacks back the charging handle and turns to Chris and Tran, a look of utter defiance on his face.

"Well, we know *his* position," laughs Chris nervously. "What about you?"

"I can't imagine they're in a prisoner-taking mood," observes Tran thoughtfully. "But even if they are, I don't like my odds in an Indonesian prison..."

Chris sighs and nods. "It looks like we fight it out."

Simple mathematics dictate the fast-moving missile boat will eventually close on the small patrol craft, but awaiting the inevitable is agony. As the Indonesians closes to within range, a brilliant flash and plume of white smoke erupts from the ship's deck; a missile climbing a few hundred feet straight up before nosing-over and tipping toward the water. Leveling off ten feet above sea level, it streaks toward the small patrol boat.

"Oh, shit," curses Chris. "Incoming!" He jerks the patrol boat into a tight turn to port; the missile adjusting perceptibly. Closing his eyes, he cranks the wheel to starboard, flinging Tran and Jon into a tangled pile on the deck. He ducks below the helm and curses. In a red-hot flash, the missile sails over with a thunderous roar, the sound fading quickly as it passes. Chris pops up and stares in disbelief as the missile streaks toward the horizon.

"Yeeeaaahhhhh!!" he shouts as Tran and Jon disentangle and struggle to their feet, wondering at their miraculous escape. The missile fades into the distance before self-destructing in a huge fireball, the shattered remains splashing harmlessly into the sea.

"Fucking Exocet!" gasps Tran. "Couldn't lock-on to such a small vessel."

The three men glance at each other and begin to laugh, the hilarity out of all proportion to their dire situation. But the laughter recedes quickly when they realize, though the failed launch seems to convince their pursuers wasting another quarter million dollar missile is a bad investment, the gap between the two vessels continues to narrow.

After an hour of intense peace, a puff of smoke announces the arrival of high-explosive rounds from the pursuing ship's 57mm deck gun. The poorly aimed shot splashes harmlessly into the sea a hundred meters off the fleeing patrol boat's starboard bow. Two more shots follow in rapid succession, neither landing anywhere near the intended target.

"Shouldn't we take evasive action?" shouts Jon.

Chris watches the drop of the shots and shakes his head. "Naw. We're more likely to wander into their sights for a lucky shot. Besides, we'd lose what little advantage in distance we have."

Two more rapid shots land well ahead of the patrol craft. Tran laughs sourly. "That's some really lousy shooting," he observes dourly. "Someone's gonna lose his rating." When no one laughs, he turns to Jon and Chris. "We'll be within small arms range in a few minutes," he announces. "Let's get the Alamo prepared."

In the cabin, they had locate a half-dozen Vietnam War-era flack vests for the boat's crew. Jon piles the vests around the machine gun in lieu of sandbags. Chris ties-off the wheel to the throttle, locking the vessel on its current bearing. He lowers himself gently onto the deck beside Jon, resting the barrel of his assault rifle on the stack of vests before taking up a position to feed the belt of ammunition into Jon's machine gun. Tran kicks open the cabin door and drops below deck, using the stairs descending into the sunken cabin as a foxhole. All weapons are trained on the approaching missile boat.

Chris' mind flashes back to a similarly desperate fight in the Salvadoran jungle nearly eighteen years before. By all reasonable accounts, he knows he should have died that day. That the final lines of his story are to be written now, in another war, in yet another foreign land, seems somehow fair exchange for the unnatural extension of his life. He thinks of Jessica and realizes he's lost something irreplaceable. It's time for him to depart. He crosses himself and prays silently that God will remember his few virtues; he adjusts the ammunition belt and looks to Jon.

"Make it count," he advises.

Jon nods, locking the stock beneath his cheek as he melds with his weapon. As the pursuer nears within range, he squeezes the trigger; spent shell casings and disintegrating links clatter across the boat's fiberglass deck. Red tracers spaced every fifth round in the linked ammunition belt provide a laser-like aid as he walks his bullets toward the target.

Standing on the bridge beside the captain, Admiral Widjaja smiles in anticipation as the missile boat closes on its prey. "They'll be surrendering soon," he announces confidently.

The exploding glass startles him.

With the rest of the crew, the admiral drops to the deck as the bullets shatter the windows encompassing the bridge. Bloodied by the flying glass, he drags himself to his feet in a blind rage.

"Kill them! Kill them all!" He shrieks, grabbing crew members and shoving them back to their fighting positions. He stumbles over a prostrate figure on the deck.

"Get up!" he shrieks, kicking the cringing captain. A sailor stoops to assist his commander. Rolling the old man onto his back, the sailor discovers two ragged bullet holes in his commander's chest. Sticky scarlet blood pools beneath the captain as the sailor gropes for a pulse. He peers up at the admiral, eyes wide in horror.

"He's dead, Sir," he announces.

From out of nowhere, an explosion; a roar so loud it punches the breath from Chris' lungs. Instinctively, he buries his head beneath his arms, an unwilling witness to his own death. But as the sound dissipates, he discovers himself inexplicably alive. Peering up from behind the flack vests, he traces the smoky trails of two jet aircraft streaking past, a mere twenty feet above the surface of the ocean.

"What the hell?" he shouts over the roar as the jets split-off in opposite directions and circle for another pass. Squinting into the sun, he can barely identify the aircraft as obsolescent American made A-4 Skyhawk attack planes.

He racks his memory. The Indonesians have A-4s, but they're stationed all the way over at Hasanuddin Airbase. "They're hell and gone from Sulawesi," he mutters.

The jets pair-up and dropped low, approaching for a second pass. "You gotta' be fuckin' kidding me!" Chris blurts, burying his head beneath his uninjured arm, waiting to be cut in half by the A-4s' 20mm automatic cannons. A string of sonic snaps announce the passage of cannon rounds overhead. Chris raises his head and spots the pursuing missile boat disappear behind a spray of white water.

He staggers to his feet, barely able to control his growing elation as the aircraft circle for a third pass. Heart racing, he recognizes on the mottled green camouflage paint the subdued outline of a lion's head. "Singapore," he chokes. He turns to Jon. "They're Singaporean!" he shouts, spotting 142 Squadron's Gryphon on the aircraft's vertical tail.

The machine gun slips from Jon's shoulder as he twists to catch a glimpse of the aircraft, eyes wide with amazement. "Singapore," he mouths in disbelief.

"OH Yeeeaaaahhh!" Tran shouts, emerging onto the deck to cheer the attack planes. Chris and Jon join him in a loud whoop as the A4SU Super Hawks drop low for another pass.

"NO! NO! NO!" shrieks Admiral Widjaja. He stumbles away from the shattered helm, clawing his way past the stunned gaggle of crewmen choking the hatch. Mixed armor piercing and high explosive rounds rip-up the composite deck, climbing the superstructure and shredding the lightweight aluminum plating that protects the bridge.

Slammed against the bulkhead, the admiral spins to see the bridge filled with a hazy white smoke and flying debris; the crew's shrieks drowned out by the roar of explosions. Gasping, he spots an escape route and staggers toward the open hatch. Something strikes the back of his shoulder; he tumbles to the floor, his arm drooping across his face. Unable to remove the arm blocking his vision, he rolls away, leaving his severed limb twitching on the deck.

"NOOoooooo!"

A fourth pass leaves the missile boat dead in the water, flames licking the aluminum structure as the crew leaps into the sea to escape the hellish heat. Black smoke belches from open hatches as the beast breathes its last.

The patrol boat continues skimming northwest toward the beaconing safety of international waters, two A4SU fighters circling protectively overhead. Soon, another ship appears on the horizon, proceeding toward them at high speed. Tran glances to the fighters for guidance and is relieved to see their protectors do not consider the approaching vessel a threat.

"Jon. Steer for that surface contact," orders Tran. He returns to where Chris has collapsed onto the port side bench and kneels beside him. He places his hand on his friend's feverish forehead. "Chris," asks Tran softly. "Are you all right?" Chris' eyes blink blurrily up at him.

"Mom? What are you doing' here?" he mumbles with a weak grin.

"I'm here to save your obnoxious lawyer ass," replies Tran soothingly. Chris' eyes open a little wider; a weak smile creases his face.

"So we're gonna' make it?"

"Yeah. It looks that way."

A thunderous roar interrupts their conversation as two A4SUs roar low over the boat, wag their wings in farewell and fade into the distance.

"There goes our escort," announces Tran with a wave to the departing fighters. "The RSN is nearby. Just hang loose for another fifteen minutes and we'll get you some medical attention."

"*Indonesian craft,*" echoes a metallic voice from the approaching ship's loud speaker. "*Cut your engines and heave-to.*"

Jon glances at Tran who nods his agreement. As the patrol boat drifts to a stop, the RSS Sovereignty, sister ship to the ill-fated Dominion, pulls alongside. Jon flings a line to the sailors reaching over the rail of the larger vessel. In response, a wooden-runged rope ladder clatters over the side and several camouflaged naval commandos drop into the boat and spread out, weapons at the ready. Jon backs away uneasily, hands in the air.

Chris glances warily at Tran, realizing immediately what the commandos are seeking. Two of the commandos disappear below deck. Chris raises himself painfully.

"Sergeant. Khalid is dead," he reports.

"Where's the body?" asks the sergeant in a business-like manner.

"On the battlefield," responds Tran. A sudden clatter announce the return of the two commandos from within the cabin.

"There's a body down there," one of them reports. Tran looks to Chris for a response. Chris begins to speak but halts, spotting Colonel Mok peering anxiously over the missile boat's railing.

A lump rises in Chris' throat; he swallows hard and announces as loudly as he is able. "That's Captain Ling's body," he chokes. A flash of horror flashes momentarily in the colonel's eyes. He turns and disappears from view.

As the commandos stand aside uneasily, a team of medics scramble aboard the patrol boat, Emergency Medical Technician kits slung over their shoulders. "Sir, you should lay back, please," urges a medic as he gently helps Chris recline onto the vinyl bench seat.

"How recent is this wound?" asks the medic professionally as he cuts away the makeshift bandage.

"About 12 hours," estimates Tran.

"Much blood loss?"

"Dunno," mumbles Chris. "I've been too busy to notice."

With a final snip, the crusty material binding Chris' wound gives way and blood oozes around the torn muscle. A wave of nausea engulfs him; his head rolls sideways as he wretches. The paramedics avoid his vomit without comment and continue to work diligently to staunch the bleeding.

"Stretcher!" calls one of the medics and the crewmen quickly pass a basket stretcher over the side.

Having temporarily curtailed the bleeding, the medics fold Chris' left arm across his body and place his right hand on top of it. "Hold your arm in place," the medic orders. "We're going to move you now." They slide a backboard beneath him and lift carefully. Delirious, Chris feels suddenly as if he is spinning out of control. He gropes for a handhold of the backboard. One of the medics catches his injured arm as it slides off the stretcher. The pain is excruciating.

"It's okay. It's okay," the medic assures Chris as they lower him onto the stretcher. Chris' vision blurs; he struggles to regain focus, but slips into merciful unconsciousness.

CHAPTER 21

Across the vast crowded dance floor, stands a woman in a simple black outfit and hijab speaking with a man in a dark suit. The stranger has his back to Chris. But the woman seems familiar, however strangely out of place among the skimpy glittering dresses draped over the subtly curved Asian figures gyrating around her. The woman in black steps aside, letting a dancer pass, her half-turn revealing familiar almond eyes and high cheekbones. Spotting him, she beams a wonderful, inviting smile fading slowly from her face as she returns her attention to the man in the dark suit.

"Jessica!" yells Chris, his voice drowned-out by throbbing dang-dut music pounding louder and louder as he grapples across the dance floor toward her. Giggling dancers close-in around him, grabbing him, drawing him away. Struggle as he might, he's getting no closer.

"Jessica!' he screams again. Her eyes turn luridly toward him as she leans forward to kiss the man in the dark suit. It's a lingering, passionate kiss. Chris freezes, the dancers gyrating around him. *How could she*? he sobs.

As she withdraws from the kiss, a bloody wound opens on the side of her face. She points accusingly at him, her eyes seething with hatred. The man in the dark suit glances at him and laughs, his yellow teeth bare in a taunting sneer.

Khalid!

She doesn't know! He realizes. *She doesn't know who he is. I've got to get to her!* And suddenly – inexplicably – he's there, standing alone before her. He glances around rabidly; Khalid had disappeared. He and Jessica are alone in the now silent room, the disco ball flinging red and gold specks of light around the black walls.

"Jessica," he croaks. "How could you?"

She smiles at him tenderly. "Why? He didn't kill me, you did," she replies with a sad look as she places her hand lightly against his cheek.

"Crack!"

A gunshot echoes through the empty room. Her brow furrows, lips quivering as blood trickles from her mouth; she stares into his eyes, startled.

"Why?" she gasps. *"Why?"*

Chris sits-up abruptly, tears streaming down his face. Sobbing like a lost child, he casts panicked glances around the sterile, white room. A rattle at the door announces the nurse who materializes from behind the curtain encircling his hospital bed.

"It's all right," she announces soothingly. "You've been having a nightmare. It's just the anesthesia wearing off." She forces him gently back against the sweat-drenched sheets. They're cold and clammy against his back.

"Wh... what time is it?" he asks for want of a better question.

"14:43," she replies precisely. "You've been out of surgery for five hours. Now please lay still or you're going to tear the sutures." It's only then he notices the thick bandages plastering his left arm and shoulder. The nurse adjusts the tube protruding from his wound and extending to a jar on the floor.

"Since you're awake," she announces, checking his vital signs by rote, "there's a man from the embassy waiting to see you. He's been here since you came out of surgery. Are you up to having a visitor?"

"A man from the embassy?" he asks in confusion. "Um. Sure. Why not?" The nurse sweeps from the room. Moments later a tall, tanned, silver haired Anglo in a Polo shirt and slacks slips unobtrusively into the room.

"How are we feeling this afternoon?" he asks.

Chris eyes him suspiciously. "*We're* feeling about as you would expect," he responds cautiously. The man stares in silence, eyes sizing him up in a manner that leaves Chris feeling naked.

"Who are you?" Chris asks finally.

The visitor gingerly places a calling card on the stainless tray table and folds himself into a chair beside the bed. Chris retrieves the card and reads it: Colonel William J. Levine, Staff Judge Advocate, United States Pacific Command.

"So what can I do for JAG?" Chris asks warily.

"You've created quite a stir, Captain," replies the colonel, peering around the curtains to make certain the nurse has pulled the door closed. "Half the command wants your head on a silver platter and the others... well they want to award you the Medal of Honor," he chuckles.

"So what camp is 'The 2'in?" Chris asks groggily.

"That remains to be seen," he replies. "She's withholding judgment until she receives my report."

Chris sighs in resignation. "So you're my judge and jury," he snorts.

"Yes, something like that."

"What do you want to know?"

The colonel rummages through his briefcase and withdraws a folding notebook. He removes the Mont Blanc pen from inside the front of his Polo shirt, flips open a legal pad and jumps right in.

"You can start by telling me who killed Khalid," he announces.

"A POLRI sniper," responds Chris.

The colonel hesitates. "Now, why *on earth* would he do that?" he asks in a voice dripping with condescension.

"Because he was a lousy fucking shot," snaps Chris.

The colonel's dark eyes cut from the yellow pad to Chris. "Your career rides on the answers you give me, Captain," he replies. "I suggest you take this a little more seriously."

"My...?" snorts Chris in disbelief. "Colonel, I have no *career*. I'm just an occasional cog in the big green machine." The colonel begins to speak but Chris cuts him off.

"You asked what happened and I told you. The sniper was gunning for Major Minh. When Khalid stumbled the shot went wild and hit him instead."

The colonel nods gravely. "Yes. That's Major Minh's story, too," he drawls.

"Where is Major Minh?" Chris asks suddenly.

"Redeployed," replies he colonel after some deliberation.

"To?"

The colonel sighs. "SOCOM required his skills elsewhere," he responds vaguely. "Besides, you are not permitted to speak with others involved in this case until after the matter is settled."

A realization strikes Chris like a bullet. "You don't really think we assassinated Khalid, do you?" he asks. Twisting in his bed, pain shoots through his shoulder; he collapses against his drenched pillow.

"I'm just here to find the facts," responds the colonel noncommittally.

"*Fine*," replies Chris coldly. "Here are some facts. First," he announces, holding up his hand and ticking-off fingers. "If we were going to kill Khalid, we could easily have done it at the hotel. Second, we risked – and lost – one of our best people trying to get the son-of-a-bitch off the island. And third, I raised the issue of killing Khalid and no one on the team – *no one* – was willing to do it."

"Except you," observes the colonel.

Chris glares at him. "Yeah. Yeah. I would've killed him," he growls. "That's what soldiers do, colonel! And I'd rather kill a hundred Khalids than risk one of my own."

"So did you?" presses the colonel. "When you found he was slowing you down? Did you decide to kill Khalid then?"

"No," spits Chris. "I - *we* - don't kill prisoners. And, for your information I was out of commission *before* Khalid was killed. Sorry, Colonel," he scoffs. "I'm not your trigger-man."

"So how were you wounded?" asks the colonel.

"The POLRI attacked the safe house. I don't exactly recall the details, but some rounds came through the window and one of them hit me in the shoulder."

"Where was Major Minh at the time?"

"He and Jon, my bodyguard, had gone to find us some transportation. The POLRI were on the lookout for our old car..."

"You mean they went to steal a car?" asks the colonel innocently.

Chris squints at him. "No, Sir. They went to Pangkalanbun's all-night rent-a-car," he snorts. "Of course they fucking stole it!"

Ignoring Chris' insolence, the colonel scribbles notes on his pad.

"So when *was* Khalid killed?"

Chris describes his recollection of how the fight unfolded, how Jon saved them by crashing the truck through the front of the house - discreetly leaving-out the part about Jon's attempt to kill him.

"So Captain Ling was treating your wound when Khalid was killed," concludes the colonel.

"Yeah," mumbles Chris.

"Then you didn't actually *see* what happened to Khalid," he observes.

"No. But I heard a rifle shot and saw Tran – I mean Major Minh – and Jon high-tail it back inside."

"But you didn't actually *see* Khalid killed," pursues the colonel.

"No, Sir. But there was a single high-powered rifle shot and Major Minh was armed only with pistol at that point."

"Perhaps you were mistaken," counters the colonel reasonably. "I mean, in the heat of battle, one gunshot must sound pretty much like another."

"Have you ever *been* in combat, colonel?"

The colonel shifts uncomfortably in his seat. "That's really not the issue," he declares.

"Yes, it is. When your life depends on who is shooting at you and from what direction, you learn to recognize the sound of every shot," explains Chris irritably. "I heard the same sniper fire four more times when we made our escape. He was the shooter," Chris insists. "And one of his shots killed Jess... Captain Ling," he insists, his voice cracking as the image of Jessica lying dead in his lap flashes in his mind.

The colonel makes a few more notes then flips his pad closed. "Captain, why didn't you leave the island when Captain Ling provided the opportunity?"

The answer doesn't come immediately. It wasn't just to keep Jessica out of trouble, he realizes. But what was it? Bloodlust? Ego? He really doesn't know.

"Sir," he answers finally. "We didn't go to Kalimantan to kidnap Khalid; we went to recover a wounded agent. But when we were on the run and found out Khalid was leading the chase, it just seemed... well... the best defense might be a good offense."

The colonel peers at Chris over the tops of his reading glasses. "You want me to go back to the admiral with a football analogy, Captain?" he asks darkly.

"No," growls Chris. "I want you to ask Admiral Lang if PACOM really intended to deploy a SEAL team to snatch Khalid, or whether the State Department intended to file another useless demarche. Or if the Justice Department would have filed another pointless request for extradition!"

"Why does it matter?" asks the colonel in mild surprise.

"Because *we* were told we are at war. If all we're doing is collecting intelligence and have no intention to act on it, then we're going to have a lot more 9/11s!"

Breathing heavily, the pointlessness of it all overwhelms him. "Colonel," he sighs. "If we were sent to find Khalid just so the admiral could upstage the other agencies, we never should have been sent there in the first place."

"So, you accept no responsibility?" asks the colonel dubiously as he removes his reading glasses and folds them into a small case.

"No Sir, on the contrary," insists Chris. "I accept full responsibility for *my* actions. My question is whether anyone else accepts responsibility for theirs."

Jessica's memorial service has already begun by the time the taxi draws up on a side street beside her family home in the exclusive neighborhood across from the soaring hills of Bukit Timah Nature Preserve. The narrow side streets are packed with parked cars.

As Chris approaches the house warily, his eyes wander across the airy three story colonial structure of a style popular in the tropics of the late 1800s. Beneath a large overhanging portico is a grand double archway. Lining the bright stucco walls are a row of tall narrow windows framed by immaculately painted blue shutters. A mottled blue tiled roof extends over wide balconies protruding from the front of the house and either side of the second floor.

He walks up the broad wooden steps, passing beneath a lumbering ceiling fan that hangs over the large portico. Stepping into the foyer, he glances around uncomfortably, his attention drawn to the darkened room on the left. Several dozen well-dressed mourners stand in a semi-circle around an altar on which Jessica's photograph is perched, surrounded by candles and burning incense.

Drawn irresistibly into the room, he approaches the altar and the open casket beyond. Shutters closed, the room lit only by flickering golden candlelight reflecting warmly off the white paneled walls, he waits patiently for the mourners to pay their respects and move away before walking solemnly before the altar and bowing deeply, his eyes fixed on Jessica's portrait. She appears in the photo as he's never seen her before. Her shimmering shoulder length black hair and innocent smile reveal nothing of the hardened case officer he knew. He realizes the portrait must have been taken about the time she graduated from college, before her innocence was shattered by the reality of the silent war she chose to fight. *I'll bet this is how her parents still picture her*, he imagines.

An involuntary sigh escapes his lips. *Is it guilt? Regret? No. It's self-pity*, he realizes with disgust. Glancing past the altar, he catches a glimpse of Jessica's profile in the open casket. Approaching reluctantly, he peers reluctantly down at her. Dressed in white she rests in peace, eyes closed as if in silent prayer. He stifles a sob, relieved her accusing eyes are no longer watching him - at least not while he's awake. He resists the urge to lean down and kiss her.

"Beautiful, isn't she?" whispers a soft feminine voice. Unconsciously aware of a presence beside him, he's unable to take his eyes off Jessica. When the delicate voice invades his silence, he turns to an attractive older Asian woman peering back at him through kindly eyes. His gaze returns to Jessica.

"Yes," he croaks, "Yes she is."

"You're Chris," the woman announces as if he can dare deny it.

He nods silently.

"Please walk with me," the woman insists as she slides her arm through his and draws him aside. With a last glance at Jessica, he allows himself to be escorted through a side door, emerging into a manicured garden of colored orchids.

"Lovely, isn't it?" she asks casually as they walk among the field of bright, fragrant pastels.

"Yes Ma'am," he responds tersely, anxiously awaiting the impending accusation: for she clearly knows who he is. The realization unnerves him.

"I'm certain you understand how difficult this is for Jessica's father," she croons. "He doesn't blame you for what happened. She was always a headstrong girl, very much like her mother," she announces with a small laugh.

Chris halts abruptly and turns toward her in surprise.

"No," the woman announces with a tolerant smile, reading his confusion. "I'm not her mother - though I would be proud to call her my daughter," she admits as they resume walking. "My late husband and I were close friends of the Mok family..."

Chris hesitates again; his jaw drops.

She examines him queerly, comprehension creeping slowly across her wise brow. "Ahhh. Of course Jessica would not have told you," she deducts shrewdly. "And you didn't suspect?"

"No," Chris insists. "My God, the colonel must despise me!"

"He does not *despise* you," she replies sternly. "Quite the contrary. He thinks of you very much as a father would toward his son. Of course he would never admit it," she adds quickly. "He is much too proud a man to confess such an emotion - even to himself."

"Then why has he been avoiding me?"

"He is hurting, Chris," she explains patiently as they resume their stroll through the garden. "Your presence is a reminder of his loss. Like any father, it's painful when his daughter forsakes him for the love of another man. That he has now lost her forever is nearly unbearable. A parent should never outlive his child," she observes sagely.

It's hard enough to accept he'd taken Jessica's heart and her life. That he's taken those things from a man for whom he has such great respect leaves him feeling strangely hollow.

A familiar voice echoes through the garden, shattering his reflection.

"Pim? Pim? Are you out here? I'm looking for..." the voice trails off as Colonel Mok rounds the corner and encounters Pim and Chris standing contritely amid the orchids.

"Jimmy," Pim purrs with an engaging smile. "I was just speaking with this *wonderful* young man."

"Hello, Colonel," Chris announces snapping nearly to attention. Colonel Mok stands, dumbfounded before stumbling backwards and turning away. Chris steps forward.

"I loved her, Colonel," he blurts. Colonel Mok stops in mid-turn, sighs, and turns to face Chris. His eyes are moist. Not gratuitous with tears, but with the dignified tears of a man unaccustomed to displaying emotion.

"... and she loved you," he responds in a tired, envious voice.

The tension in Chris' body uncoils now that the dreaded encounter has occurred. "I'm sorry, Colonel," insists Chris, his voice breaking despite his attempt to keep it even. He swallows hard. "If I could trade places with her right now... You have to believe me."

Colonel Mok peers at him queerly, as if never occurred to him otherwise. Despite Chris' six-foot-two frame, the colonel is surprised how small he appears in grief. His face is sunburned and raw, his stance awkward as he lists awkwardly to his injured left side. His red-rimmed eyes are hollow and forlorn.

"I believe you," Colonel Mok replies quietly.

"Miss... Where'd she go?" Chris asks. Glancing anxiously around the garden, he discovers Madame Kunchai has drifted silently away, leaving the two men alone to sort out their emotions. He catches a glimpse of her blue silk cheongsam as she disappears through a door and reenters the house.

"Your friend," Chris continues. "She told me. I... I never knew."

"Would it have made a difference?" asks the colonel.

"No, Sir. I suppose not," admits Chris.

A fleeting smile creases Colonel Mok's face, evaporating instantly. "I thought as much. That's why I didn't interfere," he replies thoughtfully. "A father must know when to let go."

"But our relationship could have ended her career," insists Chris.

"Chris," sighs Colonel Mok. "I have been an intelligence officer for more than forty years. When my Jessica decided to follow me into the profession, I tried to talk her out of it. But, like most children, she knew better."

"She was an awesome intelligence officer," offers Chris.

"Yes. But she was not able to put aside her personal feelings for the sake of the mission..."

Chris bites back an irrational surge of anger. "She had a right to a life of her choosing, Colonel," he replies tersely.

"Yes. I realized that too late," responds the colonel disarmingly.

Chris' fury evaporates.

"These past few turbulent months, she was happier than I'd ever seen her," he admits. His eyes stare mistily into the distance. Chris stands silently, watching the colonel. A warm breeze carries the faint aroma of burning incense past them.

"I'm an old man," announces Colonel Mok wistfully. "In Jessica's mother I was fortunate to know true love." He glances up at Chris. "And I will rest well knowing my Jessica did also."

Unable to find the words, Chris merely purses his lips and nods.

The colonel clears his throat and changes topics. "So what will you do now?"

"I... uh. I really don't know," Chris mumbles. "Apparently there is an investigation back home to determine whether I'll be court-martialed."

"Yes. I thought as much - bureaucrats looking to cover their posteriors," chuckles the old colonel darkly. "Perhaps the Republic can be of assistance in that matter," he offers cryptically.

"Thank you Sir," replies Chris gratefully. He's well versed in Colonel Mok's ability to affect events. But there remains a single burning question to which he must have an answer.

"Sir, may I ask...? What would you have done if you'd been in our position?"

The old man's eyes meet Chris' and he announces without hesitation, "I would have followed orders and returned home." Chris blanches and turns away, unable to face such a cruel judgment. For that is the crux of the matter: he disobeyed orders and Jessica died.

"... and I would have been wrong," Colonel Mok admits.

"Sir?"

"This insidious war needs committed people like you... and Jessica," he announces firmly. "There was a time when we were willing to risk everything for our freedom: during the Japanese occupation; during the Communist riots. But as with most of the supposed 'civilized nations' we have become a soft people, a people unworthy of the gifts bestowed upon us," he admits with a trace of regret. Then his face lightens. "But reading the reports of what you and my Jessica did in Kalimantan renewed my faith."

Chris flushes slightly, like a child earning the seldom-proffered praise of a stern parent.

"I hope you're right," he mumbles feebly.

"I am," replies the colonel kindly. He slips his arm through Chris' and leads him back toward the house.

As they emerge through the arched side door, Chris spots Shikha in the front row of chairs nearest the coffin. She smiles awkwardly, the smile growing in intensity as she notices Colonel Mok pass through the door beside him. The colonel squints, his eyes adjusting to the darkened room. He leans down and whispers something in Shikha's ear. She nods and moves aside, offering Chris the place of honor amid the curious stares of the other mourners, many of whom are quite obviously dignitaries.

On the colonel's cue, four robed monks step onto a platform and raise a wide red ribbon leading to the coffin. They chant in melodic tones at once uplifting and solemn.

"They are chanting the Abhidharma," whispers Shikha. "Prayers have been offered every day for seven days. Between death and rebirth, there is an intermediate period influencing the form of rebirth. If the family prays diligently and performs the required remembrance ceremonies, it will encourage a favorable rebirth."

Chris nods as if he understands the mysterious ritual. He listens intently, distracted only by sweat creeping inside his bandages. When the chanting fades, Colonel Mok approaches soberly and presents the monks a plate of various fruits. He repeats a phrase several times, bowing as the monks respond with melodious words of thanksgiving.

"That was the transference," Shikha whispers. "He has asked all the family's goodwill be bestowed upon the deceased."

Arcane though the ceremony appears to Chris, it's undeniably beautiful. The fantasy that Jessica's soul might again reside among the living brings him an irrational, if fleeting, hope.

As the chanting fades to silence, Colonel Mok steps forward and peers down into the coffin. His lips moves in silent prayer as his hand brushes Jessica's cheek; he leans down and kisses her forehead. He lifts his hand, resting it indecisively on the coffin's wooden cover, his bony fingers trembling.

Chris realizes the colonel can't bring himself to close the lid. His heavy eyes cut desperately, beseechingly to Chris, begging some intervention to relieve him of the burden or offer the strength to carry forward. Chris rises silently and steps beside the colonel, placing his hand on the colonel's as together, they lower the lid.

Colonel Mok smiles gratefully, his crinkled eyes filling with tears as he turns and wordlessly signals the pallbearers. Chris backs away as the coffin is raised to the men's shoulders and they shuffle across the parquet floor into the foyer. Children precede the coffin, spreading banana leaves on the concrete steps as the monks lead the procession into the bright sunshine, trailing the wide ribbon leading from the casket. Colonel Mok takes Chris' arm and hauls him insistently into line to take his place alongside him and Pim as they proceed solemnly down the steps following the casket.

A man carrying a pole draping a long, narrow white flag leads the procession, gusts of humid wind whipping the serpentine tail over the mourner's heads. Behind him, several elderly men carry flowers in silver bowls followed by a group of eight monks chanting the Abhidharma.

The celebratory procession continues several blocks to a large Buddhist temple nestled incongruously between the residential neighborhood and a row of modern glass high-rise office buildings.

Weak from his injuries, exhaustion compounded by the 94-degree heat, Chris would otherwise appreciate the ornately carved temple, the red and gold fixtures and reclining Buddha smiling favorably upon the hundred or so mourners as they trek up the stone steps and enter the temple.

As he enters the cool dampness of the temple, the room begins to spin. He drops to one knee on the ornately carved floor. Colonel Mok seizes his uninjured arm and helps him to a nearby bench where he collapses, pale and weak from exertion.

"I'm sorry, colonel," he announces earnestly.

He receives a familiar, pitiful smile.

"You have nothing to be sorry for, my friend."

The periphery of Chris' vision grows dim and the light fades.

CHAPTER 22

Rain drums heavily on the roof as the taxi weaves through late afternoon traffic. A roll of thunder awakens Chris from his daydream. *Rain: my constant companion*, he tells himself sourly as he watches pedestrians dart between awnings decorating the fronts of small mom and pop sidewalk cafés lining the street. Ignoring the deluge, couriers on motorcycles glide between gridlocked cars and commercial trucks vie for a clearer lane of traffic to deliver them more rapidly to their destinations.

When the taxi squeals to a stop on the wet pavement in the circular drive in front of his apartment building, Chuan, the portly young doorman, ambles down the steps and wrenches open the car door.

"Welcome home, Mr. Gates," he announces, his face betraying no surprise at the sight of Chris' heavily bandaged shoulder.

"Thanks," replies Chris self-consciously as he struggles to unfold his long legs from the compact car. "Can you give me a hand?" He stretches out his right arm and Chuan grasps his hand, drawing the taller man effortlessly from the car.

"Do you have bags?" asks Chuan eagerly.

"Just that," mumbles Chris motioning to a plastic bag in the seat containing medical supplies the hospital sent home with him. The clothes he was wearing when recovered from the Strait of Karimata more than a week ago were so ragged and bloody the hospital staff had disposed of them. Now he wears the borrowed shirt and slacks he'd worn to Jessica's funeral.

"I'll take it Chuan," announces Chris as he recovers the bag from the doorman's reluctant grasp. Chuan bows deeply and holds-open the lobby door. The frigid lobby sends a shiver up Chris' spine. He shivers as he shuffles slowly across the polished marble floor toward the elevators.

Ismah, the elegant Malaysian day manager rises from behind her desk and approaches him, hand outstretched.

"Welcome home Mr. Gates," she announces earnestly, grasping his hand in a warm, feminine grip. "Housekeeping has just finished tidying-up your room." Unlike Chuan, her eyes portray unspoken concern. "I've taken the liberty of having a bottle of wine opened for you. You'll find it on the bar."

He examines her strangely. "Thank you Ismah." She escorts him to the elevator where they stand silently, her hand on his arm until the tone sounds and the door slides open. He steps inside.

"Please give me a call if I may be of further assistance," Ismah pleads as the doors slid shut, obscuring her anxious smile.

Entering his apartment, he kicks off his shoes, drops the bag on the floor, and places his cardkey on the small table in the foyer. All the lights are on; a vase of fresh flowers adorn the coffee table in the center of the living room. As usual, the housekeeper has tuned the radio to his favorite classical radio station. He increases the volume, filling the lonely apartment with the strains of a violin concerto he immediately recognizes as Beethoven's 9th Symphony, Ode to Joy. Smiling at the images conjured by the swelling concerto, he pours himself a glass of Shiraz, slides open the patio door, and steps onto his 12th floor balcony.

The sultry air embraces him as the rain recedes to a silent trickle, the music gaining ascendancy over the sounds of the city. He recognizes the initial strains of Bach's Fugue in G-minor, "The Little," drifting eerily through the open patio door. A rumble of thunder in the distance confirms the storm has yet to run its course.

He rummages absently through his pocket, retrieving the vague, one-page order from U.S. Pacific Command. He's going home tomorrow, it informs him. Ordered back to Tripler Army Medical Center on Oahu "for medical evaluation." He stares longingly across the lights of the city, wondering how he can ever leave this place. Of all the countries he's served in during his career, he realizes Singapore will forever remain in his heart. He dangles his orders lightly against the wind, releasing them as a gust sweeps the paper from his grasp. The document levitates in the updraft, suspended in mid-air as if inviting him forward, away from the bonds of earth and into the unknown, before floating out of sight.

Somewhere into his third glass of wine comes a discreet knock at the door. He places his wine glass on the coffee table and totters unsteadily to the foyer. Glancing through the peephole, he recoils, lets out a resigned sigh and opens the door.

"Hi Shikha," he announces with a strained smile. "What brings you out on a night like this?"

"I heard you'd been released from the hospital," she replies with a shrug. "I thought you might like some company."

He eyes her warily before recalling his manners. "Of course, of course. Come in." He steps aside and she glides into the room, dressed in an embroidered black silk halter and matching slacks that hug her curvaceous body.

"I was having some wine," he announces thickly, raising the mostly empty bottle. "Want some?"

"Sure," she replies tentatively, glancing around the apartment. With a crash of thunder, the storm sweeps the building with renewed vigor, rain pouring through the open patio door and soaking the hardwood floor. Realizing he's oblivious, Shikha stalks across the room and pulls the door closed. She peers at him disapprovingly.

"You look like hell," she observes.

Standing unshaven and barefoot in an undershirt and wrinkled grey slacks, he nods. "I feel like hell." He tips the remainder of the wine into a glass and presents it to her. She retrieves it from his hand, raises the glass in a silent toast and takes a tentative sip. She lowers the glass.

"When did you last eat?" she blurts.

Something in her tone annoys him. "I had a wonderful Jell-O breakfast at the hospital this morning," he reports sarcastically. "Why?"

"Come," she responds, setting her glass on the bar and taking his hand insistently. "Let's go have some dinner."

He rips his hand from her grasp. "I don't want any fucking dinner!" he growls, finding himself inexplicably angry. "I want to sit here and drink myself into a stupor. Is that all right with you?"

"Getting drunk isn't going to bring her back," snaps Shikha.

He stares at her, unable to articulate a reasonable response, then suddenly heaves his empty wine glass at the wall. The delicate crystal shatters, its glistening shards skittering across the floor.

"No," he replies in an oddly even tone. "No, it's not." His eyes are heavy with unrealized tears.

"Chris. I know you feel guilty about Jessica. But you know what? She was drawn to you because you were *just like her*," she insists, pointedly enunciating the last three words as she jabs a finger into his chest.

"She loved you *because* you went plunging into that damned jungle after Khalid. If you had fled when she offered the opportunity, your relationship would have been over in a heartbeat. I've got news for you *Chris*: your relationship *had* to end! Because one of you was going to either cruelly disappoint the other or die proving you were worthy. It couldn't have ended any other way."

"So, what are you saying? I should be glad it wasn't me?" snorts Chris.

"No!" she snaps. "Be glad you had someone in your life that *didn't disappoint you!*"

He stares, astonished. Unsure how to process her revelation, now he's at least certain Shikha isn't here to wallow with him in his misery.

"Do you like sushi?" he asks. "I could use a bite to eat."

Shikha smiles mischievously. "Sure."

He disappears into the bedroom and returns moments later wearing a clean shirt and pair of loafers. She helps him with his buttons then takes his arm and escorts him downstairs. The couple sprint through the rain to the sushi bar across the street.

Reaching protection beneath the awning, they realize the gate blocking the entrance was partway closed. Staff scurries about the room, mopping floors and cleaning tables.

"Damn," Chris mutters. "C'mon. I've got some Gyoza in the freezer." As they turn to leave there comes a sudden shout as the owner, a frail Japanese man in his late 70s, waves them eagerly back toward the restaurant.

"You are hungry, Sir?" he asks as if receiving a "yes" response would be the crowning achievement to his day.

"No. It's all right, Mr. Sato," replies Chris tiredly. But the owner seizes Shikha's hand and leads the couple beneath the gate into the restaurant. As they approach a table, the

Malaysian employees bow deeply, flashing friendly, welcoming smiles.

"How late are you open?" asks Chris.

"Much, much later," responds Mr. Sato.

Taking their seats, Shikha orders a cask of sake' and leaves Mr. Sato to select their dinner.

"Shikha," demands Chris tentatively as the owner ambles out of earshot. "Everyone from the taxi driver to Mr. Sato seems to know *something* occurred. How is that?"

She shifts awkwardly in her seat. "Has someone said something to give you such an impression?" she asks innocently.

"Well... no," admits Chris. "But people see my injured arm and say nothing. No 'hey, what happened?' No 'how is your arm feeling?' It's weird."

"We believe in privacy here," she responds vaguely.

"Okay," Chris presses. "My room was cleaned – even though they knew I'd been away. There were fresh flowers. There was an opened bottle of wine. How'd they know I would be back? How'd they know I couldn't open it myself? Now Mr. Sato is keeping the restaurant open just for us..."

"This is Asia," she replies with a shrug. "People talk."

"About *classified operations*?" he rasps.

She gasps and erupts into throaty laughter. "Chris, there are no secrets in Asia! They know the Dominion wasn't lost in a storm," she announces with a broad sweep of her arm, indicating everyone in Singapore, perhaps even all of Southeast Asia. "And they know damned well Khalid didn't die in Aceh at the hands of the POLRI."

"Is *that* the story?" he asks.

"Yes," she responds. "But everyone knows better."

"But it hasn't been in the papers. It's not on the news..."

"And it won't be," she interrupts tolerantly. "This isn't the West. We don't publish everything we know. Our use of the media is much more subtle. We use it to send messages, to signal intentions. But informing the public regarding matters that are none of their business? No."

"But it *is* their business..."

"Yes, yes," she replies dismissively. "But we accept it without question, without discussion," she explains with the patience of a teacher reasoning with a frustrated child. "When you see a deformed man, you don't point and call out 'look at the deformed man!' You know he's deformed, but you smile and treat him as any other. And you work diligently to ensure your children and your children's children don't suffer a similar fate.

"Your press," she continues with a sour expression, "wants to announce the obvious, to call attention to it, to ask 'how does it feel to be deformed? Who do you blame?' Get photos. Interview the relatives. Complain about the injustice. Your press has no sense of... of... *propriety*," she announces, having searched successfully for the appropriate word.

Chris chuckles and shakes his head in admiration. "God, I love Asia."

Coming out of her tirade, Shikha lapses into a silence that lasts until Mr. Sato returns with the sake'. He pours them each a small cup of hot rice wine and disappears quickly to check on the status of their dinner. Chris raises his cup.

"To Singapore..."

They loiter at the restaurant for more than an hour, drinking sake' and taking pleasure in Mr. Sato's creations before realizing the employees have all been dismissed; the owner is keeping the restaurant open himself.

Chris rises shakily; Shikha's steadying hand on his arm.

"Mr. Sato," he announces thickly, the sake' providing a warm, comforting glow. "This was just the medicine I needed. Thank you." He bows deeply in the traditional Japanese fashion. Touched by Chris' praise, Mr. Sato grasps his hand and shakes it eagerly.

"You are always welcome. Please come back soon, Captain," he begs.

A fleeting smile crosses Chris' face as he recognizes the use of the title "Captain."

"There are no secrets in Asia," chuckles Chris.

"Sir?" asks Mr. Sato earnestly.

"Nothing," Chris smiles warmly. "Good night."

Shikha takes his arm and leads him into the rain, across the street, and toward the entrance to his apartment building. When they enter the lobby, Chuan springs to his feet and meets the drenched couple halfway across the marble floor before acknowledging his belated response with a weak smile.

As the elevator carries them the twelve floors to his apartment, Chris becomes intensely aware of Shikha's presence beside him. He also suspects half a bottle of wine and a cask of sake' is clouding his judgment. His musings are interrupted by a sudden flash of Jessica's dead eyes staring at him, an image that continues to haunt him during the many unguarded moments since her death. He shakes his head, trying to banish the lingering image from his imagination.

"What's wrong?" Shikha asks.

"Nothing," he replies, smiling self-consciously. "I've just had too much to drink."

The elevator door slides open. She slips her arm through his and they emerge into the hall.

Is she holding him closer? *You're drunk*, he scolds himself. *And you're an asshole*.

Shikha halts short of his apartment door, turning hesitantly toward him.

"Chris, I..." Interrupting herself, leans forward on her high heels and kisses him lightly on the lips.

"This is a really bad idea," he admits as they part, hoping she agrees. Her responding sigh provides no such encouragement as she kisses him again, her invading tongue seeking his, to which he responds lustily. As they part he looks weakly into her alluring eyes.

"Ah, Shikha…"

She places her hand softly on his lips takes his hand in hers, leading him silently inside the apartment toward his darkened bedroom. They enter the room and she nudges the door closed, leaving a sliver of yellow light cutting diagonally across the hardwoods.

Her breathing grows heavy; she draws the wet halter over her head, shaking her long shimmering black hair from the glistening silk and tossing it carelessly aside to reveal her beautiful unrestrained breasts. He steps back and watches her.

In the partial light he can make out the silhouette of her statuesque figure as her slacks slide to the floor to reveal her long, lean body and black nylon thong. She steps forward, nudging him gently against the foot of the bed. He stumbles backwards and collapses onto the cool sheets.

She climbs languidly atop him and begins unbuttoning his shirt, her warm lips pressing against his neck and moving down his body as she exposes his flesh.

"It's all right," she reassures him as her warm, naked body slides up against his.

"It's all right…"

He lay half conscious, vaguely aware of the humming air conditioner that labors against the lukewarm night. Shikha stirs beside him, her warm, moist thigh resting across his; arm draped protectively across his chest. He closes his eyes and inhales the commingled aroma of sweat from their combined bodies. A tepid breeze wafts through the room; he yawns dreamily, his body and mind sated. A crack of thunder stirs him, louder than before and un-muffled by the thick concrete walls of his apartment. *Odd*, he realizes.

Another warm gust sweeps over him and he's sure. He slips from Shikha's protective embrace and begins to rise when he hears an unmistakable metallic click. He freezes, eyes focused on a shadowy figure in the bathroom doorway.

"*Who…?*"

Something collides with his back, knocking him to the hardwood floor. The room erupts around him: sharp deafening explosions; flashes, brilliant and fleeting, like a hyperactive strobe on the verge of self-destruction; a shrill, desperate curse in a foreign tongue - then abrupt silence.

The room reeks with the acrid smell of cordite.

"Are you all right?" breathes Shikha, her voice trembling.

"Yeah," he coughs. "Yeah… what the hell?" He gropes for the bedside lamp and flips the switch. Light floods the room and he finds himself staring up at Shikha standing naked over him, a Walther PPK/S automatic pistol steady in her hand. He follows her gaze to a crimson smudge leading down the wall to a black-clad figure slumped on the floor beside the bathroom door, a smoking SIG 9mm pistol lying beside the lifeless form.

Shikha slowly lowers her pistol.

There's a loud clatter in the living room as someone bursts into the apartment. Shikha spins toward the bedroom door and crouches into firing position.

"Shikha! Chris!" booms a male voice.

"Clear!" Shikha responds. "We're in the bedroom." Lowering her pistol, she turns back toward the corpse crumpled against the wall. Three plainclothes SID counter-terrorism officers shuffle into the room, MP-5 submachine guns raised and ready. They spot the body and lower their weapons.

Colonel Mok enters behind the armed men and glances disapprovingly at the naked Shikha. She seizes Chris' robe from the hook on the bathroom door and shrugs it over her bare shoulders. One of the plainclothesmen helps Chris to the edge of the bed. He stares blankly at the corpse before looking reluctantly up at Colonel Mok, reflexively drawing the sheet over his naked lap.

"Who is it?" he croaks.

An SID officer grasps the would-be assassin's bangs, lifting a startlingly familiar face.

"*Sri?*" Chris gasps as he recognizes the haggard feminine face beneath matted black hair.

"No," Colonel Mok corrects him. "Kade Darmali. She's one of Khalid's wives."

"No... she... she was with Irwan," Chris stammers in confusion.

"Was she?" asks the colonel dryly.

"No," Chris breathes. "Irwan was already dead – shit."

"You had never met her before, had you?"

Chris shakes his head dejectedly.

"So no one can blame you for not establishing her bona fides, can they?" asks Colonel Mok reasonably.

"Sure they can," mumbles Chris, ashamed that he'd been so easily deceived.

The colonel ignores Chris' self-recrimination and continues. "We believe Irwan and Sri were captured not long after you returned him to Kalimantan in search of Khalid," Colonel Mok explains as he stares distastefully at the corpse on the floor. "They used Sri to force him to set a trap."

"For what?"

"For you. For us," he shrugs. "There are those in Indonesia who want a jihad against the non-Muslim states," he explains. "They were hoping that sinking a Singaporean naval vessel while we were supporting an American covert operation would force us into a war of which the Jihadists could take advantage."

"So what went wrong?" asks Chris.

"Apparently everything. When you and your team escaped ashore, they had to find a way to roll you up in order to make their case for war. Kade was used to bait the trap."

"But Sri - I mean Kade. She knew everything!"

He reaches into a small briefcase and drops photos of a mangled body, barely recognizable as a woman, on the edge of the bed.

"While searching for you on Kalimantan, our agents stumbled across a report of a body dumped by the roadside near Palangkaraya. Through a corrupt medical examiner we obtained DNA confirming it was the body of the real Sri – horribly tortured. The Jihadists knew everything they thought they needed by the time Jessica arrived and threw their plan into disarray."

Chris grimaces. "You know Jessica is the one who discovered Sri – I mean Kade – was in contact with Khalid," he replies. "If it wasn't for her..."

"Yes, I know," he responds sagely.

"So... why didn't it work? Why are Singapore and Indonesia not at war? I mean, they sank one of your ships and you attacked one of theirs..."

"Cooler heads have prevailed," he explains. "Honor has been satisfied. And, thanks to you and Jessica, the Jihadists have suffered a great defeat."

Chris glances at Kade, a growing pool of blood seeping across the floor. "So, why...?"

"Her failed mission resulted in the death of her husband," Colonel Mok shrugs. "She had to make recompense..."

Dawn is breaking by the time the mess is cleaned up and the body is removed from his apartment. In the meantime, Chris is interviewed by the intelligence officers who arrived to gather what little information was available before departing with their tidbits to agonize over how an armed woman illegally entered Singapore's tightly controlled shores.

Once the body is removed, the last to leave Chris' apartment are Colonel Mok and Shikha.

"You'll be flying out this morning," confirms the colonel as he approaches the door.

"Yes, Sir. I imagine that'll be a relief."

The colonel chuckles, reaching into his jacket and withdrawing a red envelope. "This is for you, if you are available."

Chris stares curiously at him then, with an encouraging nod from the Colonel, retrieves the envelope, slips his finger beneath the fold and carefully tears it open. The card within is written in Mandarin.

"Sir...?"

Colonel Mok retrieves the card from Chris' grasp and flips it over. The reverse is in English, announcing the impending marriage of Colonel James Mok to Madame Pim Kunchai. Chris smiles.

"I'll be there," he announces, extending his hand. "Congratulations."

The colonel shakes Chris' hand and smiles shyly. He glances fleetingly at Shikha and back at Chris.

"Goodbye, my friend," he announces awkwardly and disappears through the door, leaving Chris and Shikha alone in the foyer.

"You're leaving," Chris observes.

"Yes. I must," she responds softly, a wistful look in her liquid brown eyes.

"You know... you... didn't *have* to stay with me. You could have just warned me about Kade."

"I know," she replies simply. "But God gives food to every bird..." Her voice fades as the attempt to put up a brave front falters. Usually critical, her searching, case officer eyes betray the truth. She's a woman, like any other, he realizes. Or perhaps not like any other...

"Oh," she mumbles, reaching into her purse and withdrawing an envelope containing a DVD. "I... don't know if you want this," she announces tentatively. "It's from the apartment..." She presents the disc to him.

He looks at her in confusion.

"The one on Napier Road," she explains quietly. "It's of you and Jessica."

His eyes widen. "She told me the recording system was..."

"Off?" Shikha interrupts. "It's never *off*," she replies bitterly.

He accepts the DVD from her grasp, holding it as if it might shatter in his hand. "Are there copies?" he asks.

"No," she replies.

Something in the finality of her voice tells him she's telling the truth.

"So... why are you giving it to me now?" he asks warily.

"We only need such things against our enemies," she admits softly.

CHAPTER 23

Major Greg "Bear" Berewood peers anxiously over the heads of the gaggle of tour guides and hotel limo drivers crowding the terminal, vying anxiously for the attention of mainland travelers.

Chris spots him first. "Bear!" he shouts, glad to see that his friend, and not military police, is there to meet him.

"Welcome back to 'Echelons Above Reality,'" Bear grins as he crushes Chris' hand in a welcome handshake and retrieves his single suitcase. "How'd the Orient treat you?"

"Rough," Chris chuckles, shrugging his injured arm.

"What the hell happened?" asks Bear.

"I figured you knew all about it," Chris shrugs.

"Nope. The admiral slapped a lid on any discussion about what went on out there."

"That figures," snorts Chris. An intelligence veteran of two wars, Bear knows better than to pursue the matter.

"So where are we going, the BOQ?" asks Chris with a yawn.

"Crippler," grunts Bear, using the nickname soldiers gave to Tripler Army Medical Center a generation before. "You need to get checked out by our docs before they cut you loose."

"Cut me loose for what, a Court Martial?"

Bear hesitates. "Why would you think that?"

Chris shrugs. "'The 2' sent the PACOM Staff Judge Advocate to see me in Singapore," he explains. "He was quite charming; utterly ruthless, of course. Something in his manner led me to believe something I did might be illegal."

"Was it?"

Chris shrugs painfully. "Not from where I stood."

Bear thinks for a moment. "I wouldn't worry about it. Before the Admiral slapped a lid on things, the J3 was raising hell about J2 getting involved in operations. They claimed the '2 shop' didn't have the charter to conduct operations. She's probably just covering her ass."

"I hope so," Chris mumbles.

"You'll find out soon enough. After the docs check you out, I'm supposed to run you up to Camp Smith to see her."

After the examination, Chris decides not to shave or change into his uniform before heading "up the hill" to see Admiral Lang. If he's going to be court-martialed, a shave and clean uniform won't be of much help. Besides, he's in a surly mood.

"Aren't you coming up?" Chris asks as Bear drops him off in the circular drive in front of the headquarters building.

"Nope, you're solo on this one. I'll wait for you down here."

"Right," Chris responds unenthusiastically, then perks up at a sudden thought. He fishes around inside his carry-on bag and withdraws a six-pack of Tiger Beer, plopping it in the major's lap. "Here. You can drink five of them. Keep one in case things go to hell - I expect you to save a can to sprinkle on my grave."

"I'll do that," replies Bear with an encouraging wink.

Chris walks slowly up the red carpet, usually reserved for dignitaries, and enters the foyer. Adorning the walls on either side are brilliant oil paintings of the Japanese attack on

Pearl Harbor and dignified memorials to the dead. Further-on are heroic images of the battle for the Pacific and a scale replica of the Marines raising the flag on Iwo Jima. Opposite the W.W. II displays are photographs and souvenirs from the Korean, Vietnam, and Persian Gulf Wars encased in quiet dignity within glass enclosures.

I wonder what the War on Terrorism display will look like, he wonders. Thinking immediately of the DVD in his briefcase, he chuckles and continues walking.

As he enters the Admiral's suite, the ensign behind the desk rises abruptly and without comment directs him to a seat in the reception area. She disappears into the Admiral's office. Moments later, Admiral Lang emerges, her summer white uniform adorned with a dozen rows of service ribbons and awards.

"Captain," she announces warmly as she takes his hand in both of hers. "I'm so glad you're back. Please join us." She precedes him into her office. Seated on the sofa against the wall is the Staff Judge Advocate. He rises partway and perfunctorily shakes Chris' hand before dropping back onto the sofa and crossing his gangly legs. The admiral waves Chris to a chair and takes a seat behind her desk.

After a few solicitous inquiries about his injury, she comes straight to the point.

"Chris, this 'Khalid issue' raises concerns at the highest levels."

"I can appreciate that," he responds cautiously.

"The official position is that what occurred, well... never occurred," she explains. "Do you get my gist?"

"Of course," he replies honestly. *Covert means covert.*

The admiral flips open a blue file folder with the words TOP SECRET followed by a series of hash marks and a string of caveats emblazoned across the top. Glancing at the first page, she removes her glasses and drops them onto her desk.

"Now, I've read Colonel Levine's report about your team's activities on Kalimantan and I must admit I'm... well... *impressed*." Her bright blue eyes settle on Chris, his startled expression causing her to chuckle.

Colonel Levine jerks upright, his jaw dropping. "Of all the words I would have used to describe the activities in my report, 'appalling' would be most apt, perhaps even 'reckless' and certainly 'dangerous.'"

"Yes, colonel," she drawls dryly. "I read your report. But I am none-the-less impressed," she repeats. "I'm impressed this young captain and his colleagues acted when action was called for. In a nutshell, it seems to me they remembered we are at war and performed their duties in the best traditions of the service." She smiles maternally at Chris who remains sitting in stunned silence.

"But, Ma'am," sputters the colonel. "He and his team perpetrated acts of war against a friendly nation!"

"No Dick," corrects the admiral softly. "An act of war was perpetrated upon us, if you'll recall."

"But the government of Indonesia..."

"Was providing haven to a known terrorist. I believe lawyers call it 'aiding and abetting' don't they?" mocks the admiral.

"But Ma'am. The *implications*..." he gasps.

"If we're going to fight a war against a stateless enemy, some international feelings are going to be hurt. It can't be helped," she announces dismissively as she tosses the dossier onto her desk. "But if we're sending these young people out there and telling them to fight, we'd better damned well support them. Don't you think?"

"I... Of course, Ma'am," stammers Colonel Levine.

The admiral dangles the contents of the folder over her shredder, feeding them sheet-by-sheet into the gnawing contraption. As the motor grinds to a halt, she glares at the JAG officer.

"This case is officially closed, *right* Colonel?"

The colonel swallows hard. "Yes Ma'am. But... what about the Indonesian government?"

"They've already talked themselves into a corner," she replies with a shrug. "They can't admit they were harboring Khalid."

"But the POLRI... the Indonesian navy?" he sputters. "There are bodies strewn all over the island!"

"Local insurgents," she growls. "It's taken care of. Now drop it!"

Colonel Levine's mouth works dumbly; he snaps to attention and remains silent.

"Captain," she announces returning her attention to Chris. "Because none of this took place, I'm not certain how to have you and Major Minh decorated."

Chris feels a pang of guilt. *The last thing I want is something to remind me of this!*

Suddenly an idea strikes him.

"Ma'am. I'd think it's best *my* actions be forgotten. But... is it possible for a foreign national to be awarded a U.S. decoration?"

A crooked smile creeps across her face. "Captain Ling?" she asks wisely.

Chris flushes. "Yes Ma'am."

"Dick, is it possible?" she asks her Judge Advocate.

The colonel looks from the admiral to Chris and back again before responding. "I... I suppose there's precedence."

"I thought so. Look into it," she orders. "In the meantime," she announces, returning to Chris. "If you're willing to extend your mobilization for another year, I'd like to place you on my personal staff. A mutual friend seems to think you have certain... intrinsic value. And I quite agree."

Chris coughs to cover the startled laugh that erupts unexpectedly from his lips.

"Um. No Ma'am. I... uh... I appreciate the offer," he stammers, hoping she doesn't recognize the horror he feels at the prospect of being placed on staff after the events of the past year. "I've already missed my demobilization date," he explains. "I really ought to get back to work."

She nods knowingly and springs from behind her desk. "Well, Godspeed to you then," she announces with evident relief.

A brittle winter snow blankets the city as Chris arrives at Denver's ultramodern international airport, the terminal teeming with vacationers heading for Colorado's pristine ski slopes. Anonymous among the throng, he rolls his suitcase to the passenger pickup zone and hails a taxi for the ride downtown to his high-rise condo.

Arriving at dusk, he passes unrecognized through the lobby, riding the elevator with several couples returning from a day on the slopes. It's clear they have stopped at the bar en route. One of the men notices Chris' arm in the sling.

"Dude! What's with the busted flipper?"

Chris glances at his bandaged shoulder. "Snow board," he responds with a wan smile.

"Gotta keep control of the leading edge, man," the dude warns. "The ice pack is wholly unforgiving."

Chris nods. "I'll keep it in mind," he chuckles.

The couples' laughter fades as Chris departs the elevator and wanders down the hall. Fumbling with the keys, he unlocks the door and steps inside his condo. The room is lifeless and stuffy; he feels as if he's entering a tomb. Dropping his suitcase in the foyer, he wanders into the kitchen. He opens the refrigerator where he discovers a well-chilled bottle of Pinot Grigio among moldy fruit and unidentifiable vegetables abandoned more than a year ago.

Pouring a glass of wine, he slides open the patio door and steps out onto the balcony: a stranger in an alien land.

He stares across the light snow dusting Cherry Creek Boulevard and shivers against the dry, frigid wind to which he's grown ill accustomed.

Next week he'll return to his civilian job as if it's just another workday, his unknown war a brief interlude that forever changed him. He withdraws his arm carefully from the sling and flexes it painfully, working the scar tissue to re-awake muscles atrophying over the past few weeks.

Sighing forlornly, he strolls inside and retrieves his suitcase. Entering his bedroom, he spots Linda's black-stained coffee cup half-empty on the nightstand. He stoops and retrieves the mused sheets, flinging them over the mattress before heaving his suitcase onto the bed.

He withdraws a pile of mussed shirts and sniffs them; they smell faintly of the Orient, a sort of musty tropical aroma tinged with curry, mildew, and sweat. Tossing them into a pile to be washed, he returns to the suitcase and discovers something wrapped in wrinkled brown paper.

"What the hell...?" He carefully unfolds the package to discover a black leather sheath with a chipped bone handle protruding from the scarred leather. Seizing the handle, he withdraws the long curved blade and raises it up to the light; a small, yellowed piece of paper floats from the sheath, landing on top of his luggage. He unfolds the note and reads:

"To one who keeps his honor as honed as a Khukuri - Kapar hunnu bhanda marnu ramro. Jambulung."

Chris squints at the note, rereading to final sentence. "Kapar hunnu...? His eyes are drawn to the fine print in parenthesis. "Better dead than live a coward."

"Ah, Jon," he mumbles fondly as he sets aside the Khukuri and resumes unpacking. As he fumbles through the suitcase, his attention is continually drawn to Jon's sheathed Khukuri. Finally, he dumps the remainder of his clothes into a pile and flings the suitcase onto the floor. Dropping onto the bed, he adjusts his pillows and retrieves the remote; the TV glows slowly to life.

"Today, Iraq still poses a threat and Iraq still remains in material breach," announces Secretary of State Colin Powell to the UN Security Council. "Indeed, by its failure to seize on its one last opportunity to come clean and disarm, Iraq has put itself in deeper material breach and closer to the day when it will face serious consequences for its continued defiance of this Council."

Mr. Powell glances up from his notes, sweeping the assembled Security Council members with a sincere gaze.

"My colleagues, we have an obligation to our citizens. We have an obligation to this body to see that our resolutions are complied with. We wrote 1441 not in order to go to war. We wrote 1441 to try to preserve the peace. We wrote 1441 to give Iraq one last chance." He pauses dramatically. "Iraq is not, so far, taking that one last chance."

Chris works his healing shoulder unconsciously as the Secretary concludes.

"We must not shrink from whatever is ahead of us. We must not fail in our duty and our responsibility to the citizens of the countries that are represented by this body."

The Secretary's speech ends and the scene cuts to a reporter standing outside the United Nations building in New York City, the flags of member nations whipping in the brisk winter wind.

"UN insiders tell CNN France and Russia plan to veto any resolution authorizing the use of military force against Iraq," he announces. "However administration officials believe 1441 already authorizes the use of force without further action by the Security Council. This is Peter Finch reporting from New York City."

"Thank you, Peter," responds the anchor primly and turns to the camera.

"In other news, the President has asked Congress to authorize the call-up of up to 230,000 additional reserve and National Guard personnel as necessary to support Operation Enduring Freedom..."

The anchor's voice fades from Chris' attention.

He rubs his hands unconsciously on his pants legs, a nagging bloody residue still seems to cling his scrubbed hands. His eyes flow to a picture on the wall beside his bed; three soldiers in muddy camouflage return his gaze, white teeth and eyes glowing beneath camouflage paint appearing shades of gray in the black and white photo.

A tear rolls unnoticed down his cheek. He closes his eyes, picturing Jessica shrouding him from Jon's attack and suddenly he understands. *Be glad you had someone in your life that didn't disappoint you,* Shikha had said.

He smiles a fragile, tragic smile and reaches into his pocket, withdrawing the cell phone from which he'd received his alert for mobilization more than a year ago. Fingering the phone gingerly, he flips open the protective cover and presses the "Off" button.

Setting the phone on the bedside table, he closes his eyes and drifts into a deep sleep.

AFTERWORD

Though *Without Reserve* is a work of fiction, it is set against actual events. In December 2001, U.S. Special Forces found a videotape in an Afghan training camp showing U.S. sites in Singapore being cased by members of a previously undetected organization named Jemmah Islamiya. Singapore had already discovered the JI's intentions and was quietly rounding up its members when news of the tape was made public and several key JI leaders fled Singapore. Thanks to the island-state's rapid response, no attack ever took place in Singapore.

The geopolitical realities of Southeast Asia in 2001-2002, particularly Indonesia, the most populous Muslim nation in the world, are portrayed accurately in this story.

In 2003, in the wake of the 2002 Bali bombing, Indonesia cracked-down on the JI, creating a special counter-terrorism force called Detasemen Khusus 88 (Detachment 88), which has continued to hunt down and kill or capture JI leadership.

In August 2003, Indonesian Riduan Isamuddin, a.k.a. "Hambali" (on whom the character, "Khalid" was based), key JI leader and Al Qa'ida's key operations leader in Southeast Asia, was arrested in Central Thailand with the assistance of U.S. intelligence. In addition to his ties to Al Qa'ida, Hambali was involved in planning attacks in

Singapore and is believed responsible for the 2002 bombing in Bali. He was turned over to U.S. custody and was last reported held in the U.S. detention facility at Guantanamo Bay, Cuba.

Despite the fact several hundred Al Qa'ida and JI operatives have been arrested or otherwise detained throughout Southeast Asia since 9/11, the JI remains active. Besides the October 12, 2002 bombing of the Kuta Beach Resort area in Bali, killing 202 and injuring 209; the JI has claimed responsibility for the August 2003 bombing of the JW Marriott Hotel in Jakarta, killing 14 and injuring 150; the August 2004 bombing of the Australian Embassy in Jakarta, killing 10 and injuring more than 100; the October 8, 2005 suicide attacks in several Bali nightclubs, killing 23 and injuring 122; July 17, 2009 attacks on the Ritz Carlton and the Marriott hotels in Jakarta; September 16, 2014, bombing of the Rizal Monument in front of the city hall in General Santos City, Philippines, killing one person and injuring 7; and on January 25, 2015, when JI member Zulkifli Abdhir was killed in an operation that also resulted in the death of 44 police officers.

So the war continues...

Glossary of Terms

BRIMOB   Indonesian National Police Mobile Brigade. Conducts paramilitary counter-terrorist operations.

DHS   Defense HUMINT Service. The U.S. Defense Intelligence Agency's human intelligence gathering organization. To avoid confusion with Department of Homeland Security, DHS is now referred to as "Directorate for Human Intelligence."

Gehlen, Reinhard   Gehlen, a former Wehrmacht general, ran the most successful undercover intelligence organization of the Cold War on behalf of the West German government. Other than a W.W.II photograph, he was not photographed or identified in public until after his retirement in the 1970s.

GPS   Global Positioning System. A satellite-based navigation system.

JAG   Judge Advocate General Corps, the military's lawyers.

JICPAC   Joint Intelligence Center, Pacific. The organization responsible for U.S. PACOM's intelligence analysis.

J2   Senior staff intelligence officer in a joint command. Also refers to the section led by the J2. (as in: "the J2 Section")

J3   Senior staff operations officer in a joint command. Also refers to the section led by the J3. (as in: "the J3 Section")

JI	Jemaah Islamiya. An Al Qa'ida-linked Muslim extremist organization in Southeast Asia. Its goal is the establishment of Darul Islamiya, a caliphate consisting of The Philippines, Indonesia, Malaysia, and Southern Thailand. The establishment would necessarily require the absorption of the secular Republic of Singapore.
Mustang	An officer commissioned from the enlisted ranks by either attending officer candidate school or by receiving a direct commission.
PACOM	United States Pacific Command. Responsible for U.S. military deployments from the west coast of the United States to the India-Pakistan border.
POLRI	Indonesian National Police.
RSAF	Republic of Singapore Air Force.
RSN	Republic of Singapore Navy.
SID	Security and Intelligence Division. Singapore's ultra-secret and highly-effective foreign intelligence service.
SWO	Surface Warfare Officer. An officer assigned to a naval surface vessel.
TNI-AL	Tentara Nasional Indonesia - Angkatan Laut: The Indonesian Navy.